MALONE LIFTED THE LID OF THE BOX JUST
FAR ENOUGH TO CATCH A GLIMPSE OF
GOLD KID SANDALS. THEY WERE NOT
EMPTY . . .

A question occurred to lawyer J. J. Malone. "Who
knew, or might know, that these models were all working for you? That together, they added up to Delora
Deanne?"

Hazel shook her head. "No one," she said, "outside of
this very close-knit organization. You can easily understand why it would be highly unfortunate for anyone—*anyone*—to know that there was, so to speak,
more than one Delora Deanne."

Malone nodded. "It could be highly unfortunate indeed." He scowled and thought a moment. "As a matter of simple precaution, do you know where the other
Delora Deannes are right now? It might be wise to
advise them to—to take steps."

He wasn't sure what kind of steps they should take,
except that preferably they should be steps away . . .

Bantam Books offers the finest in classic and modern American murder mysteries. Ask your bookseller for the books you have missed.

Stuart Palmer
THE PUZZLE OF THE SILVER PERSIAN
THE PUZZLE OF THE HAPPY HOOLIGAN

Craig Rice
MY KINGDOM FOR A HEARSE
THE LUCKY STIFF

Rex Stout
AND FOUR TO GO
BAD FOR BUSINESS
THE BROKEN VASE
CURTAINS FOR THREE
DEATH OF A DUDE
DEATH TIMES THREE
DOUBLE FOR DEATH
A FAMILY AFFAIR
THE FATHER HUNT
FER-DE-LANCE
THE FINAL DEDUCTION
GAMBIT
THE LEAGUE OF FRIGHTENED MEN
MURDER BY THE BOOK
PLOT IT YOURSELF
PRISONER'S BASE
THE RED BOX
THE RUBBER BAND
SOME BURIED CAESAR
THREE DOORS TO DEATH
THREE FOR THE CHAIR
THREE MEN OUT
THREE WITNESSES
TOO MANY CLIENTS

Victoria Silver
DEATH OF A HARVARD FRESHMAN

DEATH OF A RADCLIFFE ROOMMATE

Max Byrd
CALIFORNIA THRILLER
FINDERS WEEPERS
FLY AWAY, JILL

R. D. Brown
HAZZARD

Sue Grafton
"B" IS FOR BURGLAR

Robert Goldsborough
MURDER IN E MINOR

Ross MacDonald
BLUE CITY
THE BLUE HAMMER
GOODBYE LOOK
THE MOVING TARGET
SLEEPING BEAUTY

A. E. Maxwell
JUST ANOTHER DAY IN PARADISE

Rob Kantner
THE BACK-DOOR MAN

Joseph Telushkin
THE UNORTHODOX MURDER OF RABBI WAHL

Ted Wood
LIVE BAIT

Barbara Paul
KILL FEE
THE RENEWABLE VIRGIN

MY KINGDOM FOR A HEARSE

Craig Rice

BANTAM BOOKS
TORONTO · NEW YORK · LONDON · SYDNEY · AUCKLAND

MY KINGDOM FOR A HEARSE

*A Bantam Book / published by arrangement with
the author's estate*

PRINTING HISTORY

*First published in 1956.
Bantam edition / November 1986.*

ISBN 0-553-26222-X

Published simultaneously in the United States and Canada

Bantam Books are published by Bantam Books, Inc. Its trademark, consisting of the words "Bantam Books" and the por-
trayal of a rooster, is Registered in U.S. Patent and Trademark
Office and in other countries. Marca Registrada. Bantam
Books, Inc., 666 Fifth Avenue, New York, New York 10103.

PRINTED IN THE UNITED STATES OF AMERICA

KR   0 9 8 7 6 5 4 3 2 1

To Dr. Elizabeth Arvad

MY KINGDOM
FOR A
HEARSE

Chapter One

The room he was in managed to be pink and green without being downright offensive. John J. Malone looked around warily, took out a cigar, wondered if he dared smoke it in such delicate surroundings, regretfully decided not, and put it into his pocket with a deep sigh.

Across the large room from him was a picture, a picture in a golden frame. Automatically the little lawyer found himself humming a line of a song he remembered from sometime, somewhere.

> *Pretty as a picture,*
> *In a pretty frame—*

Malone sighed again, but it was an entirely different kind of a sigh. He'd seen the subject of the picture any number of times before, with a succession of variations, in the colored advertising pages of magazines catering to the would-be luxury trade. Different poses, different surroundings, but always the same girl, the same exquisite face, the same delicate, half-secretive smile.

There was always the same ornately carved golden frame, and under it the same slogan that gave renewed hope to countless thousands of feminine readers, in fine, graceful script across the page—"Pretty as a Picture"— and the signature, in the same delicate script, "Delora Deanne."

In spite of the picture, Malone was unhappy. He wanted that cigar, and badly. This had been one of those mornings when the mere act of waking had been painful, exasperating and just plain terrible, to the point where he wished it was also

1

unnecessary. His bones felt as though they had been disjointed
and then put together by an amateur with a do-it-yourself kit.
His stomach felt full of damp concrete, and some practical
prankster had evidently left a dead horse in his nose and a bad-
tempered bumblebee in each ear.

But a voice over the telephone had said that Delora Deanne was most anxious to consult with Mr. Malone regarding
an urgent legal matter, and he had been on his way as though
he'd been pursued by a jet-propelled demon. It hadn't been
just a little problem that involved unpaid office rent, back salary for Maggie, his secretary, an overdue bar bill and a bank
account that had already passed zero on the way down. Nor
was it the fact that his best and oldest friend, Jake Justus, had
just become a television producer with no shows on the air as
yet but with a hopeful eye on the Delora Deanne account, and
that this visit of his might prove a valuable introduction. It was
that any moment now he was going to become one of the favored few who had met the real-life Delora Deanne face to
lovely face.

Now, however, after twenty minutes of waiting, he looked
once more around the green-and-pink room with its soft satin
furniture, and began to wonder when he was going to be in the
undoubtedly enchanted presence of the being who was the
model for beauty-seeking American womanhood, the idol of
American manhood, the inspiration for many of Malone's favorite secret dreams, and certainly the greatest cosmetic sales-
woman since Cleopatra sailed the Nile.

Delora Deanne! It would be the seraphic yet somehow
voluptuous face, haloed by hair the exact color of fresh-minted
gold, or perhaps it would be the hair alone in a soft cloud (Delora Deanne Sunshine Tint), the kind of cloud that Malone
occasionally dreamed of walking through barefoot at dawn. Or
it would be the slender, yet joyously curving body, rosy and
still somehow pale, discreetly half-seen through misty, wind-
touched veils (Delora Deanne Contour Classes), or the perfect, bare dancing feet on posy-studded grass (Delora Deanne
Special Foot Make-Up), or the pair of slim, rose-tipped hands
cupped to hold some rare and priceless gem (Delora Deanne
Manicure Magic).

Or it would be Delora Deanne's beguiling, caressing voice
from some loud-speaker, "You too can be as pretty as a pic-

ture," a voice that hinted, ever so slightly, at some remote foreign ancestry, possibly a Hungarian grandmother.

Put them all together and they spelled a lot of cold cream sales, and a lot of excellent ideas which John J. Malone preferred to keep strictly to himself.

Plus, of course, the possibility—probability, if all went well—of a wonderful, extra-super, triple-colossal television spectacular for Jake Justus to produce.

Again he hummed a bar or two of the tune which had been running through his head ever since his unhappy waking. Where *had* he heard it? He tried hard to remember. Probably in some thoroughly disreputable place the night before.

A voice behind him said, "I take it you're John J. Malone?" and the little lawyer jumped almost guiltily, got up fast and turned around.

It was not the voice that had haunted him, heard softly over the radio, nor was it the high-pitched twang that had yipped at him nastily over the telephone earlier that morning to make the appointment. No, it was just a voice, midwest prairie with a faint touch of Chicago overtones, a serviceable voice, to be used solely for the purposes of communication.

The woman who went with it was also serviceable, and as midwestern as an acre of corn. If she had been the moving, smiling original of the dream Delora Deanne he knew so well, that would have been one thing. If she had been phenomenally and spectacularly deformed and ugly, that would have been another and, in its way, every bit as enthralling. But the woman who stood before him was neither. Her face was just that, a face, with the usual components of eyes, nose and mouth, put there in their proper places for the ordinary and useful purposes of eating, breathing and seeing. Even her eyebrows, usually such helpfully expressive clues to emotion, said nothing; they were just there and that was all there was to it.

Her practical-looking hands were clean and wore a standard-color nail polish, her medium-sized feet appeared to be free from corns and bunions. Her figure was not overweight or underweight, but just standard size, and covered with a medium-blue dress that might have cost six ninety-nine in Goldblatt's basement, or seven hundred and fifty at a salon, and probably had cost forty-nine-fifty at Marshall Field's. Her hair, dressed neatly in no particular style, was just plain hair color.

She was neither likable nor disagreeable, friendly nor hostile. Malone did his best to look gallant and said, "You—are—"

"Hazel Swackhammer," the woman said, and sat down. "I am also Delora Deanne."

Malone sat down too, reminding himself firmly that more than just an introduction to the model who posed for Delora Deanne—for there had to be one—was at stake. There was his office rent to be considered, there was Jake's still unborn TV show. He settled down to making friends with the brains behind the beauty.

"My dear lady—" He took out the cigar again, decided the hell with the green-and-pink walls, and lighted it. He murmured something flattering about being extremely pleased, and looked around for a place to put his burned match. The lusciously soft carpet was a mossy green, engagingly sprinkled with pale pink and white posies, and he finally put the match in his vest pocket.

"My dear lady," he began again, in what grateful clients had complimented as the perfect cell-side manner, "what seems to be your difficulty?"

"Scandal," Hazel Swackhammer said. "Someone is trying to involve Delora Deanne in scandal, and consequently ruin me."

Two more lines of the song came back to him.

> —*but she stole my bottom dollar,*
> *And she scandalized my name.*

She told him the detailed story of Delora Deanne, from a recipe for homemade lotion learned from a New England grandmother, through the mixing of ingredients in the back room of a small-town Iowa drugstore, to the perfumed perfection of the little marble building that was the heart of Delora Deanne Cosmetics.

It was a businesslike story, told in a businesslike manner. Malone admired it, but he thought wistfully of the story as told on the radio and on the printed page and that, with any luck, Jake would tell on television, a story that had its beginning in the dreamy South. Magnolias and moonlight, soft whisperings, and an occasional glimpse of shadowy, secret gardens. The little lawyer caught himself on the verge of a quiet sigh, then mentally kicked himself for being a sentimental slob, and told himself firmly to stick to business.

"This," Hazel Swackhammer said. She handed him a small batch of clippings from newspaper columns, hinting that an unnamed beauty (very obviously Delora Deanne) was up to a lot of nonsense which, if not actually nefarious, illegal, and quite probably unchaste, was at least highly indiscreet.

"But," she said, "that is not all."

Malone felt a sudden and uncomfortable impulse to flee, client or no client, Jake or no Jake, Delora or no Delora. For days afterward, he claimed to have had a premonition all along.

"That," she went on, "is not the awful thing that made me send for you this morning." She rose, and Malone rose with her. She caught his last, yearning glance toward the picture and said, "Of course. Everyone does. But *you* shall."

Malone blinked and said, "Perhaps an introduction—"

"Simplest thing in the world," she said. "Advertising conferences go on in spite of everything, and they're all here this morning. All except one, that is."

Malone gave his head a brisk little shake in the vain hope that at least a few of his confused thoughts would find out where they belonged, and settle there. He had a grim feeling that the damp concrete in his stomach was beginning to harden now.

Hazel Swackhammer led the way into an adjoining room, this one gray, mauve and restful. Soft, pale-violet chairs were drawn up around what appeared to be a polished conference table. The man at the far end rose to his feet and Malone recognized the crisply waving dark hair, the handsome face with its smiling mouth, the dark eyes and long eyelashes that would have looked well on Delora Deanne herself, as belonging to a casual night-club acquaintance he recognized as Otis Furlong.

"Hello there, Malone," Otis Furlong said. "I suppose you want to meet Delora Deanne." He smiled and nodded to his right. "Gertrude Bragg."

It was the face of the pictures, the face of Malone's dreams, framed in the silken cloud of pale gold hair, but attached to a slightly dumpy body that rose from a pair of piano legs.

"The feet," Furlong said, "Louella Frick."

The little lawyer glanced instinctively under the table, at the pair of dainty, high-arched, slender feet in expensive beige suède sandals with fragile heels, then ran his gaze upward over a small chubby woman who looked at him through thick glasses astride a freckled nose and said, "It's a pleasure," in a voice like a discontented mouse.

"Eula Stolz," Furlong said. "Torso and legs."

Just torso and legs was too much of an understatement, Malone thought. It should have been at least The Torso, and The Legs. If only there had been a face in keeping, he would have stopped thinking about his troubles and his premonitions right then and there.

She said, "Hello," through her nose, and closed a small, pinched mouth.

"And, the voice," Furlong finished. "*The* voice. Rita Jardee."

Rita Jardee, a red-haired, haggard and skinny woman who seemed to be hurrying toward middle age, said, "Delighted, Mr. Malone," in the mellow voice that held him and untold thousands spellbound every Saturday night.

"Unfortunately," Furlong said, "the hands, Eva Lou Strauss, are missing this morning. Late again, I suppose."

A thin little sandy-haired man with rimless glasses spoke up from the other end of the table and said, "A composite. Otis, who takes our photographs, is a genius." He added, "I'm Dennis Dennis, copywriter."

Malone muttered something and was destined to wonder forever what it had been.

Jake. The Delora Deanne show. He was going to have to break this very gently to Jake. The beauty of Delora Deanne was to have been the irresistible lure to draw the eyes of goodness knows how many millions to their television screens. Now, this!

Or was it possible that a composite could be made to appear on television? He hadn't the faintest idea. Probably not. But he clung to the faint hope as though it were a life raft.

Dennis Dennis nodded toward Hazel Swackhammer and said, "We must remember the brains, mustn't we?"

Hazel Swackhammer lifted the left side of her upper lip in what, on any other face, and in any other circumstances, would have passed for a smile, and said, "My office is this way, Mr. Malone."

The office was exactly suited to her. Four walls, two windows, a filing cabinet, a desk, a desk calendar, four chairs and an ash tray. Everything perfectly practical and utilitarian, and precisely in its place.

The woman standing by the desk was tallish and vaguely beautiful. Vaguely and dreamily. Her hair was dark and soft and cloudy, her dark blue eyes looked as though she ought to be wearing glasses. Even her smile was vague, perhaps a little confused.

"Myrdell Harris," Hazel Swackhammer said.

"How do you do, Mr. Malone." The little lawyer recognized the voice he had heard over the phone. There was nothing dreamy nor vague about it. "Mrs. Swackhammer's executive assistant. Do you need me, Mrs. Swackhammer?"

"No," Mrs. Swackhammer said. "I do not."

The door closed gently behind the executive assistant— Malone suspected her employer's name for it was "secretary."

Hazel Swackhammer unlocked a desk drawer, took out a box and laid it on the desk. "This," she said, pointing to it, "came in the mail this morning."

Malone recognized the satiny white box with its silver lettering as having come from a fashionable and fabulously expensive Michigan Boulevard shop which had cost him more money in the past than he was ever going to confess to anyone. There was something ominous about it, resting there on the plain green blotter of the desk. He didn't want to open it, and he knew he was going to.

There was a pair of pale lavender suède gloves inside, so very beautifully designed and cunningly made that he could guess in an instant at their cost. But he wasn't interested in design nor cost right now. Because the gloves were not empty.

The damp concrete in his stomach began to turn rapidly into ice. Slowly, very slowly, he reached down and began to slip off the gloves until he recognized the magnificently embalmed hands that had once been Delora Deanne's, slender, graceful, ringless, and even now, lovely.

Chapter Two

It was quite a little while before John J. Malone spoke, in fact, before he even dared to try. Carefully, and with hands that were almost steady, he replaced the cover on the satiny white box, and stood staring at it as though it might suddenly spring at him.

Hazel Swackhammer sat down behind her desk and gazed fixedly at a blank spot on the wall.

"Tell me," Malone said, as soon as he felt reasonably certain that his voice would sound normal again, "why haven't you informed the police about this?"

She turned her head to look at him as though he were a slightly retarded child. "Newspapers," she told him. "I have to consider the reputation of Delora Deanne."

The little lawyer scowled and gestured toward the sheaf of newspaper clippings she still held in her hand. "It seems to me," he said coldly, "that Delora Deanne's reputation is already being chopped up in pieces for the benefit of the reading public."

The look she gave him indicated that she didn't quite like the way he'd phrased that. On second thought, he realized that he didn't quite like it himself.

"I sympathize deeply with you," Malone said, hoping he sounded as if he meant it. "Indeed I do. But you have a certain duty as a private citizen."

This time, her look told him exactly what she thought of her duty as a private citizen, as compared to her duty to the already imperiled reputation of Delora Deanne.

Malone relit his cigar, and this time he dropped his burned match on the brown linoleum floor. "Furthermore,

8

you're overlooking something," he said, as gently as he could. "The rest of—" he indicated the satiny white and silver box— "this person's person."

"Eva Lou Strauss," she said, without any expression on her face. Perhaps, Malone thought, if it had been the Delora Deanne pretty-as-a-picture and irreplaceable face, there might have been, not actually an expression, but at least a faint shadow of anxiety.

"You want her body found," Malone said sternly and righteously. "The rest of her body. Her people will want to give it proper burial. And you want her murderer to be punished."

"As far as I know," Hazel Swackhammer said, "Eva Lou Strauss had no people." Her further silence made it plain that finding and punishing murderers was definitely not her business. After a while she said, as though just faintly annoyed, "I suppose it must be murder."

"There certainly appears to be every indication of it," Malone said, trying to be delicate about it. He looked at his cigar and added, "But what I don't quite understand is just exactly what you want me to do."

"Frankly," she said, "neither do I. But I felt that you would be able to think of something. I do know quite a little about your reputation, Mr. Malone."

He wasn't at all sure whether he ought to thank her or not.

"At the very least," she went on, "I expected you to be able to tell me what to do with—*these*." She nodded toward the box. "Nothing like this has ever come up in my entire experience."

Malone refrained from commenting on that. Having a pair of beautifully embalmed hands arrive with the bills in his morning mail was hardly an everyday occurrence in anyone's life. He scowled at the box.

"I assume," he said, "that you've told none of the others here—nor anyone else—about your receiving these?"

"Obviously not," she said.

No, he reflected, she wouldn't have. She undoubtedly had simply unwrapped the box, examined its contents, put the cover back on, and thought things over for a while before doing anything. New experience or not, she had made no outcry or disturbance, had said or done nothing that would alarm her staff, her photographer and copywriter, her executive assistant and the remaining Delora Deannes. At last she'd sent for Malone. And a good idea, too, he told himself; probably the best one she'd ever had.

He wondered what kind of a fee she had in mind.

"Tell me," he said suddenly, "have you received anything besides this? Any letters, any messages, any telephone calls?"

"Nothing." She shook her head. "Just these." Her slate-colored eyes looked at Malone appraisingly. "Just what are you thinking about, Mr. Malone?"

"There is just a possibility," the little lawyer said, very slowly, turning his cigar around between his fingers and looking at it intently, "that it might not be murder." He was trying to think at least several yards ahead of himself.

She watched him thoughtfully and said nothing.

"You may get a message," Malone told her. "In fact, if it is not murder, you most likely will."

Yes, he thought, that could be the case, and there was the chance that if Eva Lou Strauss was still alive, he might be justified in not insisting that the police be notified. Certainly, this didn't seem like the right or tactful time to disagree with his new client on that point. The thing to do was wait.

"If she's been kidnaped," Malone began, and then stopped. There hadn't been any message of any kind, nothing like the conventional warning against calling the cops. But perhaps there hadn't been time yet. "If she has," he went on, "you most certainly will get a message and some kind of a demand for money."

"I," Hazel Swackhammer said, looking uninterested, "am leaving everything up to you, Mr. Malone. I know you will handle the situation with perfect discretion."

He realized that she wasn't going to be interested in putting out much, if any, money to ransom Eva Lou Strauss, who wouldn't be any further use to her without the Delora Deanne hands. Well, he would cross that bridge after the horse was stolen, and lock the barn door when he came to it.

"What did the—rest of her look like?" he asked, hoping he'd phrased it right.

By way of answer, she unlocked and opened one of the desk drawers and pulled out a portfolio of photographs. Third from the top was a full-length picture of the girl with the nationally famous hands. A tallish girl, with a generously curved figure that would have been fully appreciated in one of the better harems, but whose large-featured face showed too much and too garish make-up, and who had entirely too much frizzy hair.

"Her hair, yellow," Hazel Swackhammer said. "Not blond, yellow."

Malone understood and appreciated the distinction. He gave back the portfolio and said, "Tell me a little something about her personal life."

"As far as I have been concerned," she told him, "her personal life consisted of an address and a telephone number in my files." She gave both of them to Malone, who noted them down. "Except that naturally I reminded her from time to time of her responsibility to the reputation of Delora Deanne."

"Naturally," Malone agreed, and remembered something else. He pointed his cigar at the newspaper clippings and said, "What do you want me to do about these?"

"Put a stop to them," she said. "Find out their origin. That comes first."

Yes, it would. The little lawyer picked up the top one and read it again. Nothing remarkable nor original. What model, internationally known for her voice, beauty and cosmetic appeal, had turned from cutting up with a well-known playboy to blackmailing him? Malone sighed. He knew most of Chicago's better-known playboys, either by name or reputation, as very casual acquaintances, or as worried clients, and it was a long, long list.

On the other hand, though, he did know the columnist, Ned McKoen. But in any case, getting information was going to involve expensive and extensive buying in Chicago's best café-society saloons.

Oh well, he would be sending the bill to Hazel Swackhammer, and it had been a long time since he'd been in the *Chez.*

"There's another thing," he said thoughtfully. "These two situations—the column items and—this—" he pointed to the box again— "may be connected, and then again, they may not. That remains to be seen." He paused. "Did this girl have any particular enemies that you know of?"

"I know nothing about Eva Lou Strauss," she told him. "Nor about any of the others. Except that I do believe that Rita Jardee woman has had four husbands and has her eye out for a fifth." She looked at him squarely. "As long as Delora Deanne is not involved in any way, I have absolutely no concern about it."

Malone nodded that he understood perfectly. He said, "And how about yourself?"

"A successful woman always has enemies, Mr. Malone," she said. "I am not the exception." She paused a moment. "There is one in particular. My former husband, Charles Swackhammer. At one time he was of some assistance to me in the creation and development of Delora Deanne. Now he would like to own and control the business. Now that it is a success. It is just possible that by forcing Delora Deanne into bankruptcy and failure, he would be able to buy me out, and turn my loss into his gain. Or at least," she added, "so he may think."

Win, lose or draw, Malone reflected, he did not envy Charles Swackhammer.

He could imagine someone deliberately planning just such a newspaper column for such a purpose. But Malone could hardly imagine him going to the length of mailing Hazel Swackhammer a beautiful box containing the hands of Delora Deanne. No, not even for the purpose of frightening her. If he knew her, he would know better than to try to frighten her. And anyway, assuming that, one way or another, he did gain control of Delora Deanne, he too would need her famous and photographed hands.

At last he said, "Is there anything else you have to tell me?"

Before she answered, she put away the portfolio. She found the brown wrapping paper and the string which had come around the white satiny box, rewrapped the box, tied it securely, put it away on top of the portfolio, and shut and locked the drawer.

Then she said, "I have told you everything, Mr. Malone. I shall mail your retainer to your office. And I trust I shall hear from you before long."

Malone went away unhappily, with only the vaguest ideas as to where he was going, and what on earth he was going to do when he got there.

He peered wistfully into the mauve-and-gray room and saw that all the Delora Deannes who had been there had disappeared. He wished he knew where Eva Lou Strauss had been. Even more, he wished he knew where she was now. Most of all, he wished that he knew just how he was going to find out.

Dennis Dennis was there, leaning against the conference table, his arms folded, talking to Otis Furlong who was still sprawled in his chair. They waved cheerily to Malone to come in.

"I suppose Hazel called you in about the scandal," Dennis Dennis said.

The little lawyer tried to look surprised. "Scandal?" he repeated innocently.

"Don't try to be coy," Otis Furlong said. He took out his pipe and began filling it, ignoring the mossy green carpet which, in this room, was sprinkled with tiny violets. "We too read the daily newspapers."

Dennis Dennis lit a cigarette and said, "Which is she going to do about it? Sue, or stay shut up?"

"Stay shut up," Malone said blandly. "Which girl is it, if it really is one of the Deloras?"

Otis Furlong shrugged his shoulders, and Dennis Dennis said, "Search me. Might be any or all of 'em. Though I can't exactly see the Deloras ganging up together, even to take a sucker."

"They aren't exactly *en rapport*," Otis Furlong agreed. He finished tamping his pipe and reached for a match. "Hazel must be fit to be tied in a bowknot, though she'd never let on. What I can't figure is, how did any Delora latch on to a playboy? They live about as secluded lives as top-secret atom scientists."

Malone said smugly, "Youth will find a way," and brushed hopelessly at the cigar ashes that had just fallen on his vest. It was true, Delora Deanne, the beautiful, the enchanted, the well-nigh legendary, never showed herself in public. That, he had always assumed, had been part of the magic legend. Now he realized that none of them could possibly have appeared publicly. The Delora Deannes, he reflected, must have led one hell of a dull life.

"I wonder who the playboy is," he asked very casually, not really expecting an answer, but hoping for the best.

The handsome photographer shrugged again, and again Dennis Dennis said, "Search me." He added, "I'm glad Hazel isn't going to make a great big thing out of it. We have enough troubles around here as it is."

"Any particular kind of troubles?" Malone asked lazily, with a great show of disinterest.

"Oh, no. Just the usual run of mild upheavals that result from handling a bunch of highly jealous females," Otis Furlong said. "And poor old Hazel always worrying for fear her ex is going to try and take her precious business away from her. And Dennis here worrying for fear his ex will find out how much money he's winning at the races and try to get her alimony increased."

Dennis Dennis snorted. He added, "And Otis here worrying for fear his ex is going to get laryngitis and lose her job, or get drunk and fall on her face in a Delora Deanne broadcast."

"My ex being Rita Jardee," Otis Furlong explained. "But our pal here exaggerates my worries." He lit his pipe, put away the matches, got to his feet with amazing, catlike grace for so tall a man, and said, "Drop in at my place some time, Malone, and have a drink. It's right in the neighborhood. I've got something cute to show you."

"And drop in at my ivory tower here some time," Dennis Dennis said. "I'll whip up a poem or something."

Malone said a yes and a thank you to both of them, and went on to the little blue-and-gold reception room. The breathtaking lovely who had already told him her name was Tamia Tabet, and whose telephone number he had already obtained, smiled at him warmly, from behind her gilt-and-ivory desk. Malone made a mental note to do much, much more research about the whole Delora Deanne organization, and soon.

"Well, Mr. Malone," said Myrdell Harris' shrill voice. "What's going to happen now?"

He turned to look at her, wondering again how that voice, and that misty, dreamy beauty ever got together. "Sorry, I'm not a soothsayer," he said amiably.

"Come now, Mr. Malone, I know all about you." Again she favored him with that vague, lovely smile. But there was nothing vague about the way she said, "Who is going to be murdered? Or, has she been?"

Chapter Three

"Come in quick, Malone, and lock the door," Helene Justus said.

The little lawyer obeyed and stood looking at her dejectedly. For once, even looking at Helene didn't raise his spirits. Not more than a little, anyway. Delora Deanne might have his secret dreams, but it was Helene who had a very special place in his secret heart.

Worries or no worries, he looked admiringly at her smooth, pale hair, nearer the color of pure cornsilk than even Delora Deanne's, at her caramel-colored fur worn carelessly over her shoulders more perfectly than even Delora Deanne could ever wear anything, at her long, slim legs, more beautiful than anyone's, anywhere.

But the very sight of her smooth perfection only deepened his gloom. He walked over to the filing cabinet and pulled out the drawer marked *Confidential*.

"No, thanks, Malone," Helene said. "It's too early in the morning." She looked at him closely. "What's the matter?"

Malone helped himself generously to the cheap gin, shut the file drawer, growled, "My grandmother died," and sat down behind his desk.

"I know," she said unsympathetically. "Your grandmother died in 1886, and this is no time for cheap vaudeville jokes, Malone. I need your help." She lit a cigarette, frowned, and said, "It's Jake."

"I know," Malone said, as reassuringly as he could. "But look. Remember Rome wasn't burned down in a night. Building a TV production company takes time."

"I'm not so sure about Rome," Helene told him, "but I

15

know all about TV production companies taking time. I know something else, too. They take money. Jake has a beautiful office, but the rent is due on it."

Malone caught himself on the verge of remarking that two could play at that game. "What can I do?"

"You can lend him some money," Helene said calmly.

The little lawyer looked at her as though she'd been suddenly taken with a form of insanity. He opened his mouth.

"Shut up and let me talk," she told him. "There isn't much time. I told Jake I'd meet him here for lunch. But I got here early, and I'm going out through your back door in one minute. When he gets here, you're going to lend him the money. A thousand ought to see him through." She was fumbling through her tan alligator purse. "Tell him you won it. Tell him a client paid you. Tell him anything. But do it." She shoved ten hundred-dollar bills into his limp hand.

"But—" he began, and stopped. He would do anything in the world for her, and she knew it.

"You said yourself it was just a matter of time."

Malone hadn't said anything of the kind, but he refrained from mentioning it.

"He'll get a show pulled together and sold. And then he'll pay you back and you'll pay me back, and he'll be a highly successful TV producer, and everything will be rosy."

Malone thought about the Delora Deannes that added up to one composite, and about one of them being missing, and winced inwardly. Still, there would be other possibilities for Jake. All he needed was a start. And Jake would never take the money from Helene herself.

As though she'd been reading his thoughts, she said, "Anyway, I expect to be an ex-heiress any day now. Pa's courting a red-haired widow he met in Palm Springs."

On the other hand, there was the chance that Jake might find out about the transaction. Malone shuddered. Then Helene smiled at him, and he would have promised her a round-trip rocket trip to the moon if she'd asked.

Anyway, he told himself after she had gone, he'd as good as committed himself. He stared indignantly at the money and finally stuffed it away in his wallet.

Maggie O'Leary, his black-haired, blue-eyed secretary, came into the office. "Malone—"

"Please," Malone said wearily. He raised a feebly protesting hand. "I know all about everything. The office rent. The bank. The bill from Saks." He drew a long breath. "I have a new client. A very rich client. Less than an hour ago she said she was putting a check in the mail." Though, he thought unhappily, she hadn't mentioned the amount it would be for.

"Malone—" she began again.

"Don't worry about a thing," he told her valiantly.

"It's something else," she said. "Malone, I want you to meet my brother Luke."

"I've met your brother Luke," Malone said. "Charming guy."

Maggie drew a long, patient breath. "He's inventing a camera."

"Nice of him," Malone said. "Might come in handy for photographers. Now go away, I want to think."

She said, "And von Flanagan called. Three times."

The little lawyer stiffened. A call from his long-time bosom friend and bitter opponent, of the Homicide Division, just might be ominous right now.

"He said it was important," Maggie added.

Yes, very possibly ominous. Had the—the rest of Eva Lou Strauss's body been found, had the matter of the hands in the gloves been found out already? Hardly probable, Malone tried to reassure himself. It couldn't have happened that fast. Von Flanagan did move, and eventually in the right direction, but ponderously. That was supposed to be a cheering thought, but somehow it didn't seem to do much for him.

He considered calling von Flanagan back. He considered not calling von Flanagan back. He put one hand on the telephone, but left it there. One good way of staying out of trouble was not calling anyone back, especially von Flanagan. And then again—

Jake's arrival made the happier decision for him. If there was trouble, he'd rather hear about it after lunch.

The tall red-haired ex-newspaperman, ex-press agent, ex-night club owner and possibly ex-television producer if something didn't turn up, looked tired and worried. He sank into a chair and managed what was a passing imitation of a smile.

Maggie brightened visibly. "Mr. Justus!" she exclaimed happily. "I want you to meet my brother Luke."

Jake blinked and looked a little vaguely around the room.

"He's not here," Maggie said hastily. "But I want you to meet him. He's inventing a camera with a lot of eyes."

"Later," Malone said in a firm voice. "We'll get to your brother Luke later. Right now, we both want to think."

She sniffed and flounced out, closing the door hard.

Jake sighed deeply. "Mr. Jake Justus is a television producer," he said nastily. "Mr. Jake Justus is a big shot. Everybody wants to meet Mr. Justus. Everybody has a relative who wants to meet Mr. Justus. Mr. Justus has a lovely office in the Wrigley Building with his name on the door. In gold letters yet. Mr. Justus has a telephone answering service that says Mr. Justus will call you back, only Mr. Justus never does. And pretty soon Mr. Justus won't have the lovely office with his name on the door—"

"Stop it," Malone said. He walked over to the filing cabinet and came back with the bottle from the *Confidential* drawer and two glasses. As Jake gratefully downed his drink, he added, "You know yourself it's just a matter of time."

"Time," Jake said in a bitter voice, "is the thing I don't have the money to pay for."

Malone cleared his throat. "How about a little loan to tide you over—" He reached for his wallet.

Jake looked suspiciously at Malone, and even more suspiciously at the gin.

"I am not," Malone said indignantly. "Nor out of my mind." He took out the hundred-dollar bills. "I know I'll get it back. Just a matter of time. If this will tide you over—"

"Malone," Jake said, fingering the bills. "You didn't win this much at poker."

"I could have," Malone said. "And have, too, in my time. But as it happens, a client paid a big bill." Jake still looked a little dubious, and he added quickly, "A long overdue bill. Don't think you ever knew about the case."

"Well—" Jake said. He still looked dubious.

"Just consider it a little investment," Malone told him, "in the Justus Television Production Company. Probably turn out to be the best one I ever made."

He shoved the bills farther across the table, Jake picked them up gingerly as though he were afraid they might vanish, and put them away.

"And absolutely no need to tell Helene about this," Malone added.

"Definitely no need," Jake said. He poured himself another drink, said, "Thanks, Malone," and lit a cigarette. "Now about this morning—?"

Malone was silent for a moment. Sooner or later Jake was going to have to be told about the composite. But not just yet. And as far as what he preferred to call the Other Thing—that he shoved firmly into the back of his mind. Right now he'd rather pretend it didn't exist at all.

"I met Mrs. Swackhammer," he began slowly. "A very interesting woman—"

"Swackhammer," Jake said, frowning. "Sounds familiar."

"Funny. It does to me too," Malone said. "But anyway. She's the owner and the boss and the brains of Delora Deanne."

He was still trying to think what to say next when Helene made her second appearance. Her eyes were bright, her cheeks were faintly pink, and there were tiny glistens of snow on the caramel-colored fur. She's done a nice, quick job, Malone reflected admiringly, of running around the block after she'd seen Jake enter the building, to collect that faint glow and the snowflakes.

She kissed Jake enthusiastically and said, "Well! Am I in time to hear all about Delora Deanne?"

Malone repressed a slight shudder and said, "You are."

She glanced at the bottle on the desk and said, "A fine idea, but let's adjourn to Joe the Angel's, where the glasses are cleaner."

Instead of indignantly defending his housekeeping, Malone gave her a feeble smile and said, "I'll meet you there in ten minutes. Got a very important telephone call to make first."

At the door Helene paused and said, "Malone, did you know that Maggie's brother—"

"I do," Malone said. "He's inventing eyes like a camera. Or something. Later." He waved them toward the door.

The question that had suddenly come into his mind might not mean a thing, and then again, it might. Anyway, it wasn't going to do any harm to find out. He picked up the telephone and dialed the number of Rico di Angelo's strictly high-class undertaking parlor on North Avenue.

He was still wondering just how to phrase the question when Rico came to the phone. "Listen," he said at last, after spending as much time as he could on idle pleasantries, "I want to know something about your business. Can you cut off a person's hands? A live person, that is. And then embalm them?"

"I say no," Rico said, a little coldly.

"You mean it can't be done?"

"I mean I don't cut off anybody's hands, Malone."

"You don't understand," Malone said desperately. "It's a hypothetical question. I mean, is it possible for something like that to be done?" He heard only silence, and drew a long slow breath. "Look, Rico. Suppose somebody has somebody's hands. Never mind what's happened to the rest of the somebody. Could this somebody take this somebody's hands and take them to somebody—not you—and have them—?"

"Malone," Rico interrupted. His voice was very gentle and almost pleading. "I am your good friend. My cousin Joe the Angel, he is your best friend. You go home. Drink coffee. Lie down. You feel better. Malone, go home." He hung up.

The little lawyer sighed, replaced the receiver and struggled into his overcoat. He'd make another try at getting the information as soon as he felt a little stronger.

He was halfway to the door when the telephone rang. For a minute he hesitated, finally gave in and answered it. Rico was calling back. But this time his voice was indignant, almost angry.

"Malone," Rico said. "I just think it all over fast. I am your good friend, yes. My cousin Joe the Angel is your best friend, yes. But Malone, I will not do it. Not even for you. Whatever it is, I will—not—do—it." And he hung up for the second time.

Chapter Four

Joe the Angel interrupted an animated conversation with Jake and Helene to regard Malone coldly. Far more coldly, the little lawyer thought, than a mere overdue bar bill called for.

"Malone," Joe the Angel said. "My cousin Rico called. He told me you are either drunk or you are crazy."

Malone said, "I never felt better in my life."

"He told me you wanted him to cut off someone's hands."

Helene gasped. Jake turned an anxious face toward Malone.

"I told him nothing of the sort," Malone said indignantly. "I asked him a purely hypothetical question, that's all. Whether something was or wasn't possible."

"Was it?" Helene asked, and Jake asked, "What was it?" and Joe the Angel came in with, "Why?"

"I was trying to fill in a word in a crossword puzzle," Malone snapped crossly. "And don't bother me. I've got things on my mind."

He became uncomfortably aware that someone was regarding him coldly and decidedly unfavorably in the bar mirror, and recognized Gus Madrid. Malone nodded and turned away uncomfortably. The big, glowering gunman wasn't anyone he wanted to be on unfavorable terms with.

Joe the Angel poured three ryes and three beer chasers. Helene tactfully changed the subject to next week's fight card, and this inevitably led to the subject of television. A gleam came into Joe the Angel's eye.

"The television business!" Joe said enthusiastically, lifting a glass to Jake. "You know, I got a little niece. Just seventeen and beautiful like—this! And she sings—" He warbled a few notes.

A resounding and ill-tempered chirp came from somewhere on the other side of the room.

Malone jumped, turned around, and said hoarsely, "What's that?"

A dejected small white bird sat alone in a wire cage on a table, looking at them with a gloomy stare.

"My parakeet," Joe the Angel said. "My good friend, the city hall janitor, he gave it to me."

"Parakeets are green," Helene objected.

"Not this one," Joe the Angel said proudly. "An albino. Very rare."

Jake said, "Parakeets talk."

"This one doesn't," Helene said. "That makes him even rarer."

Malone strolled across the room, poked an experimental finger into the cage and said, "*Tweet!*"

The parakeet gave him one silent, scornful look, and turned his back. Malone reported, "Not friendly," and went back to the bar.

Joe the Angel glared at him, and said to Jake, "My beautiful niece, her name—"

The booth telephone rang. The parakeet jumped on his top perch and chirruped, "Ring! Ring, ring, ring!" as a weary *Examiner* reporter got up to answer the phone.

"See," Joe the Angel said triumphantly. "Already he learns one word. Any time, he will talk."

"If he repeats the language he probably hears around here," Helene commented, "he'll be a social outcast for life among parakeets."

Joe the Angel pretended he hadn't heard and went on, "Jake, my niece, she dances like she sings."

"I want to meet her," Jake said, trying to sound enthusiastic about it. "But later. Not this week. Later."

Joe the Angel beamed and said, "I will telephone and remind you."

And, Malone reflected gloomily, the telephone answering service will announce that Mr. Justus will call back.

It was Helene who suggested that they adjourn to a booth in the back room. Malone barely had time to get a new cigar lighted before she demanded, "Now. All about Delora Deanne."

"Well," Malone said, stalling desperately, "I met a very interesting person. Hazel Swackhammer."

This time it was Helene who frowned and said, "I think I've heard that name before somewhere."

"It's a name you'd remember if you ever had heard it before," Malone said.

He managed to keep the conversation on memorable names for several minutes, covering, along the way, Mr. Addison Sims of Seattle, and the science of memory association in general.

"But Delora Deanne," Jake said.

"There were two interesting people there too," Malone said, "Dennis Dennis. He writes the advertising. And Otis Furlong. He takes the pictures."

"Also easy names to remember," Helene said coldly, "and we've both met Otis Furlong. Now about—"

Malone decided it was time to order another drink, and conversation lagged until Joe the Angel had come and gone away again.

"Myrdell Harris," Malone mused. "Interesting girl. Hazel Swackhammer's executive assistant. And the receptionist, Tamia Tabet. Now there's an interesting girl for you."

Jake glared at him. "I've no doubt they're all interesting people, and they all have names that are easy to remember. And I have no doubt the receptionist's telephone number is easy to remember. But—"

"It is," Malone said. "In fact, she—"

"Leave your love life out of this," Jake said.

"Well, you see," the little lawyer said miserably, "it isn't just Delora Deanne. It's, well—" He paused and relit his cigar, very slowly. "I met four of them this morning. The other one was—she wasn't there."

Jake and Helene stared at him for a very long moment of silence. Finally Helene said accusingly, "Malone, you're —"

"I am not drunk," Malone said in an unhappy voice. "I just wish that I were."

"And I just wish you'd explain," Jake said.

Malone drew a long breath and dived in. He told them about the Delora Deannes he had met and described them: Gertrude Bragg, the face, Louella Frick, the feet, Eula Stolz, the torso and legs, and Rita Jardee, the voice. He mentioned that Eva Lou Strauss had been absent from the conference and skimmed over that lightly.

"I don't believe it," Helene said at last.

"I wish I didn't believe it either," Malone told her. "But I saw it myself." He went on about the genius of Otis Furlong who had created the composite, but nobody was paying attention. Then everyone was silent, brooding over another rye.

At last Jake sighed, and said, "Oh, well. Maybe I can think of a new twist for a quiz program."

Helene snorted in frankly unladylike derision. Then her eyes looked at Malone in a brief question. Malone gave her a faint nod of assent. She smiled her thanks.

"You'll think of something," she told Jake consolingly.

"Maybe a new angle on a Western," Jake muttered bitterly.

Malone said nothing, plunged in gloom.

Finally Helene wondered something vague about Maggie's brother's invention.

Jake said, "Let's not make life any more complicated than it is right now. Right as things stand, I'm practically obligated to sign up Joe the Angel's niece. Sign sight unseen."

"If she's really beautiful," Malone said, "and if she really sings like—that, and if she really dances like—so," he gestured gracefully, just barely missing his beer, "at least she'd be a novelty."

"But not Delora Deanne." Jake sighed.

There was another long and even more dismal silence.

"I can always go back to being a press agent," Jake said at last.

Suddenly Helene said, "Otis Furlong!"

"What about Otis Furlong?" Jake asked, not caring much.

"The genius that made the composite Delora Deanne photographs. Why couldn't the same thing be done on television?"

The two men stared at her. Finally Jake said, "It's impossible," and Malone said, "Now you're drunk."

She ignored Malone and told Jake, "How do you know it's impossible when you haven't tried it? Think of the Wright brothers."

"Think of Benjamin Franklin," Malone said, "and Robert Fulton, and Alexander Graham Bell."

Jake was staring intently and thoughtfully at nothing at all. "It's just barely possible," he said, very slowly. "Just barely. I haven't any idea how it could be done, but then, I haven't any reason why it couldn't be done, either."

That called for one more drink and they drank it enthusiastically to Otis Furlong, to Joe the Angel's niece, to Maggie's brother Luke, to Delora Deanne, and for no reason anyone could think of, to the Smith Brothers.

"A composite," Jake said. "The voice—dubbing it in is a cinch, of course. But the other girls—"

Malone described them all over again, going into more details.

Helene proposed that they visit Otis Furlong immediately after lunch.

Suddenly Jake paused in what he was saying, and looked searchingly at Malone.

"The girl that was missing this morning—?"

"Eva Lou Strauss," Malone said, not daring to look up. "She's the hands."

Jake said nothing. After one of the longest minutes he'd ever lived through, Malone finally met his eyes.

He knew perfectly well what the red-haired man was thinking about. Joe the Angel's quote from his cousin Rico. And Eva Lou Strauss on the missing list. Jake had figured it all out for himself.

Chapter Five

Otis Furlong's studio was on the same pleasant street as Delora Deanne, just off Michigan Boulevard. Soft snow was falling, the air smelled fresh and clean. The lake that showed beyond the Drive was gray and placid now. A delightful world to look at, Malone reflected, but right now a damned difficult one to live in.

A chaste metal sign beside the door of a small but flawless three-story house read *Furlong and Furlong*. Jake pushed the bell; a moment later the tall, handsome photographer greeted them warmly. He gestured toward the sign.

"An idea of my own," he explained. "If anyone bothers me about anything I don't want to be bothered about, I just say that the other Mr. Furlong is the one to see about that." He added, "Studio's upstairs."

Jake decided that changing the name on his office door to *Justus and Justus* would be an excellent idea, and made a mental note of it.

There was a short flight of stairs with a polished mahogany banister and, at their top, an enormous room, occupying a good two-thirds of the whole floor. At one end was another staircase, this one with intricately patterned bright tile steps, leading to a balcony where two carved wood doors indicated rooms beyond.

"Bedroom and bath upstairs," Otis Furlong said. "Kitchen

and darkrooms downstairs underneath. Designed it myself, re-modeled it myself. What are you drinking?"

They said that rye would be fine and yes, beer on the side even finer. Malone made himself comfortable and glanced around the big room.

It managed to be large and spacious, and still cozy, care-lessly cluttered and yet with an orderly comfort, highly util-itarian, with its lights, cameras and other equipment of the photographer's trade, and at the same time decorative.

Malone sighed and began to relax a little, momentarily putting all the Delora Deannes and Jake Justus Television Pro-duction Company out of mind. The ice in his stomach had gradually been warmed back into the damp concrete, and even that was beginning to disappear under the beneficent influ-ence of the rye.

There was one item in the room that bothered him, how-ever. He found himself continuing to stare at it, wondering if he ought to mention it or just ignore it completely. That was an enormous rose-colored porcelain bathtub in what was approx-imately the center of the vast room, and even to Malone's un-practiced eye as far as photographic studios were concerned, it didn't quite seem to belong there.

There was plenty more to look at in the room. A life-size portrait in oils of Delora Deanne on one wall, a collection of Oriental gods and their girl friends on a set of teakwood shelves, and on another wall a group of Japanese prints that indicated that their owner possessed not only artistic sen-sitivity and a fine eye for details, but a very broad mind as well. There was all that and more. *And*, the rose-colored bathtub. Even the rye didn't make it go away.

"Beautiful, isn't it," Otis Furlong said, following Malone's gaze. "Absolutely beautiful!" He sat down on a fat leather hassock, his elbows on his knees, his glass in one hand and his pipe in the other. "Borrowed it from that place with all the lovely plumbing fixtures down in the *Tribune* Building. But brother, if you think that's beautiful, just come and take a look at the water in it!" He gestured with his pipe.

Malone walked over and looked, fascinated. The water was indeed beautiful, of a delicate green, translucent hue, spangled with little white sparkles and feathers of rippled foam.

"Feel it," Otis Furlong said.

Malone felt, with one hesitant finger. It was cool, smooth, and yet springily solid to his touch.

"Lime gelatin," the photographer said. "A discovery of my own."

"Lovely!" Helene breathed.

"Not only that," Jake said almost reverently, "but it's probably the only body of water Florence Chadwick hasn't swum across."

"It's supposed to be Delora Deanne bath oil, or some such damn thing," Otis Furlong told them. "But slide Eula Stolz's torso into that, and—"

Malone knew what he was going to add. The rest of Delora Deanne. But the final photograph, he reflected with an uncomfortable pang, was going to be minus a pair of hands. And the artist didn't know that yet. Or—did he? Malone returned to his comfortable chair, reached for a fresh cigar, and picked up his glass.

The tall photographer looked uncomfortable, trying to decide how to talk his way out of what he'd unfortunately said. But it was Jake who spoke first.

"That's all right," Jake said. "About the composite. In fact, that's one reason we dropped by. Don't worry, we're the last people in the world who want it to leak out. But we do know everything about everything."

The little lawyer looked away hastily.

"Everything about the composite, I mean," Jake went on, and Malone breathed again.

"It's a work of genius!" Helene said, in a tone of voice that had melted stronger men than Otis Furlong would ever be, including half the police force of Chicago.

He beamed at her. "A very simple process," he told her. "Lots of photographers do it. But I do have a method of my own, one that I worked out myself, of course."

Jake took a long breath and asked, "Could such a process be applied to television?"

Nobody spoke for a while. Everybody looked hopefully at the photographer.

"Theoretically, yes," Otis Furlong said at last, a dreamy look in his eyes.

"Naturally," Jake said quickly, "if such a process could be developed for television, you'd get the full credit for it."

The dreamy look intensified. "I see no reason why it

couldn't," he said. "That is, theoretically. I'll have to do some thinking about it. Some real thinking about it." He paused. "I'll do that. I'll do some real, real thinking about it. Then I'll make some notes about it. And then we'll talk about it." He smiled at Jake.

Jake said that was fine, and yes, he would have another drink. Helene said that was wonderful, that Mr. Furlong was really a real, real genius, and yes, thanks, she would too. Malone held out his glass.

When the photographer was settled on his hassock again, Malone said, "Tell me all about these girls."

"The girls?" Furlong shrugged. "They're all right. Bunch of pretty good kids, but sort of dumb. Gertie's the dumbest of the lot. She's damn near classic. Steady, though; never blows up. Eula's a pest. Always yipping and yapping about something, she's too warm, she's too cold, she wants this, she wants that. Louella has a nasty temper and you never know when she'll get the old claws out. And Eva Lou is about as lazy as they make 'em, but basically she's just a good-natured, generous, lusty slob. I wonder where she was this morning."

So do I, Malone thought, so do I. He said, keeping his voice very steady, "She certainly has wonderful, beautiful hands."

"You said it, brother!" The photographer rose and went to a carved wood cabinet that stood against the wall. "Just made a very, very dream shot of 'em yesterday." He took out a large colored photograph and held it out to Malone.

This time the famous hands held a delicate crystal bowl, every exquisite finger perfectly posed, one wearing the huge opal ring that had become almost a trademark. Its colored lights seemed to be reflected, again and again, in the swirling mists and half-hinted flowers that formed the background.

"Funny thing about that opal," Otis Furlong said, indicating it with his pipe. "Hazel didn't like it at first. But Eva Lou couldn't get it off without having it sawed off. She wouldn't do that. So for once, Hazel gave in, and now it's famous. It certainly hasn't brought Eva Lou the customary bad luck."

Malone repressed a shudder and said nothing.

"Yeah, they're pretty good kids," Otis Furlong said again, replacing the picture and closing the cabinet. "Don't get along too well together, but we keep 'em apart as much as we can."

"How about their personal lives?" Malone asked.

Otis Furlong laughed. "Personal life? A Delora Deanne?" He laughed again. Then he turned to Jake. "Speaking of television, Dennis Dennis is anxious to meet you. Very anxious."

"I'm very anxious to meet him too," Jake said politely. "As soon as I get things a little more organized."

"Good man, Dennis," Furlong said. And to Malone, "And that was no joke about his alimony troubles. Wish he had a good lawyer."

"I wish so too," Malone said heartily. "But out of my line. Crime is my specialty."

"May come to that yet, if she doesn't stop bothering him," Otis Furlong said, relighting his pipe. "She's a pest. She's the kind of woman who inspires articles on marriage counseling in the women's magazines, with all the sympathy on her poor, abused side. Also, the kind that reads all the articles and takes all the advice. She worked so hard at making a go of their marriage that finally Dennis went."

He grinned at them, his good-looking face lighting up. "Me, I'm lucky in my ex-wife. Known her a long time. I was only her second. Rita's a swell kid, bit of a lush now and then, but lovely on the air. Never asks me for a dime."

For no apparent reason he went on. "I met Charlie Swackhammer once. Not a bad guy. Dennis knows him a little better, he's been around the outfit a lot longer than I have. Dennis says Hazel used to call him Cuddles. Swackhammer I mean, not Dennis."

"Is that really his name?" the lawyer asked.

"Dennis Dennis? Naturally not. Used to be Stubblebottom, or Flipstitch, or Featherfloof, or something like that. He was suddenly taken with poetry writing some years ago, and 'by Dennis Dennis' looked good at the top of a piece of paper. But he ended up being Delora Deanne's ghost writer just the same. Maybe Hazel picked him for his initials, I don't know. But he's a good guy. Not sour. Nothing can be sourer than a disappointed poet, but he's all right."

Except, Malone reflected, that sometimes the sourness didn't show on the surface, like a rosy apple that puckered your mouth when you bit into it unwarned.

They finished their drinks and rose to go. Otis Furlong went downstairs with them to the front door.

"Nice seeing you. And—about that composite, on television." His handsome brow puckered. "Very tricky. Very difficult. Maybe impossible. Probably very, very, terribly expensive. But I'll really think about it, I really will. And watch your foot on that bottom step, it's tricky."

They said thanks and good-by and started on their way. Malone promptly tripped on the bottom step, bruised his shin and swore.

"Cheer up, Jake," Helene said. "There's always Maggie's brother's camera. With eyes."

"Or you can always think up a new twist for a quiz program," Malone growled.

Jake told them both to go to hell and hailed a passing taxi.

Again Malone felt vaguely unhappy, without purpose, without destination. He supposed he might as well go back to his office, where Maggie had probably laid a folder of first-of-the-month correspondence on his desk. He wondered how soon Hazel Swackhammer's check would get there and how big it would be.

"I'm going to the office," he told them in answer to their questioning look. "And alone. I've got to think."

"Malone," Helene said accusingly, "you're worried."

He denied it furiously.

"If it's money," Jake said wickedly, "if a little loan will tide you over—"

The little lawyer repressed an indignant impulse, and just in time.

It ended with their dropping him at the office, with a promise to see him soon. And very soon.

Maggie looked up from her desk as he walked into the anteroom. Her eyes were anxious. "Malone, there's someone here to see you. He insisted on going right on in." She seemed a little pale.

Gus Madrid rose from a chair as Malone entered the office. He looked much more menacing than he had in Joe the Angel's City Hall Bar, and considerably taller. At the moment, Malone felt, something just over seven feet.

"Well, Malone," he said grimly, "let's don't horse around. I don't waste any time, understand?" He thrust his huge hands in his pockets. "So tell me right off, where's my girl? And what do you think you're going to do to her?"

Chapter Six

"Now let's both be perfectly reasonable about this," Malone said very calmly, leaving the door to the anteroom wide open. He walked over and sat down behind his desk and began unwrapping a fresh cigar without any noticeable tremor. "I not only don't know where your girl is, I don't even know who she is."

The gunman said that Malone was a liar, with a number of adjectives.

"You're wrong," the little lawyer said, "though if you were right, I'd be leading a very interesting life. No, you've come to the wrong missing girls' bureau, pal."

Gus Madrid's answer was another grim look.

Malone sighed. "But I'm always glad to help. Just what girl are you so concerned about?"

"I only got the one girl," Gus Madrid growled. "She's all at once gone. I want to know where she's at. I don't want nothing to happen to her. And if anything has happened to her, by any chance, already—" He broke off with a threatening scowl.

"I sincerely hope nothing has happened to her, or will," Malone said, and meant it from the bottom of his heart.

Gus Madrid looked puzzled. "You're mixed up with that face-powder outfit somehow," he said. "And I heard what Joe the Angel was shooting off about a while back, about cutting off her hands."

"You misunderstood," Malone told him smoothly. "Do I look like a man who'd go around doing things like that?"

The gunman didn't say no, but then, he didn't say yes either. "Well, anyway, she's gone, and nobody knows where she's went to." His eyes narrowed. "You know who I mean. Evie Lou."

31

"Oh, her," Malone said. He waited for more information. Finally he gave up and said, "So she's your girl, eh?"

Gus Madrid answered with an angry look, as though Malone should have known it all along.

"Well," the lawyer said after another long wait, "how did you expect me to know she's your girl when I've never so much as seen her?"

"Evie Lou," Madrid said. "Last name's Strauss. Works in that face-powder factory. Some kind of modeling. Now she's gone. You was there this morning and then you asked Rico di Angelo to cut off her hands."

"Believe me," Malone said earnestly, "I went there on other business, and I didn't ask Rico to do anything of the sort." He considered calling Rico for confirmation and decided against it. Rico was sure to come up with the wrong answer.

"Then why did you go there this morning?"

Malone sighed. "About some newspaper stories. Some model has been getting her name in the papers and her boss doesn't like it. But not Eva Lou." He felt certain that was the truth. From the picture he'd seen of the missing model, she didn't seem the type who could be taking a rich playboy for his extra cash-type spending money. And from his knowledge of Gus Madrid, he doubted that anybody, rich playboy or not, would go fooling around with his girl.

"Y'know," the big gunman said grudgingly, "y'got me almost, but not entirely, about half-convinced." Just as Malone was beginning to breathe a little easier, he went on, "But just the same. Me, I'm sticking closer to you than a brother, Siamese type, until she shows up." He seemed to be settling into the big leather chair as though he intended to stay there for the duration, however long that might be.

Malone said, "That's going to play hell with my love life, chum." He added, in a hopeful voice, "What's the matter, don't you trust me?"

"I trust ya, and I don't trust ya," Gus Madrid said. "And me sticking right with ya is how much I don't."

Malone sighed, and hoped something would turn up. It did. There were faint sounds in the anteroom. Maggie called, "Mrs. Justus is here," and Helene appeared in the doorway, a pale vision of fabulous furs and breathtaking loveliness.

"A confidential client," Malone explained to the gunman. "Do you mind?"

"Not at all, friend, not at all." Madrid lumbered to his feet and started for the door. "But I'll be right out in the hall, remember." The smile on his heavy face was a leer.

For the second time that day Malone repressed an aggressive impulse just in time.

Helene waited until the door was closed, and then said, "I just stopped by to ask how you made out with Jake this morning."

"Fine," Malone said.

She gave him a smile that he wouldn't have sold for a Texas oil well. "It's just a matter of time, Malone."

"Sure," he said, "sure, sure, sure. Don't worry about Jake. If this composite thing doesn't work, something will." He managed a weak smile and added superfluously, "Don't worry about a thing."

"Just so he doesn't ever know," she said. "And I can't thank you enough."

"Oh, yes you can," Malone said. "Did you see that oversize orangutan that just went into the hall?"

She nodded.

"He's still out in the hall. He's keeping a very determined eye on me."

"Why?"

"That's his business. But do you think you could lure him away from here so that I can get down the freight elevator?"

"Easiest thing in the world," Helene said, with a blithe assurance she hadn't learned at Miss Bridges' Finishing School. "I'll lure him so far away you could come down the front elevator with a brass band, if you wanted to. But what's the occasion?"

"I've got to go find a girl," Malone told her.

She lifted one delicately arched eyebrow. "So early in the afternoon? And you don't want your oversize pal along?"

"Damn it," Malone said. "It's his girl I'm looking for."

"Why can't he find his own girls?"

Malone looked at her helplessly and said, "You wouldn't understand."

She shrugged her shoulders and said, "All right, John Alden, play it your own way. You did me a favor, now I'll do you one." She smiled again and was gone.

He sat frowning at his ash tray, collecting his thoughts. Obviously, the place to start was Eva Lou's apartment. He didn't really expect to learn anything, or perhaps even to get in, but at least it would give him something to do until those formless thoughts began to jell.

He'd heard from Hazel Swackhammer—Delora De-anne—at ten o'clock that morning, and now, only a few hours later, he was beginning to feel the discomforting presence of something very wrong indeed. He didn't quite know what it was, but it was something far more annoying than mere scandals in newspaper columns, and even more horrible than a pair of embalmed hands in the morning mail.

He cursed himself for a superstitious Irishman, and started for the door, just in time to meet Jake coming in. At exactly that moment the telephone rang, and both men stood still while Maggie answered it. Malone could hear von Flanagan's deep rumble, and shook his head furiously.

Maggie said smoothly, "I'm sorry, I don't know what time he'll be back," and hung up. She turned to Malone and said, "Well, when will you be back?"

"I don't know," the little lawyer growled. "I forgot to read my horoscope this morning." He grabbed Jake's arm and hurried him down the hall to the freight elevator.

Jake finally caught his breath and said, "Creditor chasing you?"

"Right now a creditor chasing me," Malone said between his teeth, "would be like a bloodhound chasing a turnip!"

Outside the dingy old building that had housed his office through more triumphs and troubles than he cared to remember, he peered warily up and down the street. The coast was clear.

"Come on," Malone said. "Washington Street is no place to hold a quiet conversation." He led in the direction of the sanctuary of Joe the Angel's City Hall Bar. Whatever she did, Helene wouldn't have lured Gus Madrid there.

A quick peek through the window showed he was right. He settled down in one of the back booths with a comfortable sense of safety.

"Now," Jake said. "Give."

"Believe me," Malone said. "One drink and I can explain everything."

They waited until Joe the Angel had come and gone away again, and then Jake said, "One of the models was missing from this morning's chummy little get-together. The one who posed for the hands. Then there was this business about your talking to Rico. It goes together, and yet it doesn't."

"It does," Malone said. He added fervently, "But I wish it didn't."

There was nothing to do but tell Jake the whole story, and Malone immediately did, omitting only the details of Gus Madrid—no point in worrying Jake unnecessarily—and some personal plans regarding Tamia Tabet, the cuddly blond receptionist—that was none of Jake's business anyway.

He finished with, "I didn't tell any of this in front of Helene, because you know how Helene is."

Jake said, "Very wise," nodding at his glass. "Very, very wise. I do know how Helene is."

"So don't you tell her," Malone warned him. "I have enough problems to cope with, without Helene helping me to solve a possible murder case."

Jake nodded again, and said even more solemnly, "But I'll help you. You helped me, and now I'll help you. And it certainly does look like murder. Where do we start?"

"Where she lived," Malone said. "The missing girl, I mean. That's where I was going when I ran into you."

This time Jake's nod was positively owlish. "Very, very sound reasoning. Unless I'm drunk." He looked at his wrist watch. "No, I'm not. Let's go there before we are."

Out in the street, there was still no sign of either Helene or Gus Madrid. Malone hailed a passing taxi, consulted his notebook and gave the driver Eva Lou Strauss's address.

"It's there not being any kidnap message that bothers me," Malone said. "Because there should have been."

Jake agreed that there should. "The usual routine," he said thoughtfully, "would have been a disappearance. Then a message with a demand for money. And then the little gift of hands."

Malone shuddered.

"Of course, there may have been a message by now."

"I doubt it," Malone said. "Hazel Swackhammer would have called me."

They worried in silence for the rest of the brief ride. Malone said, as the cab slowed to a stop, "If I don't hear from her in the meantime, I'll go over there in the morning and ask some more questions." Including, he reminded himself, a polite financial demand of his own.

The Brindle Arms, a seven-story brick apartment building set flush with the sidewalk, boasted a small lobby crowded with bits of imitation medieval art, a desk and a switchboard in front of pigeonholes for mail, an aging potted fern, and a self-service elevator. Jake and Malone strode blithely past the desk with its magazine-reading occupant, carelessly tossed ashes at the potted fern and reached the elevator.

"So far, so good," Jake said in a congratulatory tone.

Neither of them had noticed the sleek black sedan that had slid to a quiet stop just across the street.

Chapter Seven

A cart full of linens stood at the open door of apartment 312, and the sound of a lazily pushed vacuum cleaner came down the hall. Malone and Jake walked up to the door and peered in at a furnished apartment that was like practically every other furnished apartment in its price range in the city of Chicago. It was just a little too elaborate and just a little too shabby, but it was comfortable. The pictures on the wall obviously went with the apartment, the television set just as obviously didn't. There was a faint and not at all disagreeable aroma of tobacco smoke, long years of coffee-making and cooking, perfume, gin, and human habitation.

A large-bosomed, red-faced cleaning woman switched off the vacuum, took a limp cigarette from her mouth, and gave them a well-what-do-you-want? look.

"I'm John J. Malone," he said. He waved vaguely. "This is Mr. Justus."

The broad red face blossomed into a smile like summer sunrise. "I've heard of you, Malone. If you're looking for Eva Lou Strauss, she's not in. But come in and sit down just the same." She abandoned the vacuum cleaner. "My name's Geragthy, Mary Geragthy."

They said they were pleased to meet her, came in and sat down.

"I know she's not in," the little lawyer said. "I wonder where she's gone."

"No knowing," Mary Geragthy said. She shrugged her shoulders. "Here, there and everywhere she goes. Gone on a trip most likely, this time. She left yesterday."

Malone sighed. "If I knew what clothes she'd taken with her, I might be able to figure out where she's gone. I don't suppose you'd know?"

She flung open a closet, glanced through dresser drawers. Malone and Jake glanced with her. Not a great assortment of clothes, gaudy for the most part, fairly good, but none expensive. There was lingerie in exuberant hues and lavish with lace. And a lot of cheap but elaborately seductive housegowns and negligees.

"Funny, it's her summer suit that's gone." Mrs. Geragthy said, "and in weather like this, too." She shook her head and clucked her tongue.

"Florida?" Jake suggested hopefully.

"Most like," she said. "Or California, or Cuba."

Another verse from that song popped nonsensically into Malone's mind, ending with:

> But she ran away to Cuba,
> The weather was to blame . . .

"She sure didn't take much with her," the jovial woman said. "Suit, blouse, and some underwear. Most like she'll be back before too long."

Malone winced, said nothing, and kept his eyes away from Jake.

Mary Geragthy paused suddenly in the act of opening another bureau drawer. "Well! She didn't take her gloves!"

The two men peered with a kind of fascinated horror at the satin-lined drawer the cleaning woman had just opened. It was full of gloves: suède gloves, kid gloves, silk gloves, all kinds of gloves, embroidered, spangled, and even jeweled. And all of them very obviously, to Malone's practiced eye, of a cost way out of proportion to the rest of Eva Lou Strauss's wardrobe.

"Not one pair of them did she take!" Mrs. Geragthy said. "Not one! And her fair wild about gloves, she was. Always buying new ones, never throwing the old ones away. Queer, she'd

not take at least one pair. Wouldn't you think she'd need them,
even with a summer suit?"

This time, Malone not only winced, but shuddered.

"It is cold, at that," Mrs. Geragthy said. She went into the
kitchenette and came back with a bottle of Scotch and three
glasses. "Eva Lou won't mind. Generous as the world is round,
that girl."

With the drinks downed, she sat down comfortably and
rambled on amiably about Eva Lou.

No, she didn't know much about what Miss Strauss did for
a living, but she didn't make much, poor dear. Lovely girl, and
always friendly and more than good-hearted.

"Men friends?" Jake asked.

Oh yes indeed, she had men friends. Two of them, and
both well-fixed. She could have lived a lot better than this, she
could. But she didn't like to take presents from them, except
little things.

No, it was seldom if ever that she went out with them, no
indeed. Most always she and one of her friends spent the evening here with the television and a good bottle of Scotch.

Yes, she might have gone away on a trip with one of them,
but she never had before. In fact, she'd never gone away on
any kind of a trip before. Funny thing that she would, and not
leave one word for anyone.

No, Mrs. Geragthy didn't know who either of the men
friends were, except that one of them looked tough.

There wasn't much else to be learned about Eva Lou
Strauss, and after a while the two men went away. Malone still
felt unhappy and vaguely purposeless. Eva Lou Strauss's
Scotch hadn't really helped much. The snow was coming down
a little faster now, beginning to cake crisply on the sidewalks,
but Eva Lou had gone away in her summer suit, leaving all her
cherished gloves behind.

They walked up to Division Street and hailed a passing
taxi.

"The office?" Jake asked.

Malone shook his head. "No. Not yet. I want to stay away
from there for a while."

Jake frowned. "I really mean it," he said. "If it's a matter of
a creditor, you might as well borrow some of your own dough
back."

"It isn't," Malone said laconically.

"Von Flanagan?"

"Now why on earth," Malone said, with a faint show of irritation, "would I be dodging von Flanagan?"

"Why indeed," Jake said blithely, "except that the rest of Eva Lou Strauss may have turned up, and he just might have stumbled on the fact that her boss called you in this morning."

Malone said, "Shut up," and added, "anyway, that isn't it."

Jake sighed. "Somebody's boy friend?"

Malone nodded and let it go at that. He said a quiet thanksgiving that Jake didn't know anything about Gus Madrid. And, even more important, that he didn't know what Helene was up to right now.

"The apartment then," Jake said. He gave the address and the taxi started through the snow. The black sedan moved out from the curb and followed, discreetly and unnoticed, at a distance.

For once, Malone didn't feel the immediate comfort and security that usually enveloped him when he stepped inside the apartment Jake and Helene had lived in since the eventful, and in some ways, terrible, day of their wedding. Instead, he found himself wondering if the rent were paid. He glanced around unhappily. Everything looked exactly the same, and yet the feeling of everything was different. A lot had happened here, not all of it pleasant, but all of it exciting, and he had an uncomfortable feeling that a lot more was just about to happen.

Jake came back from the kitchenette with a tray of drinks and said, "Helene'll be along any minute now and make dinner. She's taken up cooking for a hobby."

"Very domestic of her," the little lawyer said. He began worrying not only about the rent, but about how long the groceries would be paid for.

Something would work out. Something had to.

Finally he said, "Better call my office. Maggie might just be worried."

Or that check from Hazel Swackhammer might have come in.

No, nothing in the mail. But von Flanagan had called. And a Miss Myrdell Harris wanted him to call her back. Said it was important.

Malone mentally told von Flanagan to go to hell, and dialed Myrdell Harris' number.

The voice that came over the wire with, "Yes, this is Myr-dell Harris," was soft, flutelike, and almost alluring.

"You are not Myrdell Harris," Malone said accusingly.

There was a laugh. Then she said, "Would you really rather I sounded this way, Mr. Malone?" in the yipping twang he'd heard first thing that morning.

Malone stared stupidly at the telephone and said, "I beg your pardon?"

"Or perhaps you'd rather I sounded like this, Mr. Malone?" It was a more than passable imitation of the famous and well-nigh golden voice of Delora Deanne.

"I'll be damned," Malone said. "I mean—I'll save the questions till later."

"A little later this evening?" she said, in what he de-cided—and hoped—was her own voice. "At my apartment?" She gave him the address, a famous one on Lake Shore Drive.

Malone promised he'd be there, and hung up.

Jake raised eyebrows like question marks.

"Bad enough," the little lawyer growled, "that Delora De-anne turns out to be five girls, one of them missing. Now Myr-dell Harris turns out to be one girl with at least three voices." He paused and drew a long slow breath. "I just hope the com-parison ends there!"

Chapter Eight

Malone repeated it glumly. "Five girls with one name. One girl with three voices. One guy with two names. One guy with one name who's two guys."

Helene kicked the door shut, put down a shopping bag, and asked the little lawyer very solicitously if he'd like to lie down for a while before dinner.

Jake sighed. "I peg the one guy with two names. Dennis Dennis. But the other, no."

"Otis Furlong," Malone explained patiently. "Furlong and Furlong, only there's only one Furlong."

Jake said, "Oh, that," and scowled.

"All at one time," Helene said blithely, "we've got quintuple, triple, and two sets of double schizophrenia. And if you count Maggie's brother's camera with all the eyes—"

She vanished into the kitchenette before Malone had a chance to suggest that she might like to lie down before dinner.

Dinner was not an outstanding success. Not that Helene didn't, surprisingly, turn out to be a more than adequate cook, but the effort of avoiding the mention of Delora Deanne, composites, murder, disappearances and hands got heavier and heavier. It was disconcerting, Malone felt. Or better, disconcentrating. Lovely word. He brightened up at having thought of it, muttered it out loud, and received two startled looks and utter silence for a while.

Then too, Helene worried him. She seemed anxious, and at the same time, secretly pleased with herself. He'd seen similar looks before on her exquisite face, and knew he had occasion for worry. Then too, there was her smile. Usually whenever Helene smiled, the effect was as though someone had just turned on all the electric lights in a room, but this time it seemed a little too smug to suit him.

Finally he finished his coffee, said good night, added that he was going to see a girl about three voices, and went away moodily, hoping that Jake and Helene would mind their own business for the evening. Though, he remembered with a slight wince, this was their business too.

This time he didn't miss the black sedan. It was parked conspicuously at the entrance to the building.

"Get in, chum," Gus Madrid said, opening the door.

The little lawyer hesitated a minute, decided that this was a time for wisdom rather than valor, and got in.

"Good," the gunman said. "Me, I don't like trouble. I'm a very peaceable type person. This way you don't scram down no dark side streets, and you don't fool me with no blonde."

Malone counted to ten very carefully, and then said, "Blonde?" in an innocent but slightly squeaky voice.

"Never no mind," Madrid said. "I know all about that blonde." His attitude made it plain he had no more to say on that subject. He started the car and said, "So where are we going?"

"I'm going to see a girl," Malone said cautiously. He gave the Lake Shore Drive address.

Madrid snorted and drove silently through the softly falling snow. At the impressive apartment building he parked the car, remarked that Malone's babes had nice, expensive tastes in dwelling places, and got out with Malone.

"Look here," Malone said desperately, "you can't come in with me."

"And just who," the big gunman demanded, "is going to stop me from coming with you?" He glowered down at Malone.

"It—" Malone paused. "On this particular date, I don't need a chaperone."

Gus Madrid produced another leer. Then, "How do I know it's not my girl?"

"Because it isn't," Malone said, wishing he had a slightly less inadequate answer.

"How do I know my girl isn't hidden wherever you're going?" He added, "I got a suspicious type mind."

After some discussion, they reached a compromise. Gus Madrid would accompany Malone to Myrdell Harris' apartment, satisfy himself that Eva Lou Strauss was nowhere on the premises, and then wait outside.

Upstairs, the little lawyer looked appreciatively around. Executive assistants evidently did better for themselves than secretaries. The big living room was not only gracefully but expensively furnished; Malone also knew something about the rents in that particular building. Furthermore, Myrdell's smoky taupe hostess pajamas, that came close to matching the color of her eyes, had undoubtedly come from one of the shops that had cost him entirely too much in the past.

She looked inquiringly at Gus Madrid, and Malone hastily introduced them. "My bodyguard," he explained.

Myrdell Harris lifted delicate eyebrows and said, "How quaint!"

The gunman glared at her, announced that he was going to look through the apartment, and did. "I'm just looking for my girl," he said after he finished. He added, "Eva Lou Strauss," and Malone's heart hit bottom.

"How coincidental!" Myrdell Harris said with a misty smile.

That one went so far over Gus Madrid's head that he didn't even swing at it.

"Well," he said, "she ain't here." He paused. "Well—" At

last he said, "Well, I'll be waiting downstairs, Malone," and went out.

The little lawyer drew a long, relieved breath and sank down in the satin chair Myrdell Harris had indicated with an airy, floating gesture.

"He isn't exactly chatty, is he?" she said. "Drink?"

Malone nodded. A minute later the feel of a tall glass in his hand gave him a little reassurance. He decided that she had been talking in her natural voice at last. It was a pleasant one.

Evidently she'd guessed what he was thinking about. "Always," she said, "I've been very good at imitating voices," sounding exactly like Hazel Swackhammer.

Malone jumped and said, "Don't do that!"

She smiled again and relaxed against the blue-gray cushions of her chair. Malone found himself relaxing with her. Here he was, he reflected, with a whole evening to spend, with nothing—well, with very little—on his mind, a drink, a pleasant companion, a charming apartment. If only she had been his type. Delora Deanne, for instance. Or even better, the cuddly little pink-and-white-and-gold darling behind her desk in the blue-and-gold reception room of Delora Deanne.

"Your bodyguard," she said dreamily, bringing him right back to nasty reality. "It is coincidental, isn't it? That Eva Lou Strauss was his girl." She sighed faintly and said, "Oh, well, she always was the earthy type."

Malone noted her choice of tenses and was very quiet, waiting.

Myrdell Harris shrugged her shoulders and breathed, "She'll turn up, one way or another."

John J. Malone didn't like the way she'd phrased that, no, not one little bit. He wondered if executive assistants opened their employers' mail in the morning. He went right on keeping very quiet.

"They always turn up," she went on, "that kind of girl. Frankly, I think Hazel is wasting her money, hiring you to look for her."

"I beg your pardon?" Malone asked politely. He wondered if she called Mrs. Swackhammer Hazel to her face.

"But it's her business." This time her smile was a shade more definite. "Enough of all that. Do tell me all about yourself."

"My dear lady," Malone said. "My dear girl—" He spread his hands in a deprecating gesture and did his best to look as though he were her abject slave. "Tell me all about you. The voices—"

Again the dreamy smile. "I planned to be an actress. But I was best at imitations. Then I decided the business world held a more lucrative future. So—"

Definitely lucrative, Malone reflected with another look around the apartment, at the hostess pajamas, and at the diamond bracelet that was too modest to be anything but real. He wondered why she'd sent for him and just how he was going to go about finding out.

"I used to tease Rita Jardee no end by imitating her," she said, and she sounded exactly like the golden voice. "Then one day she got furious, and Hazel made me stop it." That was Hazel Swackhammer to the last clipped consonant. "Rita's hated me ever since. Jealousy."

Malone said nothing and looked curious.

Myrdell smiled. "Otis and I are nothing but friends," she half-whispered. "And Rita's through with him anyway." She changed the subject and the voice abruptly. "I talk this way to strangers and creditors." It was the unpleasant twang.

She lit a cigarette and blew a cloud of smoke around herself. The effect was pleasing and, Malone observed, she knew it. He remembered the interested and appraising way she had run her dreamy eyes over Gus Madrid's muscles, and almost wished he didn't prefer blondes.

"Tell me, Mr. Malone," she shot at him suddenly, "do you really think you can find Eva Lou Strauss?"

"Why does everyone assume I'm looking for her?" Malone snapped. "Why do *you* assume that I am?"

Myrdell added a little more smoke to the effect and said, "Leave it at 'everyone.' Your bodyguard—"

"Mr. Madrid," Malone said stiffly, "happens to have a girl named Eva Lou Strauss. His business is none of my business."

"Which is?"

He almost said, "Looking for Eva Lou Strauss." The conversation was getting him nowhere. "My business is the honorable practice of law."

Something about that seemed to amuse her.

"Look," Malone said, "what gives you that impression?"

"That you're a lawyer?"

"Damn it," Malone said. "You know exactly what I mean."

"Oh," she said. "That." She paused. "This morning Eva Lou Strauss didn't show up. Hazel gave me your name and told me to send for you."

"It was about another matter entirely," Malone said. He wished he knew whether or not she knew about the little package in that morning's mail, and looked intently into her eyes. It was like looking into a shadowed mist. "About some column items that had upset Mrs. Swackhammer."

She said, "Oh, that," again, as though Delora Deanne got involved in scandal every day of the week. "Your gangster friend—your bodyguard—"

"Has a girl named Eva Lou Strauss," Malone said. "All right, the same Eva Lou Strauss. Let's not go into all that again. Now you tell me, what do you know about Eva Lou Strauss?"

"Nothing," Myrdell Harris said. "Except that she's missing."

They seemed to have completed a circle, Malone reflected, and he wasn't going to go around it again.

Suddenly she said, "I do know a lot of things. Other things, I mean."

"Such as—?" Malone asked hopefully.

"Just things." She put her half-smoked cigarette out lazily. "I'm not just Hazel's executive assistant, I'm her confidential assistant." She let it go at that and gave every indication that she meant to keep right on doing so.

Malone sighed. "If it's any of my business, why did you ask me to come over tonight?"

Again that vague, dreamy smile. "Shall we leave it—that I wanted to get better acquainted?" She reached for another cigarette. "It's possible as this goes along, I might be helpful to you. And you might be helpful to me."

Any time she was helpful to him, Malone told himself, it was going to cost him money.

"As what goes along?"

"Oh—" her gesture might have meant anything—"all this."

"Including Eva Lou Strauss?"

She nodded. "Including Eva Lou Strauss."

"Do you know where she is?"

"I've already told you that I didn't. But she'll turn up sooner or later."

No, he very definitely didn't like the way she said it. "What do you know that might be helpful?"

"Oh—" Again the gesture. "Just—things." And again the smile. "I'll keep in touch with you as things go along."

The little lawyer rose, briefly considered shaking her, and decided to give up.

At the door she said, "I need to be very careful. You see, everybody—nearly everybody—hates me."

He managed to say something in the way of a gallant protest and headed down the corridor. It had been a thoroughly unsatisfactory visit from every viewpoint. He tried to console himself with the fact that she hadn't been able to find out anything from him either, but it didn't help. He felt irritated. Frustrated. What was that beautiful word? Disconcentrated, that was it. To get undisconcentrated, he needed a drink, several drinks, and a quiet place to do some heavy thinking. What would the cuddly receptionist be doing this evening? Then he remembered Gus Madrid.

The big gunman was almost friendly as they got in the car. "Where next?"

Malone said, "I don't know."

"And Malone, don't you go telling babes I'm your bodyguard, understand. Me, I'm not nobody's bodyguard. Okay you tell 'em I'm your chauffeur. But no bodyguard."

He slammed the car door and went on. "Okay, drive you where to next?"

"At least," Malone told him glumly, "you're saving me a lot of taxi fares."

That brought him to an abrupt and hasty review of his finances. Something under twenty dollars, he estimated, not counting a possible extension of credit at Joe the Angel's City Hall Bar.

He glanced at his uninvited companion. Yes, Gus Madrid looked prosperous. And something had to be done about those finances, fast.

"Tell you what," he said almost happily. "I know where there's a good all-night poker game—"

Chapter Nine

"Never mind what happened," the little lawyer growled. "And never mind giving me any sympathy. Just say that last night I made the biggest mistake of my life."

Jake closed the office door behind him. "Who's the big goon sitting out there?"

"Him?" Malone winced. "A damned good poker player."

"You may not need sympathy," Jake said, "but you look as though you needed a drink. And what was the mistake?"

Malone looked at him through tired, red-rimmed eyes and said, "Jake, there are times when I begin to think it was a mistake ever being born at all."

"If it's a matter of money—" Jake began.

Malone considered borrowing back a hundred from Jake. After all, it would be an investment in Jake's future success, in a sense. He considered borrowing from a long list of people who probably wouldn't have it anyway. He considered a lot of things, including going to bed and sleeping all day. Then he shook his head.

"It isn't that bad," he said bravely.

True, the check from Hazel Swackhammer might come in a later mail.

"How's Helene?" he asked, hoping she was still asleep.

"Fine," Jake said. "She was up at the crack of dawn, and she's been gone since breakfast."

Malone scowled. There was nothing to do but hope for the best, but he had a feeling it wasn't going to do any good.

"She said she was going shopping," Jake said. He looked worried. "Malone—whatever happens, Helene mustn't find out about—this. It's something she shouldn't be mixed up in."

The little lawyer nodded. True, in the past, Helene had been mixed up in a lot of things, of which murder had sometimes been the mildest, but he knew how Jake felt because he felt the same way. Helene sometimes had a way of complicating things, which he didn't like to contemplate in connection with the present tangle.

"Anyway," Jake said, "if she were to find out about it *now*—after we've already kept it a secret from her—" He didn't need to say another word.

Malone sighed. It would probably take a miracle to keep Helene in the dark, but at least he could hope for one. He said, "How's the television business?"

"Fine," Jake said bitterly. "Now look, Malone. Something's going to have to be done about all this. I called the Strauss girl's place. She hasn't come back."

"So did I," Malone said.

"She's got to be found, Malone." Dead or alive, his tone added.

Malone made a sweeping gesture that included not only Chicago, but the North and South American continents. "Where? Where do we look? Where do we start?"

"Don't be a defeatist," Jake said firmly. He added in a milder tone, "Though it's going to be like looking for a needle in a haystack."

"A haystack," Malone said in a gloomy tone, "entirely composed of last straws." He glowered at Jake as though he were personally responsible for most of them. "If you're going to just sit there and brood, you might as well go do it in your own office."

Jake said, "At this hour, the corridor outside my office is littered with actors, writers, musicians, and odds and ends of people waiting for Mr. Jake Justus, very important producer."

"Maybe Eva Lou Strauss will be there," the lawyer said. "Maybe she's just a frustrated actress." He thought about Myrdell Harris and wondered if he ought to tell Jake about his completely fruitless visit with her. No, no point to it. Then he thought about Myrdell Harris imitating the golden Delora Deanne voice. In a pinch, she could do the same job on a Delora Deanne TV show, if there ever was one. That is, if anything happened to Rita Jardee. As far as he knew, nothing had, yet. He found himself wondering how Rita Jardee's voice could be sent through the mail to Hazel Swackhammer, and found the thought so disquieting that he abandoned it at once.

He decided to drive the thought out of his mind by telling Jake all about Myrdell Harris, complete with voices. Also, complete with lack of information.

Jake scowled and said, "If you'd stayed there and tended to business last night, instead of getting mixed up in a poker game—"

"It wasn't for pleasure," Malone said wearily. "Just call it an ill-timed investment."

Jake looked at him suspiciously. "And by the way, since when do you keep a spare poker player sitting around in your front office?"

Malone sighed. "Oh, all right. He's keeping an eye on me because he's looking for Eva Lou Strauss, and he thinks I know where she is." He explained the details.

"Well," Jake said at last, "with enough people looking for Eva Lou Strauss—" He paused, looked sympathetically at Malone and said, "Maybe he'll get tired of waiting and go looking for her himself."

"If he doesn't," Malone said, "I'm staying right where I am. He's not only an expensive person to play poker with, he's a terrible driver."

"Well," Jake said again, "well—" He rose, adjusted his topcoat and started for the door. As he reached it, a sudden inspiration seized him. He flung the door open wide, and said loudly to Malone, "Then I'll go right over and see this Strauss girl. Maybe she'll listen to reason and come back."

He closed the door quickly before the little lawyer could say a word, leaving him sitting behind his desk in popeyed protest.

"Mr. Justus," Maggie said hopefully, "my brother Luke—"

"Later," Jake said. "Definitely, but also, later." He pushed on into the corridor.

The elevator door opened. Jake stepped in, noting with pride that the big gunman had stepped right in behind him. Getting rid of him might prove a problem later, but at least for the moment he'd gotten him away from Malone.

He paused a moment on the sidewalk, blinking in the sunlight reflected on the already soot-smudged snow. A place to think seemed to be called for, and fast. Luring Gus Madrid away from Malone's office had seemed like a brilliant inspiration at the time; now he was beginning to look dubiously and uncomfortably at the immediate future. He decided that it was something like having captured an untamed water buffalo.

He realized that he was heading in the general direction of Joe the Angel's, and went on a little more purposefully. That was as good a place to think as any.

A few minutes later he settled down on a bar stool and noted, with a mixture of satisfaction and discomfort that Gus Madrid had also settled, a few stools down. He ordered a rye and sat staring at it. There was a possibility that he might go out through the door leading to the storage cellar, thence to an opening into the uncharted—for him, at least—labyrinth that lay under Chicago's Loop.

After a second rye he discarded the cellar exit plan as both impractical and undignified. Joe the Angel wouldn't lift a fraction of an eyebrow if he were to go exploring, but he certainly wouldn't permit the big gunman to follow. Besides, Jake thought, he would probably get lost himself.

With the third rye, Joe the Angel propped his elbows confidingly on the polished bar. "Jake. My niece—"

"Sings like the birds," Jake said. "Dances like a spring breeze. Beautiful as the stars, but friendlier."

"You said it." Joe the Angel glowed.

"But," Jake said firmly, "later. When I have my show a little more organized."

Joe the Angel sighed, and changed the subject. "Malone. I worry about him."

"Me too," Jake said. "I worry about him all the time."

"But not like I worry, Jake. My cousin Rico—" he paused, shook his head. "I don't like this. This cutting off of hands."

Jake became very uncomfortably aware of Gus Madrid four feet away. He said, very confidentially, "Just between us, Malone's been working too hard. Don't worry about whatever Rico said. Nothing to it. But Malone gets little fancies, sometime. Nothing serious." He hoped he sounded convincing, and felt like Judas.

The booth telephone ringing was a welcome diversion. Again a sleepy-eyed *American* reporter got up to answer it. Again the dingy white parakeet said, "Ring, ring, ring," in a nasty voice.

And again Joe the Angel glowed. "Very smart, that bird. Very rare bird."

"If he's so smart," Jake said, "why don't you teach him to answer the phone instead of talking about it?"

Joe the Angel looked at him coldly and went away to wipe up a purely imaginary spot at the far end of the bar.

Jake sighed and went back to considering his next move. He couldn't stay here indefinitely. For one thing, Malone himself would show up sooner or later, and the luring away of Gus Madrid would have been wasted. On the other hand, there seemed no place else to go. Certainly not back to the apartment. He wasn't going to let the big gunman find out where he lived, and possibly encounter Helene.

Well, as Malone had pointed out, there was always his own office. Gus Madrid would be welcome to park outside in the corridor as long as he liked.

He ambled slowly up to Wacker Drive and across the bridge to the Wrigley Building. There he moved more briskly, giving the briefest of greetings to the assorted hopefuls in the lobby.

Two more hopefuls were outside his office when he arrived, with Gus Madrid lingering down the corridor. He recognized them as unemployed actors and managed another brief greeting.

"'Lo, Jake, just dropped by in case you were in—"

"Mr. Justus, I happened to be in the building, and—"

He waved at them, muttered something about having to make a few phone calls and seeing them later, and went on in. He felt a little more secure with the office door closed behind him, and not just from Gus Madrid, either.

The anteroom needed dusting. For that matter, so did his own office. He located a cloth in an otherwise empty drawer and spent a few minutes housecleaning. Then he arranged and rearranged papers on the desk. Finally he opened the door and motioned to the two actors.

"Sorry my secretary isn't here. Home with a sprained rib or something."

He interviewed and soothed the two actors without promising them anything. As the day progressed, he did the same with other actors, three announcers, an ex-rodeo star, the manager of a troupe of acrobats, a belly dancer, and an assortment of writers, directors, musicians, and miscellaneous singers. All of them expressed proper concern over his secretary, and all of them went away properly soothed.

He checked with his telephone-answering service and found that there had been no telephone calls. He called down to the restaurant for a sandwich, coffee, and the newspapers.

At last he peered into the corridor, saw no one but the slouching figure of Gus Madrid leaning against the wall. With a feeling of relief, he locked the door, turned out the lights and settled down to spend the afternoon. He glanced at the front pages of the trade papers and laid them aside. He looked over half-a-dozen magazines in the anteroom and discarded them. Finally he located a dictionary and went to work on all the crossword puzzles in all the newspapers.

By the time he had finished with them, the office was beginning to grow dark. He glanced at the window and saw that the sky had clouded and that it was snowing with real enthusiasm now.

There was no reason on earth, he thought suddenly, why he couldn't go downstairs, grab a taxi, and with a series of street directions he'd long ago learned from Helene, lose Gus Madrid completely. In fact, there was no reason why he couldn't have done that long ago, or even in the first place.

Oh well, Malone had been free from his shadow for the day, and for his own part, he'd learned a lot of new and interesting words.

He opened the door into the hall. Gus Madrid was no longer by the elevator, he was in the doorway. "I'm coming in," he said, and did, kicking the door shut behind him. He glared at Jake with suspicion and said, "Where's Eva Lou Strauss?"

Jake hesitated an instant between "I don't know who you mean" and "Will you please get out of my way," and finally said inadequately, "She isn't here."

"I see she ain't here," Gus Madrid said irritably. "What I want to know is, where's she at?"

Jake shook his head.

"Distinctly," Gus Madrid told him, taking a step forward, "I distinctly heard you tell that guy Malone you was going straight to where she was, and you come straight here, well, a'most straight here, and she ain't here. So—"

"Oh, an eavesdropper," Jake said.

The gunman promptly stated that Jake was several things, all far more unpleasant than eavesdropper.

"Look here," Jake said, hanging on to his temper by a rapidly thinning thread, "I'm a respectable businessman—"

Gus Madrid's comment on that reflected objectionably on a number of Jake's personal habits. "If you wasn't going to where she was, why'd you say you was?"

"Oh, that," Jake said, trying for a very light touch. "That's just a little joke Malone and I have. Instead of saying, 'I've got to see a man about a horse,' we say, 'I've got to see Eva Lou Strauss.'"

This time, Gus Madrid not only commented, even more unpleasantly, on Jake's personal habits, but on his origin and veracity as well.

Jake forgot himself and answered with two succinct words.

That was his first mistake. His second was very bad aim with his right. But as he went down, at least he knew what hit him.

Chapter Ten

For a little less than a minute, Malone considered going after Jake and Gus Madrid. Then he thought better of it. Jake's impulse had been well-meant, and it behooved him to take advantage of it as best he could. Anyway, Jake could take care of himself in any situation. At least, he mentally added, he always had.

He decided to go back to the remodeled and redecorated little gem of a house that enclosed the heart and soul and, most importantly, the brains of Delora Deanne.

The breathtaking lovely in the little blue-and-gold reception room greeted him more than warmly. "You got here very quickly, Mr. Malone. We just called your office a few minutes ago." Her smile made him forget almost half of his troubles.

Hazel Swackhammer met him in the green-and-pink

lounge, and led the way to her office. Her expression was as close to grim as it was to anything.

"You've heard something?" Malone asked hopefully. "A message?"

She closed the office door and said, "You might call it that, I suppose."

There was a box, still in its brown paper wrapping, on the desk. Malone looked at it silently, and the uncomfortable chill landed in his stomach again. The shape of the box told him perfectly well what it was.

"By messenger," Hazel Swackhammer said. "I called you at once. And I decided to put off opening it until you got here."

Malone nodded, still silently. He didn't need to open it, but he knew he was going to. He untied the string slowly and pushed aside the brown paper wrappings with fingers that, he suspected, were registering somewhere three thousand miles away on a seismograph.

The pale mauve shoebox proclaimed, in graceful black lettering, that it came from a shop whose name was not only known at least halfway around the world, but whose prices were spoken of in awed hushed whispers.

Malone lifted the lid just far enough to catch a glimpse of little gold kid sandals with a multitude of tiny straps, and high, slender heels. They were not empty.

He closed the box, rewrapped it fast, and retied the string in a whole series of knots. Then he stood staring at it, drawing every breath as though he expected it to be his last.

At last he said, "Well, at least this one came by messenger. So you ought to be able to trace it. Or rather, I ought to be."

"I doubt it," Hazel Swackhammer said. "It was brought by a shabbily dressed man who smelled to high heaven of cheap gin, and refused to deliver it to anyone except myself. He'd been paid half a dollar to bring it here, and I tipped him a dime." She paused. "Well, Mr. Malone, what do you propose to do about it?"

Malone decided against telling her that he didn't know. He said nothing and did his best to avoid looking at the box.

Finally she put it away decisively in her desk drawer and said, "Naturally I immediately telephoned Louella Frick at her apartment. Her roommate didn't know anything except that she was not in."

Malone went right on saying nothing. There was no point, he already knew, in asking questions about Louella Frick. He would simply be told that the private lives of the Delora Deanne models were none of Hazel Swackhammer's concern, as long as they didn't create unpleasant disturbances in the newspapers.

Finally he did manage to ask for Louella Frick's address, and wrote it down. On a second thought, he included the addresses of the remaining Delora Deannes. Then one question did occur to him.

"Who knew, or might know, that these models were all working for you? That, together, they added up to Delora Deanne?"

Hazel Swackhammer shook her head. "No one," she said, "outside of this very close-knit little organization. My secretary, Miss Harris. Mr. Furlong and Mr. Dennis, of course. My receptionist, Tamia Tabet. And naturally, they knew each other." She added, "You can easily understand why it would be highly unfortunate for anyone—*anyone*—to know that there was, so to speak, more than one Delora Deanne."

The little lawyer nodded. "It could be highly unfortunate indeed." He scowled and thought hard for a minute. "As a matter of simple precaution, do you know where the other Delora Deannes are right now? It might be wise to advise them to—to take steps." He wasn't sure what kind of steps they should take, except that preferably they should be steps away.

"Quite naturally," Hazel Swackhammer said, "I thought of that." There was just a tinge of reproach in her tone. "I telephoned, but none of them were at home. I shall continue to telephone." Her eyes said, "And just what are you going to do?"

Again he decided against suggesting that the police be called in. And again he wondered exactly what he was going to do. He could go to Louella Frick's apartment, and probably find that she had gone away on a trip, leaving a large collection of beautiful and valuable shoes behind.

On a sudden impulse he made up his mind to get a little better acquainted with Dennis Dennis, and asked where he would be found.

Mr. Dennis had an office on the second floor, and was in. "But," Hazel Swackhammer said, her eyes narrowing a little, "of course, you won't say anything to him about this."

"Oh, no, no, no," Malone hastily reassured her. "I only thought I'd just make some excuse to see him, and hope he might accidentally drop some information that might be helpful."

"I doubt," she said, "that he knows anything. Anything helpful, that is. But go ahead." She managed to give the impression that at least Malone would be doing something besides standing about and saying nothing.

He murmured something noncommittal and wandered away. The full-length portrait of Delora Deanne that decorated the staircase, with its delicate gilded metal railing, only depressed him more. The whole affair seemed to be confused beyond confusion. And probably still more confusion lay ahead of him.

Had two of the Delora Deannes been kidnaped, or murdered, or both, and their hands and feet sent to Hazel Swackhammer either as a preliminary to an extortion message, or as a grim warning? A grim warning of what? And which one was going to be next, the torso and legs, the face, or the voice? And just how was he going to prevent it, assuming that it hadn't taken place already?

Myrdell Harris appeared at the foot of the staircase, almost as though she had been watching for him. She gave him the dreamy smile.

"New trouble, Mr. Malone?" she breathed.

He wondered if he really detected a hopeful note in her voice. Her oval face, with its vague, sweet smile, told him nothing. "No, nothing new." That was practically the truth.

The smile intensified but, if anything, grew more vague. "I know I'm going to be a great deal of help to you, before everything is over with."

What everything? He started to speak, but she was already on her way. He reached for her arm, but it eluded him like a shred of mist.

"Your check went out in the mail to you this morning." Another smile. Then she seemed to fade away, to dissolve rather than actually move.

Well, that was one helpful thing she'd done, at least. Except that the check wouldn't be at his office until the next morning. He had plans for the evening, and something was going to have to be done about them.

One thought struck him as he reached the top of the curving stairs. Even without hands and feet, Delora Deanne could go right on doing a lot of cosmetic business, and if Otis Furlong did come up with a workable idea for producing her *in toto* on a television screen, there was one problem less. It might take a little searching, but other beautiful hands, other exquisite feet could be found. Even the luscious torso and legs could undoubtedly be duplicated in time. But the angelic, wistful and alluring face of Delora Deanne, nee Gertie Bragg—never!

Could some especially adroit kidnaper have thought of just that fact, and be leading up to a threat of sending *that* to Hazel Swackhammer, if a sufficiently large sum of money was not immediately forthcoming? It was his first thought so far that began to create some kind of a pattern.

Then there was another thought. Charlie Swackhammer. Cuddles. Where did he fit into all this? According to his ex-wife, he had designs on the Delora Deanne business, and was quite possibly responsible for the campaign in the columns. Still, he would hardly go to the enthusiastic lengths of murder, mutilations, mailings and messengers, to gain control of a business. Or would he?

The little lawyer made a mental note to put Cuddles Swackhammer high on his list of persons to be visited that day.

One way or another, he had to earn that check that was in the mail. To say nothing of getting a lot of puzzling problems out of his own mind.

He saw Myrdell Harris crossing the room below, some businesslike-looking folders in her hand. She looked up and gave him the same dreamy smile. For an instant, her cloud-colored eyes suggested that she did know everything about everything that was going on, and that it was perfectly possible for Malone to learn it from her. But before he could speak to her, she had maddeningly vanished again.

Chapter Eleven

Malone found Dennis Dennis in a small, uninteresting office that was hardly in keeping with the rest of the Delora Deanne decor. It was at the back of the building, and its one window looked out in the general direction of Lake Shore Drive and the lake front. The furnishings and their arrangement were similar to Hazel Swackhammer's private office downstairs, save that a standard-size typewriter stood on the desk, with a pile of unused paper on one side of it and an overflowing ash tray on the other.

Dennis Dennis himself was sitting with his back to the desk, his coat off, and his feet propped up on the window sill. He seemed to be gazing not only at the snow-screened lakefront, but all the way to Milwaukee, and possibly points even further north. But he wheeled around when Malone came in, and smiled a greeting.

"Snow slips," he said mellifluously, "with soft sweet sibilance, inseparable with the silver streaks of shining streams." He made a hasty note with pencil on the top sheet of paper and said, "What can I do for you, Malone?"

"Go right on with what you were doing," the little lawyer said.

Dennis Dennis gave him a wry smile. "Twenty years ago, and I might have. But it's much too late now, much too late." He looked at the penciled note. "It'll come out something like this. 'Sweet silver dreams, Delora. Snow will not harm your soft smooth skin, protected by Delora Deanne silver lotion.'"

The smile became a macabre, unpleasant grin. "Neither snow, nor hail nor sleet, and who the hell knows what sibilance is anyway, except you and me, Malone. Draw up a chair and park."

Malone obediently drew up a chair and parked.

"Time was," the ex-poet said. "Time was. Ah, yes. But that was before Delora Deanne's dollars turned out to be silver to the touch, and I made the horrible mistake of marrying a good woman. Tell me, Malone, do you think I could get away with a murder?"

Malone jumped and then said, "Easily. But be sure to engage a good lawyer first."

"Consider yourself engaged," Dennis Dennis said, a little less bitterness in the grin. "But for the love of heaven, don't ask for money in advance. That woman has tied up my last telephone slug."

He leaned back in his chair, hands clasped behind his head. "And she was a toothsome little wench when I married her, too. College graduate she was, sociology major, plus courses in domestic science. I should have known. Bad enough to make mistakes, without going ahead and marrying them, Cigarette?"

Malone shook his head and took out his fifth cigar of the day.

"Oh, well, it may not actually come to a lethal act. I have high hopes of marrying her off to an old college chum I never really liked. Sent her a birthday present of a very erudite tome entitled *The Successful Second Marriage*. That ought to do it; she loves to do the right thing. Then I can go back to writing what I really think about snowfall."

"Tell me about Hazel Swackhammer," Malone said. He slid the cellophane wrapper from his cigar, held it to his lips, and blew it with amazing accuracy at the wastebasket. "I only met her yesterday morning."

"You probably know as much about her as I do," Dennis Dennis said. "She's like a tigress with a deep sense of insecurity, where Delora Deanne is concerned. Especially about her reputation. So damned afraid someone might find out that there are five of them. More damned afraid that someone might insinuate that Delora Deanne was not quite all that she should be."

"Is she?" Malone asked innocently. "Or, are they?"

The last trace of bitterness was gone from the grin now.

"I've too much on my mind to worry about any private lives except my own." He went on, "If Hazel hadn't been the type to fly into a great calm, there would have been an inordinate amount of jumping up and down and running about and yelling and screaming and ringing bells, when those column items appeared. I suppose that is the reason she sent for you, Malone."

It sounded more like a question than a statement. Malone answered it with a noncommittal nod and said, "I don't think it's anything to worry about. Those things just come and go, and nobody really remembers them. Which one of the gals do you think it was?"

"Hell," Dennis said, patting all his pockets in search of a match, "none of them." He finally located one and lit a slightly bent cigarette. "None of 'em ever looked at a man except Eva Lou, and I guess she just looked at all of 'em—but in sweet seclusion. Eula's too money-mad and she doesn't like men anyway. Louella's much too respectable and too fat, and Gertie is just plain too dumb. Rita, of course—well, she's just Rita. But she's just another little homebody hell-raiser like Eva Lou. When she does step, she's the saloon type anyway, and not the playboy nightclub type."

This time Malone grinned, and hoped it wasn't a sickly one. "Somebody must have been thinking of another Delora Deanne."

"Or another five of them," Dennis Dennis said. "Oh well, they're not a bad bunch to get along with. Rita always beefs about the radio copy, but give her a couple of slugs and a chuck under the chin, and she reads it like a chorus of Ethel Barrymores."

"Too bad she and Furlong couldn't get along," Malone said, very, very casually.

"Oh, Rita never could get along for more than a year or so with anybody on a matrimonial basis," Dennis Dennis said cheerfully. "I guess they parted friends, at least there haven't been any fireworks when I was around. She's a lot of fun, but she must be hell at breakfast."

Well, that appeared to settle that, Malone thought. So far, the interrelationships of the Delora Deannes and the staff didn't produce anything worthy of murder, or even mild mayhem.

"Swackhammer," he said, slowly and thoughtfully. "The name sounds familiar."

"It should," Dennis Dennis said. "You see it every time you ride a streetcar or pick up a newspaper. If you read advertisements, that is. Swackhammer Brothers, Morticians. They've got a whole string of high-class, low-pay undertaking parlors. Must make a fortune."

Now Malone remembered. His blood wasn't actually running cold, but it did seem to be a little cooler.

"He's good at it," Dennis Dennis said. "Embalming's an art, like everything else, and he's a real artist. I saw one of his jobs once, and it was a pip. Beautiful!"

Yes, decidedly cooler. Malone said, "He couldn't possibly have been the person who set up those column stories, could he?" as though it was the farthest thing from his mind.

Dennis Dennis laughed. "Hell, no! Good old Cuddles? He wouldn't be bothered. I imagine he was glad to be rid of Hazel and her damned goo for the face and bear grease for the hair. Hasn't been heard from around here in heaven knows when. Just sticks to his embalming and lets them as wants be beautiful."

He lit a new cigarette from his half-finished one, threw away the empty pack, took out another one from his desk drawer and began tearing at its cellophane. "I met him a few times, long while back. Sort of liked the old lecher."

Malone lifted a questioning eyebrow and Dennis Dennis added, "Oh, no, nothing serious. He's just the usual foolish fifty, only a little more usual than usual."

"Oh," Malone said, wondering if Dennis Dennis had said exactly what he meant. "Well, as I remarked, it isn't anything too serious."

"Maybe one of the Deloras did it herself," Dennis Dennis said. "Just to heckle poor old Hazel."

That was a new idea, and Malone turned it over a few times in his mind. "Possible," he said a little dubiously.

"Rita's the only one who would think of it, though," Dennis Dennis said, running a thin, nervous hand through his sandy hair. "And now that it comes to mind, I wouldn't put it past her." He took off his rimless glasses, began polishing them, and chuckled. "Next time I take her out on the town, I'll beat the truth out of her and let you know."

Malone muttered something about biting the hand that fed, and immediately wished he hadn't mentioned the subject of hands. But it seemed to go right past Dennis Dennis without making an impression.

"Not too well fed," Dennis Dennis said. "Hazel isn't one for conspicuous waste, even where fancy decorations for the joint are concerned. Always wonder if she doesn't slip down here at night and sling a paint brush herself." He put the glasses back on.

"But these column stories," Malone began, getting doggedly back to the subject or at least, he reflected, one subject.

"Could be one of the Deloras, yes, could be." The ex-poet began pleating a scrap of notepaper. "Not all sweetness and light around here. Just the other day Hazel got sore and threatened to fire all the Deloras. They made the mistake of asking for more dough. In fact, that's what the big confab was about yesterday morning."

"Did they get it?" Malone asked.

"No," Dennis Dennis said. Before Malone could think of anything else to ask, he went on, "Say, you're a friend of the television producer, Jake Justus, aren't you?"

Malone nodded.

"Like to meet him," Dennis Dennis said. "Like to very much. I can write other things besides cosmetics advertising, you know."

The little lawyer murmured that he was sure Jake would be more than delighted.

"Too bad all the Deloras aren't combined in one girl. She'd be a natural for television."

Malone said that yes, it was indeed too bad.

Dennis Dennis tossed the pleated paper at the wastebasket and said suddenly, "How do you like this to go with Furlong's pink bathtub, spoken in Rita's maple-syrup voice? 'Silken soft—and sweeter than your sweetest dreams.'"

"Swell," said Malone, getting into the spirit of it.

"Just so Rita doesn't develop a lisp overnight."

Or a cut throat, Malone thought. And that reminded him that he had to be up and doing. Just what, he wasn't at all sure, but doing.

He finished his cigar, said his good-by, and went away, pausing at the door leading to the reception room to admire the golden-haired doll-like girl behind the gilt-and-ivory desk.

"My dear, how did you get such a delightful name?" he inquired in the tender tones he reserved for golden-haired, doll-like girls.

"I picked letters out of a hat," Tamia Tabet said. He noticed happily that she had a pert dimple in one cheek. "And no, I haven't any plans for the evening."

Fifteen minutes later Malone went out into Oak Street with her address in his pocket and a warmer glow in his being than he'd had all day.

He wondered if it had occurred to Hazel Swackhammer to put a special delivery stamp on the envelope that held that check.

With an important evening ahead of him—all, he told himself, in the interests of business and Delora Deanne—something immediate was going to have to be done about the financial situation. Quite possibly Joe the Angel would consider it a worthwhile investment.

He'd get to that problem later. He ignored the beckoning nods of several taxi drivers, crossed Michigan Boulevard and took a bus to the border of Evanston. The snow was coming down steadily now, and in Lincoln Park it lay silvery and crisp and soft.

It hadn't made his life any materially brighter to learn that Cuddles Swackhammer was a mortician by trade. Rather than making any pattern emerge, it had only added more confusion. If there was any pattern, he reflected. The matter of the Delora Deannes was beginning to seem more and more like several jigsaw puzzles mixed together, with new pieces, of a strange color and design, being added every few minutes. And also, more and more he was beginning to feel that he wasn't going to like the picture if it ever did finally appear.

Nor had it brightened his life to learn that Hazel Swackhammer was one for stringent economy He remembered Myrdell Harris' chance remark about creditors. Or had it been chance?

He tried to dismiss the matter of that check from his mind, and concentrate on Louella Frick. The address Hazel Swackhammer had given him was just over the boundary line of Evanston, one of a series of comfortable, homey-looking apartment buildings, all more or less alike. In the summertime, Malone reflected, there would be green leaves on the vines and window boxes at all the windows. Right now the vines were brown, and there was snow on the little square of lawn, but the effect was still a pleasing one.

One effect, however, was not as pleasing, and for a moment he stood still, staring. The big, two-tone convertible in front of the building could belong to no one but Helene Justus.

Chapter Twelve

The plain-faced, graying-haired woman who opened the door smiled at him agreeably and said, "Miss Frick's not home. Are you a friend of hers?"

Malone said, "Yes," and waited hopefully.

"Well, come right on in and get warm. There's another friend of hers just got here. My, but isn't it getting cold outside!"

Malone agreed that yes, it certainly was cold outside, as he gratefully stepped into an apartment that was as comfortable and as homey-looking as its outside had been. There were bright potted plants in the glassed-in sunparlor, and invitingly cushioned wicker chairs. Helene looked at him serenely from one of them.

The little lawyer sank down in the nearest chair and told himself he might have known. Just how Helene had gotten into the act he didn't know, but there she was, not only with every intention of staying there but probably taking center stage.

"We're old friends," Helene said brightly to the smiling-faced woman.

Malone nodded agreement, and looked around him. Just good old-fashioned comfy and cozy, with a restful, soothing warmth. The furniture showed signs of wear, and none of it had cost very much in the first place, but it seemed exactly right for where it was, as did the friendly little clutter of family photographs on the old-style radio.

"I'm Mrs. Titchner," the gray-haired woman said cordially. "Mrs. Florence Titchner. I've been a friend of Lou's for years and years. Why, she's been living here with me ever since she first came to Evanston, and my, I'm going to miss her something terrible. Did you know she decided to go back to the farm?"

Malone said cautiously, "She's been thinking of it for some time, hasn't she?" Helene was gazing dreamily out the window.

"Oh, my, yes, ever since she first came to Evanston, she just didn't talk about anything else. Evanston's my home, really, you know, I came here when I married Mr. Titchner in 1919, I lived in Grand Forks before that, and I've gone right on living here in this apartment ever since he died in 1940 of a heart attack. I just don't know what I'm going to do without Lou, but I suppose I'll get along all right somehow. Yes, she was always talking about going back, you know, she used to say to me, 'Floss, I'm just going to stay here long enough to save a little money, and then I'm going back to Ohio where I belong.' She never did get married, you know, and my, she did miss all her old friends something terrible, so I guess I ought to be glad for her sake that she's gone. Did you say you'd been a friend of hers long, Mr.—"

"Malone," he said hastily. He felt a little out of breath. "No, not very long."

"Well, Lou was a wonderful woman, it's too bad she never did save up as much money as she'd intended to, but then you know, she never did make very much. I never did figure out what she did, but she said it was something to do with cold cream, though my, she never used very much of that stuff any more'n I do. But I've known her and her family all my life. I'm quite a bit older'n she is, and my, I've known her ever since she was born, I guess. Used to visit back in Ohio every summer, that's how I come to know her folks." She paused just long enough to smile. "Well, I don't know how many times she's said to me, 'Floss, I've made up my mind that someday I'll just get on a train and go back whatever happens, and when I do, as far's my things are concerned you just give 'em away, I won't need 'em down on the farm.' The furniture's mine, you know, and she never did have very much of her own, poor dear, just a few dresses and the one good coat she wore this morning, except for shoes. My goodness, I never saw anybody had so many pairs of shoes, and such nice ones, too, but she always said she wouldn't ever need them where she was going to go, Mr.—"

"Malone," the little lawyer repeated feebly. Helene was still staring out the window, even more dreamily.

"Oh yes, Malone. I never was much good at remembering names. Don't you feel well, Mr. Malone? You want to take care of yourself in this kind of weather. You know, I feel real guilty about her leaving all those shoes behind, I couldn't wear any of 'em myself, of course, and my, I just don't know who could, and I wonder, would you like to take a look at them, seeing you're right here. Maybe you know somebody they'd fit, and seeing you're an old friend of Lou's I know she'd like you folks to have them if you do know somebody they'd fit, and if you'd like to look at them I'd be glad to show them to you—"

Malone said, "Yes, I would," and regretted it even while he was saying it. But Helene was already on her feet.

Mrs. Titchner led the way into a cheerful little bedroom bright with chintz, and opened a closet door. The back of it was one enormous shoe-rack that held enough shoes, Malone reflected, to make even a centipede happy. All were delicate, all were graceful, and all had cost enough to make a Texas oil man think twice.

"My *land*, it does seem such a shame, spending all that money just on shoes, why you know I believe there's pairs there she never wore more'n once or twice, and then going off and leaving them all behind, but then, I don't suppose she would need that kind of shoes where she's gone, would she?"

"No, she wouldn't," Helene said softly. Malone glanced quickly at her. There was a kind of hushed look on her face, and he knew she was thinking the same as he. Eva Lou, and a satin-lined drawer of beautiful, beautiful gloves. Louella, and a closet rack filled with beautiful, beautiful shoes.

Or did Helene know about Eva Lou? Malone had an unpleasant suspicion that she did, that she knew all about the gloves and shoes being left behind because they weren't going to be needed any more.

He managed to avoid the reproachful look he expected from her eyes. Somehow he made his escape, explaining that the shoes, unfortunately, were far too small to fit the party he had in mind. Mrs. Titchner was effusively sorry, also sorry that they had missed seeing her old friend Lou, and that they didn't have time for a nice hot cup of tea.

Outside, Malone and Helene said, "What are you doing

here?" simultaneously, and then Helene beat him to the next punch.

"You might have known better than to team me up with your gangster friend last night. Though I'd have figured it out myself anyway."

He hedged with, "What did he have to do with it?"

Helene sniffed. She motioned to Malone to get in the convertible and slid in herself under the wheel. "Simple. Walking away from your office, I turned my ankle. He gallantly helped me down to the drugstore. There it turned out the damage wasn't serious, but I wanted a cup of coffee to calm my nerves."

"An old trick," Malone said scornfully.

"Still one of the best," she told him serenely. "Anyway, he told me he was looking for his girl, Eva Lou Strauss, and he had to keep an eye on you because you knew where she was." She looked at the miserable Malone coldly and thoughtfully. "Naturally I remembered the name. Naturally I remembered your mentioning that one of the models was missing. So naturally, I told him that I was looking for Eva Lou Strauss myself, but that I was keeping an eye on you because you didn't know where she was."

The little lawyer looked unhappily out the window.

"After all," Helene said, "I had to protect Jake's interests. So we settled down to keeping two eyes on you, one for each of us. Then Jake turned up and both of you went up to her apartment." She paused meaningfully.

"We just went to see if she'd come back," Malone said, wishing he were anywhere else in the world, preferably Bermuda. "And she hadn't."

"I know she hadn't," Helene said. "We went up too, after you'd gone. Then Mr. Madrid took me home."

Malone managed to hide a sigh of relief. At least, Helene only thought Eva Lou Strauss and now, Louella Frick, were missing. She didn't know about the packages that had arrived, and might still be arriving, at Hazel Swackhammer's desk. It turned out, though, that he was congratulating himself too soon.

"And that's not all," she said almost accusingly. "I did a little bit of arithmetic all by myself. Eva Lou Strauss posed for Delora Deanne's hands. And Joe the Angel said you asked Rico de Angelo about—about—"

"You're a bright little girl," Malone said. He threw the

remains of his cigar savagely out the window. He unwrapped another one and lit it slowly and carefully. Then he explained it all to her, leaving out only a few personal plans that were nobody's business but his own.

Helene started the motor and drew a long, sighing breath. "Thank God, Jake doesn't know anything about all this!"

Malone thanked God and several saints that Jake didn't know Helene knew about all this. He foresaw an immediate future that was not only going to be difficult, but fraught with peril. His last hope was that Jake and Helene could keep secrets from each other better than he'd ever been at keeping secrets from either of them.

"Malone, what are we going to do?" Before he could say a word she added quickly, "I think, first of all, we'd better start looking for Eva Lou Strauss. And fast. Because that's a very familiar-looking car parked down the block."

Malone looked. Difficult and fraught with peril, he reflected.

Suddenly Helene started the convertible and slid alongside the black sedan. She waved a cheerful greeting to Gus Madrid. "How did you get here?"

The smile that almost invariably answered one of Helene's appeared on the dour face. "Same like you did. The dame that lives here used to work where my girl did. I found her name in the phone book. It was easy." He looked extremely proud. "Only I saw you was here."

"Well, I can tell you," she said with disarming frankness, "your girl isn't here. And nobody here knows anything about her." She leaned a little out the window and added a little more candlepower to the smile. "I think we ought to join forces. You see, Malone here is looking for Eva Lou Strauss too. And so am I. Because my husband wants to use her in a big television show. In fact," she added, "I think you ought to hire Malone to find her for you. He's wonderful at finding people."

Gus Madrid looked thoughtful and said, "Oh." He was thoughtful for a few more minutes and then said, "You could maybe be right."

"Of course I'm right," Helene told him warmly.

This time, after another period of intense thinking, Madrid said, "Well." And at last he sighed and said, "How much?"

Malone sighed too, and it was with relief. "I'll meet you at the office and we'll talk it over."

"You see?" Helene told Gus Madrid. "Now you haven't a thing to worry about." She gave him one more smile as a clincher. Helene had convinced far more skeptical men than Gus Madrid would ever be.

"It's as simple as that," Helene said a few blocks later. "In fact, I ought to ask you for a cut."

The little lawyer was silent. He had a feeling he was going to get a fee—assuming he got it—for promising to do something that he already suspected couldn't be done.

Halfway to the Loop he asked Helene to drop him at the Wrigley Building. He realized immediately it was a mistake, but it was too late to do anything about it now.

"I'm going there myself," Helene said. She gave Malone a suspicious glance from the corner of her eye. "I want to be along and make sure you don't say the wrong thing to Jake."

Malone reflected that all he wanted was to make sure Jake didn't say the wrong thing to her. He pointed out that there were other people in the Wrigley Building, and he might want to see any one of them. Helene answered him with a scornful sniff.

"Jake mustn't know anything," she said firmly. "It's bad enough he knows that Delora Deanne is five girls. Otis Furlong may come up with a solution for that. It's worse he knows one of them is missing. But if he knew two of them were missing, and that somebody apparently has started murdering them—"

"That's enough," Malone said. He muttered aloud that too many cooks made light work.

"You mean," Helene told him, "too many hands and we'll all be in the soup."

Chapter Thirteen

"You'll be all right," Malone said reassuringly, "as soon as you can keep your balance."

They helped Jake to his feet. He stood swaying for a minute and then fell flat on his face again.

"The trouble is," he complained, "I can't seem to keep my balance even lying down."

"Concussion!" Helene said in a horrified voice. Obviously, she declared, Jake had to be rushed to a hospital, and at once.

Jake sat up and began rubbing his head gingerly. "Water," he whispered. "Next office."

Helene rushed off. Jake whispered fiercely to Malone, "Don't you dare, ever, say one word to Helene."

Malone was about to whisper, "And don't you," when Helene came back. She spilled most of a paper cup of water over the stricken man and said, "Darling!" Jake groaned, but made another and successful try at standing up. Helene promptly shoved him into a chair and announced that Jake still had to be rushed to a hospital.

"I tripped," Jake said at last. "I tripped and hit my head on the corner of the desk. Right there."

Helene rushed over and examined the corner of the desk. As long as she didn't examine the mark on Jake's head, and its location, Malone reflected, everything would be well. He announced that he had to be getting along. Jake and Helene both had an I'm-coming-with-you look in their eyes, and both of them kept quiet, each warily watching the other.

Finally they compromised; Jake would go home and lie down for half an hour, and Helene would keep him company.

Malone breathed a little easier and hoped they'd keep off dangerous conversational topics, that neither of them would let a whole litter of kittens, all named Delora Deanne, out of the bag.

He stood in front of the Wrigley Building, thinking things over. The sky had begun to clear and the sun flirted in and out from clouds that had become fluffily pale and opalescent around their edges. The snow crunched and chirruped satisfactorily underfoot, and the air was snapping with cold.

At last he hailed a passing taxi. What he had left of his bankroll, after discovering that Gus Madrid was one of the best poker players in the city of Chicago, wasn't going to make even a slight dent in the future evening's activities anyway. That problem he would get to later. He noticed the black sedan in traffic, but right now that didn't worry him either.

Malone was headed for the office of Inspector Daniel von Flanagan, Homicide, and he hadn't the faintest idea what he was going to say, or ask. Things were now at that delicate and perilous stage where he had to be highly considerate of his client's wishes, and at the same time, he had a feeling that any hour now he might need at least information and, quite possibly, help.

The box that had come through the mail yesterday morning could just possibly be traced. But that would have to be done through official channels, and he wasn't ready for that yet. Also, it would take time, and time was one thing he didn't think he had.

Somewhere in the confusion of all he had learned in the last two days there were a couple of facts that belonged together like Romulus and Remus, or Damon and Pythias, or gin and beer. Separately, they meant nothing. Taken together, they might mean something important, something he badly needed to know.

The only trouble was that he couldn't remember what they were.

He closed his eyes as the taxi whipped through traffic, and tried to think. Then he gave that up, and tried to doze. He was just beginning to succeed when the taxi stopped.

He found von Flanagan in an amiable mood. The big police officer yawned, put his newspaper aside, stretched, and said, "Been trying to get you on the phone for two days."

"Been busy," Malone said, and waited warily.

Von Flanagan said, "Tickets for the fights Thursday night?"

"I'll take care of it," the little lawyer said. "It's as good as done."

Von Flanagan yawned again. There seemed to be nothing else in particular on the calendar of his mind. He said, "Everything quiet 'n peaceful, 'n then you come in. So why don't you just go away and leave it like that?"

"Just a purely social call," Malone said, taking out a cigar. "With a purely hypothetical question to put to you."

"Shoot it," von Flanagan said, "and I'll probably give you a purely imaginary answer."

"Hands and feet," Malone said. He looked thoughtfully at the cigar. "Suppose somebody sent a pair of human hands through the mail? And then sent a pair of human feet by messenger?" No point, he told himself, in adding the details of gloves and shoes.

"Dead?" von Flanagan asked.

"Naturally," Malone told him.

Von Flanagan thought for a moment. "Wrapped up?" he asked.

"Also, naturally," Malone said.

"Breaking the law," von Flanagan said. "But not in my department." He scratched the side of his nose. "Through the mail, that would be a federal matter. By messenger, that would be transporting a dead body, or any part thereof, through the streets without a permit. I can get it looked up for you, if you want me to."

"It's not that important," Malone said lazily.

"Just a minute," von Flanagan said, suddenly sitting up straight. "Did these hands and these feet come off of the same person?"

"That," Malone said airily, and blowing a cloud of smoke toward the ceiling, "remains to be seen."

A suspicious look came slowly over von Flanagan's broad, red face. "Presumably this person, or persons, is or are dead?"

"Or in damned bad shape," Malone agreed.

"This is in my department," von Flanagan said. He scowled at Malone. "Malone—" his eyes narrowed just a little—"exactly what is going on?"

"I told you it was a hypothetical question," Malone said amiably. He added, "A friend of mine just wants to know."

"Well, advise your friend not to do it," von Flanagan said, relaxing again. "And don't forget the fights Thursday night."

"A date," Malone said. "Gadenski still over in Missing Persons?"

Von Flanagan nodded. The look of suspicion began to come back. "More hypothetical questions, Malone?"

The little lawyer shook his head. "Owe him a little money," he lied cheerfully.

He located Gadenski, a tall, thin, dark, perpetually worried-looking man, and explained that this was purely a personal favor, very strictly unofficial, and to be treated as such, and that he, Malone, would be delighted to return with practically any favor, practically any time.

It was a matter of a girl. Well, several girls. He went on with names, descriptions, probable clothing, where last seen, previous addresses and possible destinations of Eva Lou Strauss and Louella Frick. Then, while he had the unofficial service available, he added Gertie Bragg, Eula Stolz, and Rita Jardee for good measure.

Gadenski noted it all down, promised he'd do his best, and said in a cheerful grumble that certain persons seemed to think he had nothing better to do than keep track of their women for them.

Malone went away, thinking gloomily that he didn't expect anything really helpful in the way of information, but at least he'd proved that he was still right in there trying.

Gus Madrid was waiting for him when he returned to the office. The check from Hazel Swackhammer wasn't. Jake had telephoned that he felt much better and would be down in a little while. Nothing had been heard from Helene.

He ushered the big gunman into the inner office, broke out from the emergency drawer a bottle he reserved for important clients and visiting dignitaries, and said cheerfully, "I assure you, as a client of mine, you haven't a thing to worry about."

Gus Madrid accepted the glass, sat down, and said, "Thanks, Malone. I always heard you was the very best lawyer type guy. Only I never knew lawyer type guys went around finding missing girls for their guys."

"You'd be surprised at what some lawyers have to do for their clients," Malone assured him, and wondered if the big gunman could guess at even a fraction of it. He decided to let the subject of fees wait till a little later, and said, "Tell me about her."

In the next half-hour he learned that Eva Lou was a real swell type girl, didn't like to go out, but liked to have a swell time to home, that her folks were Polish and she didn't know where they were at and hadn't for years, that she'd married a no-good type guy named Strauss who'd left her stranded in Milwaukee, that she'd come to Chicago and got her this job with this cold-cream factory, he didn't know what it was, that she'd had another guy on the string, a businessman type guy but he, Madrid, had pretty well cut him out, and that was all he knew. He was willing to spend some real cash type money to find this girl, but also he was a careful type guy and there would be some strings to it.

Malone sighed and hoped that Eva Lou wouldn't turn up a deceased type corpse.

That was about all the information Gus Madrid had. He hadn't dated Eva Lou night before last, he'd had some important business to take care of. Malone caught himself about to ask what type business, and decided it was none of his concern. There was nothing else Gus Madrid knew, including the name of the businessman type guy, and from here on in, it was all up to Malone.

Malone cleared his throat delicately and brought up the little matter of money. Gus Madrid took out his wallet but held on to it.

"It's like this, Malone. I'm a cautious type guy. I give you money now. But this is not such a simple business type transaction. Maybe you don't find my girl." He laid five hundred-dollar bills on the desk. "Down payment."

Not finding Eva Lou Strauss was probably considerably beyond the mere *maybe* point, Malone reminded himself. He looked very thoughtfully at the bills.

"Maybe I find her myself," Gus Madrid went on. "Every half-hour, all day and all night, I call up account maybe she's come home." He paused. "And maybe somebody else finds her." He paused again. "And maybe she never does get found at all."

Malone had winced at every "maybe." He said nothing.

"So in that case," Gus Madrid said, "in any one of those cases, then I get my money back."

He rose, looked at Malone. "Tomorrow," he said. At the door he turned back and added, "Meantime, I keep my eye on you, Malone."

After he had gone, the little lawyer sat looking at the money for quite a while. The bargain had been made, and he knew that it was irrevocable now. But suddenly he'd remembered Gus Madrid's particular occupation. He was what was known popularly—more often, not so popularly—as an enforcer.

Chapter Fourteen

"No matter where you're going," Jake said, "I see absolutely no reason why I can't go with you. After all, we're in this together." His expression added, "To the finish, and up to the neck."

"Oh, all right," Malone said in a cross voice. There simply was no way to tell Jake of the danger that Helene might turn up at the most inopportune moment. Jake had said she'd gone to visit a friend, and immediately Malone had begun to worry about whose friend it was.

There was nothing to do about it now. He struggled into his topcoat, brushed at a few cigar ashes on his vest, made a determined effort to straighten his tie and led the way into the anteroom.

He paused there to hand Maggie a hundred-dollar bill. "Pay yourself some salary and pay a little on the rent." He hurried Jake through the door, avoiding Maggie's startled eyes. There went the first of Gus Madrid's money. With a sigh, he realized that he was now entirely committed to doing the impossible.

A search through the telephone book had told him that

the main location of Swackhammer Brothers, Morticians, was out on Milwaukee Avenue and he gave the address to a taxi driver.

Jake looked at him curiously. "Malone, do you—"

"Shut up, or go away," the little lawyer growled. "I want to think." He chewed angrily on his cigar.

The façade of Swackhammer Brothers resembled a cross between a small-scale national monument and a branch bank, and they stood admiring it for a moment before going in. The whole Swackhammer family, ex-wives included, obviously had a great leaning toward decorative fronts. Malone tried again to straighten his Sulka tie and brush a few more cigar ashes from his badly wrinkled hand-tailored suit.

Charles Swackhammer was a large, cordial man, with grayish hair that had once apparently been sandy, cheerfully bright blue eyes, a briskly businesslike air, and a warm handclasp. He had indeed heard of John J. Malone, and of Mr. Justus, and was delighted to meet them. He certainly hoped that Malone was not there either on sad personal business of his own, or as the bearer of unpleasant legal tidings.

Malone said with hearty assurance that he was neither, and, with Jake, followed the big man into his private office.

"If it's legal business," Charles Swackhammer said, offering Malone an expensive Havana cigar, "it's probably Hazel. It almost always is. But I'm used to it."

"Well," Malone said hesitantly, "it is, in a way, and in a way it isn't." He was wondering exactly just how much he dared to confide.

"Well, don't worry about it, whatever it is," Swackhammer said expansively. "Because it isn't important." He pushed a button on the intercom box on his desk and said, "Darling, bring me in that folder on the Deanne stuff."

He beamed at them both and said, "You gentlemen called on a very happy day. Tomorrow there will be a new Mrs. Swackhammer."

They murmured something congratulatory, and Malone wondered if the future Mrs. Swackhammer called him Cuddles. Then a pert-looking brunette popped in with a manila folder of papers, laid it on the desk, and popped right out again.

"This is something Hazel will never forgive, when she knows about it," the big man went on. He opened the folder on his desk and pointed to it. "I trust you. And anyway, it doesn't matter now whether Hazel knows about it. She may already, for all I know." He added to Malone, "You're a lawyer. Go ahead. Look it over."

Malone went quickly through the contents of the folder. Brief and to the point, they made it very plain that Charlie Swackhammer owned forty-five per cent of Delora Deanne.

"Hazel only has forty-five per cent," Charlie Swackhammer said. "And I can lay my hands on the other ten per cent any time I want to. Fact is, I'm planning to do it before I leave on my honeymoon."

That was something new to think about. Malone scowled. Obviously Charlie Swackhammer was in a position to oust his ex-wife from her enameled and gilded nest any time he felt in the mood.

"Simplest thing in the world," Swackhammer said. "After I left her, she had to have money to keep the business going. Easy for me to see that friends of mine put it up, and then quietly buy 'em out. And don't look down a moral, legal nose at me, Malone, if you're planning to. Because I could—at any time—have had lawful possession of the formulas she got from me."

The little lawyer lifted his brows and said, "Formulas?"

"Naturally," Cuddles Swackhammer said, gesturing with his cigar. "You don't just whip up a little batch of some so-called magic cosmetic like you were stirring up a cake. Not that they aren't practically magic at that. I'm the one who ought to know. Because I developed 'em."

"But—" Malone said, and then stopped. Confusion seemed to be piling up. At last he went on to repeat a condensed version of the story of Delora Deanne cosmetics as it had been told to him the day before, beginning with the old New England grandmother. "Of course," he finished, "the story used in the Delora Deanne advertising, about the lovely Southern belle—"

"New England grandmother, my foot!" Cuddles Swackhammer said. "And sweet Southern belle, my other foot! Far's I know, Hazel never had a New England grandmother. But those formulas came out of one of the finest embalming establishments in the country, if not in the world!" He emphasized this point by bringing a pink, well-manicured fist down on his desk, hard.

There was a little silence. Jake cleared his throat. "Of course," he began tentatively, "I know from my own experience in the advertising business—"

"The advertising business," Cuddles Swackhammer said, "would make a liar, if not a damned liar, out of George Washington. No offense meant, Mr. Justus. I use advertising myself." He beamed at Jake, and then said, "When I married Hazel, she worked right along with me and helped me. We had a lot of use for special cosmetics, you understand. Just by way of example—now you take this special make-up that's supposed to hide every facial blemish except cross-eyes."

"Delora Deanne Magic Mask," Jake remembered out loud.

"That was Hazel's first hit," Swackhammer said, nodding. "All her suckers went for it, whether they needed it or not. Well, that was developed right in my little back room, with her looking on. You see, in a case where I'm confronted with multiple bruises and contusions—"

"I understand perfectly," the little lawyer said hastily.

"Of course," Cuddles said. "And then there were lip colorings and—well, about everything you care to name. All good stuff—it has to be good in my business. And all kinds of formulas for the hair, naturally. No matter how bad the hair is, matted, tangled, stained, I have to turn out a good-looking result. Then, for instance, sometimes we get a case where there's been a prolonged immersion in water—"

"I'll take your word for it," Malone said.

The big man grinned. "Happens all the time. But as I was saying, I never wanted to have any big dust-up with Hazel. Running her little business kept her happy and kept her from doing too much worrying and stewing about Maybelle and me. Otherwise, she'd have figured out some way to get even with Maybelle, if I know Hazel. And as it worked out, I could just sit back and collect my percentage of the proceeds without her knowing it, and she did all the work and worrying. Nice deal."

Yes, Malone thought, a very nice deal. Except that it only made his present problem more complex than ever.

"Well, anyway," Cuddles Swackhammer said, "just what did Hazel want you to see me about?"

"Nothing," Malone said truthfully. He hesitated a moment. "She called me in because she's been a little disturbed—annoyed—by some items in the newspaper columns—a newspaper column—that might have been construed as applying to her Delora Deanne." He paused, still choosing his words carefully. "I should say, or one of them."

Swackhammer chuckled. It was a friendly, heart-warming chuckle. "Know the item you refer to. Saw it myself. Disturbed! Annoyed!" He chuckled again. "I'd like to have seen Hazel's face when she read it."

Malone felt himself grinning. "I asked Mr. Justus for help," he said, relieved that at last he could explain Jake's presence, "because of his newspaper connections. And it just occurred to us," he went on cautiously, "that you might have some idea who was behind it. Someone who doesn't like her."

"Gosh," Swackhammer said. "That would take in too many people for me to list."

"Well," Malone said, "it's nothing very important. I was just a little curious myself." He got up. "Thanks for all the information."

"Think nothing of it," Cuddles Swackhammer said. He beamed at Jake. "So you're the big television feller. Like to have a talk with you sometime. Always thought I could do something myself."

Jake said, "Sure. Any time."

"Soon as I'm an old married man," Swackhammer said happily. "Sorry Maybelle isn't here. Like you to meet her. Maybelle Bragg, that is. Maybelle Swackhammer to be. Used to work for Hazel. Wonderful, wonderful girl." He glowed like a postcard sunrise, and invited them to come in again, adding with a professional laugh, "But not as a customer."

They managed a hollow laugh between them, and went away. Outside in the taxi, Malone said, "Bragg. Used to work for Hazel Swackhammer."

"Gertie Bragg," Jake said.

Malone said, "Face."

They were silent halfway to the Loop.

"The thing about this," Jake said at last, "is that the more you find out, the less you know."

"And the less you know," Malone said, "the more confused it all gets." He noticed that the black sedan was still discreetly following them, just as it had all the way to Swackhammer Brothers.

"Myrdell Harris," Jake said, out of the blue. "You couldn't find out anything from her, but I bet I can."

The little lawyer muttered something scathing about Jake's way with women.

"You forget," Jake said, "she's a thwarted actress. And I'm a big-shot television producer."

Malone conceded that Jake might have something there. At any rate, it wouldn't do any harm for Jake to try.

The taxi stopped in front of Joe the Angel's City Hall Bar. Evidently the owner of the black sedan had used a shortcut and found a parking place, because he was waiting on the sidewalk for them.

"Look here," he said coldly to Malone. "There's too much business with undertaker type guys getting mixed up in this." He spotted Jake getting out of the taxi.

"Listen, you," he said, "I am not a type guy who goes around apologizing. But—"

"Neither am I," Jake said happily. This time, he swung first.

For a minute, Malone looked down at the fallen gunman. Then he looked up at Jake. "Millions of people in the world," he said bitterly, "and only two of them are my clients. And you have to sock one of them."

Chapter Fifteen

"All right now," Malone said. "It's all settled. You've had one punch each, and you're even. Neither of you has apologized, so you're still even. So let's have no more trouble."

"Not in here," Joe the Angel added, in an ominous voice. He said in a milder tone, "Drinks on the house."

Gus Madrid's nose had stopped bleeding. He put his handkerchief away in his pocket and sat down on a bar stool. Jake stopped rubbing his knuckles and sat down on another. Malone sat down between them and hoped for the best. The small cluster of curious pedestrians had gone on their way, the customers of Joe the Angel's City Hall Bar had returned to their various occupations. The city hall janitor hadn't even looked up from his beer.

"Just the same," Gus Madrid said glumly, "if it wasn't for your wife—"

"What's that about my wife?" Jake demanded.

"He just means," Malone said hastily, "he's treating you with the respect due a married man."

There was a cold and indignant silence.

At last Jake said, "Well, I'm going to phone Myrdell and make a date for after working hours."

Gus Madrid said, "A nice type wife like you got, you oughtn'ta go making dates."

"You leave my wife out of this," Jake said furiously.

Joe the Angel reached under the bar. Malone said, "Shut up, guys, or you'll get me thrown out of here." The parakeet suddenly yelped, "Ring, ring, ring," and Malone added in a rage, "And you keep out of this!"

"I throw you all out," Joe the Angel said. He yelled at the city hall janitor, "And you too!"

Malone decided it was time to leave anyway and managed a dignified departure, Gus Madrid close behind him. Jake had headed into the telephone booth. The city hall janitor hadn't paid any attention.

At the anteroom to Malone's office, Gus Madrid paused. "Malone. Undertakers—"

"Have their living to earn, even as you and I," Malone said. He added in what he hoped was a mollifying tone, "Charles Swackhammer was Hazel Swackhammer's husband. I went to see him just in case he might know anything. He didn't. But somebody will. And don't worry."

"Oh," Gus Madrid said. He showed every intention of settling down to stay.

Malone met Maggie's puzzled gaze. He said, "And don't *you* worry." He went on into his private office and slammed the door.

Late afternoon sunlight glared at him across the snow-topped roofs outside his window, and he glared right back at it, suppressing a childish impulse to kick the wastebasket. Finally he sat down behind his desk, looked at the fine Havana cigar he'd allowed to go out no more than half smoked, threw it in the wastebasket, and reached for one of his own two-for-fifteen cent brand.

Everything he added together seemed to leave him more on the minus side. Charles (Cuddles) Swackhammer owned a large piece of Delora Deanne, and he was hardly one to go around deliberately damaging his own best interests, especially to the point of possible murder and mutilation. Cuddles was playful, but not that playful.

Cuddles was just about to marry one Maybelle Bragg, ex-employee of Hazel Swackhammer, and a sister, cousin, aunt, mother or daughter of Gertie Bragg, the face. For some reason he couldn't explain to himself, the imminence of the Bragg-Swackhammer nuptials bothered him. He didn't know, and couldn't even guess why, but he was bothered and apprehensive just the same.

He looked up the telephone numbers of Gertie Bragg, Eula Stolz and Rita Jardee in the telephone directory and called them all. No answer. He slammed down the telephone and scowled at it, wondering what he'd have said if there had been an answer. But there was no one at home. No one at home anywhere any more. And right now there might be a new and even more terrible offering on its way to Hazel Swackhammer by mail or by messenger. Worst of all, there didn't seem to be a single thing he could do about it.

He rose and began to prowl restlessly around the room, straightening the large steel engraving of Stephen A. Douglas and the framed photograph of the Oblong Marching Society, moved the ash trays around, stared unseeingly out the window, tore last week's pages off the desk calendar, eventually did succumb and kick the wastebasket.

Hazel, and her jealous, grasping ways, and her almost mad devotion to the Delora Deanne she had created. Otis Furlong, and the curious note that had crept into his voice when he spoke of his ex-wife, Rita Jardee. Dennis Dennis, and his unpublished lyrics, and his alimony payments to a good woman. Cuddles Swackhammer, and his bride-to-be. The beautiful hands of Eva Lou Strauss, the generous wanton, and the beautiful feet of Louella Frick, the farm girl and home-body. And all five of the Deloras missing.

The photographs in Otis Furlong's studio, and the softly falling snow transmuted into words in Dennis Dennis' typewriter. Myrdell Harris, and her vague smile and her too many voices, and her untold knowledge of—something. Tamia Tabet, who would probably giggle and grow affectionately tender at a touch. Ned McKoen and his sly column items. Cosmetics used in embalming. *Damn!*

It all added up to something, but he seemed to be working all the wrong problems in the wrong arithmetic book. Something that was right there in the confusion and fear and premonitions of terror yet to come. Some one fact, intangible, tantalizing, maddening. He knew it, and still he didn't know it; he could feel its frightening and revealing presence, and yet he just couldn't put his finger on it.

The telephone rang sharply, and he jumped. Maggie came in to announce anxiously that it was von Flanagan. The little lawyer looked apprehensively at the instrument, sighed deeply, rubbed a hand over his sweating face, and finally answered.

Von Flanagan just wanted to know if Malone had gotten the tickets for the fights yet, because if he hadn't, he had a friend on the sports desk of the *Tribune* who wanted a couple of traffic charges fixed up. He added, just a shade too casually to please Malone, "And what goes on with your friend, the practical joker?"

"I told him I'd see him in jail," Malone said, and hung up fast. He said to Maggie, "I will, too." Right now, though, he didn't have the faintest idea who, or when, or how.

"Malone—" Maggie began in an unhappy voice, "Malone, that Mr. Madrid—"

"Don't worry about him," he told her, hoping he sounded more reassuring than he felt. "We're playing on the same team."

"And Malone." He was pleased to note the anxiety was gone. "My brother Luke—"

"Tomorrow," Malone said, waving her away. "Right now I have things to do. A great many of them."

He telephoned Gadenski. Gadenski was gone for the day. He telephoned Otis Furlong; there was no answer. He telephoned Dennis Dennis; he had gone to the broadcasting studio. He telephoned Hazel Swackhammer. No, there had been no messages, nor—anything. And what was Malone doing?

"A great deal," Malone told her confidently. He telephoned Myrdell Harris, at the office and at home. She was at neither place. Once more he telephoned Gertie Bragg, Eula Stolz and Rita Jardee. Once more there was no answer.

Finally he telephoned Tamia Tabet to remind her of tonight's date, and hung up feeling better. He patted the wallet in his pocket, and felt still better. True there was still tomorrow to worry about, and Gus Madrid to worry about, but that was another day.

"Tomorrow is tomorrow," he told Maggie, "and Tamia is tonight. The devil fly away with Hazel Swackhammer," Malone said almost gaily. "And with Dennis Dennis, and Cuddles, and with Otis Furlong, Ned McKoen, von Flanagan, and Delora Deanne. And with all the hands and feet in the city of Chicago, except those belonging to Tamia Tabet."

"Malone," Maggie said, in a worried voice, "do you know what you're talking about?"

"I do indeed," Malone told her, "and stand aside for a man in a hurry." He put on his overcoat, set his hat at a jaunty angle, and headed for Joe the Angel's like a whole flock of homing pigeons.

Forty-five minutes later, he settled accounts with the owner, manager, bartender and headwaiter of Joe the Angel's City Hall Bar. Now, no matter what happened next, he'd re-established credit where he was likely to need it most.

Two hours and a shave, haircut, massage and manicure later, he paused briefly to admire his freshly pressed suit and new Countess Mara tie, and was on his way. Now the snow fairly sang merrily underfoot, a half moon was already adding glistening magic to streets and buildings, and Tamia Tabet was ready and waiting for him when he rapped softly at the door of her little apartment in a remodeled mansion on upper Rush Street.

She had on an entertainingly cut dress of more or less the same color as Otis Furlong's borrowed pink bathtub, and so extremely simple in design that he immediately knew either she hadn't bought it on a receptionist's salary, or had made it herself. She also wore a smile that made him momentarily consider abandoning the evening's plans for the suggestion of a quiet evening at home. But, he reminded himself sternly, this evening was planned to be more than a purely social one, and he still had to earn that check, regardless of how much or how little it might be. Moreover, there was the little matter of the task he'd taken on for Gus Madrid—

Right now he refused to think of those items, as he tucked Tamia Tabet's arm in his own and waved down a taxi. In fact, he almost waved a cheery greeting at Gus Madrid in his black sedan.

Nothing was going to interfere with his definitely unmouselike but best-laid plans for the evening ahead. And he simply refused to remember how many times he'd been dead wrong about such predictions in the past.

Chapter Sixteen

"It isn't that you're being unreasonable," Jake said, "it's just that you won't listen to reason."

He suddenly realized that he'd come perilously close to being cross with her, and gulped. Finally he added, realizing its inadequacy, "Darling!"

Helene smiled at him and said, "I'm perfectly willing to listen to reason. It's just that I don't quite see what Myrdell Harris has to do with it."

"Look," Jake said with something like desperation. "It's like this. Myrdell Harris—she's this Swackhammer woman's executive assistant."

"Secretary," Helene said.

"All right. She's her secretary. As such, she's obviously an inside track to Hazel Swackhammer. As such, she can obviously be a help in selling a Delora Deanne television program. And as such—" he stopped himself just in the nick of time.

"As such," Helene said very calmly, "it's imperative that you talk with her tonight. Alone. When you haven't even assembled a show yet. When you don't even know if Otis Furlong can come up with a means for doing a composite on television. Otis Furlong, or anybody."

"Well," Jake said, "there's Maggie's brother Luke's camera."

The expression on Helene's face told exactly what she thought of both Otis Furlong and Maggie's brother Luke's camera. But she said warmly, "Of course, Jake. Something's bound to work, sooner or later."

Jake breathed easier. "Another thing," he went on, trying to divert the course of the subject while still staying on it.

"Malone told us she has a perfect imitation of the Delora Deanne voice. Suppose something happened to Rita Jardee. Like laryngitis or something." Or sudden death, he thought.

Helene thought the same thing and hoped Jake had meant exactly what he'd said, and no more.

Jake looked at her. Deloras or no Deloras, there was only one Helene in the world. Right now she wore a smoothly sleek dress of some shiny, satiny stuff with unexpected tiny sparkles here and there, a stuff almost the exact color of her soft, corn-silk-color hair, and not a bit more glowing. In that one look he seemed to see her again in every time he'd ever seen her, from the very first sight of her, clad then in ice-blue lounging pajamas, a fur coat, and loose galoshes. He saw her busy, indolent, happy, anxious, loving, furious, and even frightened, and all one Helene.

"Darling," he said again. Repetitious and inadequate or not, it was exactly what he meant. "I'll give it all up for you. I'll give up the whole damn television business for you. Anything." Anything, except give up and live on her father's fortune.

"Don't be silly," Helene said briskly. "You'll do nothing of the sort. You know perfectly well I'm having more fun than two ants at the same picnic, and if you ever dare give up television, I'll leave you."

The brief moment in which they were several universes apart had passed.

Helene picked up a sleek brown wrap for which hundreds of small animals had lived and loved, threw it carelessly around her shoulders, and said, "Get going, you lazy bum. Locate your Myrdell Harris. What's more, I'm not going to insist on your taking me with you."

The tall, red-haired man cocked an eyebrow. "Oh," he said, "you trust me."

"No," Helene said serenely, "but I've got plans of my own."

For just one moment, Jake hesitated, ready either to confess the whole thing, or to give it up. Whatever happened, even if he had to go hunting for a press-agent job, Helene mustn't get mixed up in this—this thing, whatever it was. But if he confessed even a part of it, Helene would exuberantly insist on plunging right in to help. He couldn't guess at what the results of that could be, indeed, he didn't even want to.

Helene said, "I'm going to call on a perfectly respectable lady." Her kiss was as quick and as light as a snowflake, and yet as warm as sudden flame. Then she was gone.

Down in the car, she began to worry about the whole situation. She felt reasonably sure that Jake's reasons for seeing Myrdell Harris were exactly what he'd said they were. But if Myrdell Harris did know anything of what was going on, there was always the chance that she'd confide in Jake. Women of all ages were inclined to confide in Jake, given the slightest opportunity.

Oh, well, there was nothing to be done about it now. She told herself she was getting to be a worse worrier than Malone, and started the car.

The address, far out on the northwest side, was a shabby, two-apartment building, of badly weathered wood. There was an infinitesimal yard, where there might have been grass and even flowers, a very long time ago, and a sagging flight of steps. Helene looked at it for a few minutes before she left the car and went up to ring the doorbell.

It was a little while before the door was opened by a big-bellied man in carpet slippers, baggy slacks, an undershirt and one suspender. He looked at Helene as though she were personally responsible for all the troubles he and everyone else had ever had, and said, "Well?"

"I'm looking for Miss Eula Stolz," Helene said.

"Eula ain't here," the man said. He continued to block the door with his body and didn't seem disposed to add anything more.

A thin complaining voice from somewhere inside said, "What is it, Frank?"

"Lady here wants to see Eula," the man called back, still eyeing Helene unpleasantly.

"Well, tell her to come in," the voice called, "Eula ain't here, but tell her to come on in."

The man stepped aside. Helene hesitated a moment, and then went on in. There was a dark, narrow hall, and a lighted kitchen at the end of it, a kitchen that apparently, from its well-worn furniture, served as a general sitting room. There were dishes in the sink, a cluster of empty quart beer bottles to one side, and a freshly opened one on the table.

An enormously fat woman with streaky gray hair was squeezed into a rocking chair beside the table. She looked at Helene suspiciously and said, "You a friend of hers?"

"In a way, yes," Helene said. She tried to look like a friend of Eula Stolz.

"Well, Eula ain't here," the woman said, "not since yesterday morning."

"Left for work and ain't come back," Frank said. His voice suggested that it was all Helene's fault, too. "Never heard from her since. Never look to hear from her." And didn't care much, his expression added.

"I'm her Aunt Rose," the fat woman volunteered. "Eula, she boarded here. Paid her board, too," she added defensively.

"Didn't pay much," the man growled.

"Well," Aunt Rose said placatingly, "she didn't make much. Worked in some bath-soap factory somewhere, but she didn't make much."

Helene tried to think of something to say; she wished Malone were along.

"She probably took off for Hollywood like she always said she would," Frank said. "Every time she got mad, she said she would. Said she'd be appreciated out there."

From Malone's description of the torso and legs of Delora Deanne, Helene reflected, she probably would be.

"But she left all her clothes behind," Aunt Rose said.

Helene perked up and said, "Would you mind—I wonder if I could see them?"

"Why not?" Aunt Rose said. She pointed to a door. "That's her room there. Turn on the light for the lady, Frank."

Frank grumbled, and turned on the light.

Eula Stolz's room was small, with one window that opened onto the wall of the house next door, and lighted with one bulb hanging from the ceiling. It wasn't particularly neat, it wasn't particularly messy, in fact, it wasn't particularly anything. There were a bed, a bureau, a dresser, a chair, a rug, and two pictures; none of them had cost very much to begin with, and none of them had received very good care.

She opened the closet door, and caught her breath. There were dresses and dresses and dresses. Dresses for evening, for afternoon, for the street. There were slack suits and playsuits and bathing suits. All of them were gay and lovely and costly.

Helene looked at a few of the labels, and caught her breath a second time.

The bureau drawers were overflowing with exquisite, filmy, lovely lingerie and stockings.

Helene almost fled back to the kitchen.

"Maybe you'd know someone who'd like to buy 'em?" the man named Frank said.

Helene shook her head. Finally she managed to say, "I'm sorry. I don't know anyone they'd fit—"

She shook her head and said a thank you to Aunt Rose's invitation to have a beer before she left, and groped her way down the hallway of the building that smelled as though a lot of different people had been living there over a long period of time.

Once out in the car, she lit a cigarette and sat very still for a few minutes. She'd found out exactly what she'd expected to find out, but it had still shaken her.

Beautiful gloves, beautiful shoes, beautiful clothes, all left behind because they weren't going to be needed any more.

Suddenly she started the motor and fairly shot down the street. Right now, she wanted to find Malone, and fast.

Chapter Seventeen

The evening began by proceeding according to plan, though dinner at Jacques' produced nothing except a good-sized check and some very, very pleasant memories that were not entirely composed of excellent food. Malone observed Gus Madrid eating gloomily at a table by himself; once during the meal he left it to make a telephone call.

The early show at the *Chez* took his mind briefly off murder and the cosmetic business, and got him and Tamia on first-name terms. If there was any jarring note, it was that Gus Madrid didn't seem to enjoy the show. For one fleeting sympathetic moment, Malone found himself wishing that, as long as

Gus Madrid didn't have his Eva Lou to keep him company, he did have some cuddly little blonde of his own.

On their way to the next important stop, they paused at a quiet little spot where Malone switched from champagne to rye and soda, Gus Madrid brooded alone in a rear booth, and Tamia shyly confided that the color pink always made her think of making love. For that matter, so did blue and green.

But a radio was playing softly in the quiet little spot, and the program was "Delora Deanne Dreams."

"—sweet silver dreams, Delora! Snow will not harm your soft, smooth skin—"

A sudden nasty prickle ran over the little lawyer's skin, and he sat bolt upright on the upholstered bench. The words were the words of Dennis Dennis, but the voice was not the voice of Rita Jardee.

It was like it. Yes, it was very like it. So much so that—as Malone observed in a quick glance across the table—Tamia Tabet didn't seem to notice the difference. But Malone had listened to that voice too many times, on the radio and in his own favorite dreams.

He excused himself, and this time it was he who headed for the telephone booth.

Rita Jardee's number did not answer, though he let it ring for a long time. Neither did Cuddles Swackhammer's, nor Delora Deanne's, nor any of the other numbers he called.

The bored-voiced operator at the broadcasting studio didn't know anything about anything, and couldn't, or wouldn't, connect him with anyone who did.

Well, he told himself, there was nothing he could do about it now. He went back to their booth, took Tamia's soft little hand again, and managed to pick up the conversation right where he'd left off.

"—but how about magenta? Or purple?"

The Pump Room produced more businesslike, if less delightful, results, Gus Madrid, who had made another telephone call, hovered near the door. From across the room, Ned McKoen signaled them that yes, he would be very happy to join them at their table. Ten minutes later the short, plumpish columnist slid into a chair and said, "What's new?"

"I'm the one who asks you that," Malone said.

"Then read about it in the newspapers," Ned McKoen said happily. "New development in the model-playboy affair."

He patted Tamia's knee, smiled at her vaguely, and said, "And how are you, my dear? That's good." He picked up his glass and went on, "Turns out she isn't suing him, never intended to sue him. All been sweetness and light all the time. Turns out she's marrying him instead." He hiccuped quietly and said, "P'arm me."

"Would you call Charlie Swackhammer, of Swackhammer Brothers, a playboy?" Malone asked.

"Four will get you seven," the columnist said, "that's exactly what he's doing right now. Well, happiness to him." He lifted his glass again. "And what legal business are you doing for his ex, Malone, or don't I ask you that yet?"

"You don't," Malone said. "And how did you know?"

"I protect my sources," Ned McKoen said with injured dignity. "Thanks for the drink, Malone, and good luck to you." He emptied his glass and wandered away in the general direction of a Hollywood starlet Malone found hard to recognize without a bathing suit.

Well, it didn't matter so much now what Ned McKoen's sources had been. In fact, the chances were that the columnist had simply relied on his own shrewd powers of observation. Must have, or he wouldn't have made such a bad guess, confusing possible breach-of-promise with what had turned out to be pure and probably simple object matrimony. Or else May- belle, the cute little thing, had tipped Ned McKoen off herself, with the idea of luring a possibly coy Cuddles Swackhammer to the altar.

He silently toasted the bride-to-be and her Cuddles. Gus Madrid chose that moment to return from one of his fruitless telephone calls and stop at Malone's table.

"What I want to know is," he said glumly, "are you doing anything to find my girl, or aren't you doing anything to find my girl?"

"In my own way," Malone said, "I am. You've just got to have confidence in me, that's all."

Gus Madrid gave him a look showing all the confidence he would have given a coiled rattler, but he went away.

"Just a guy wants me to find his girl for him," Malone told Tamia.

"What was that you just said?" Tamia Tabet asked, pouting prettily.

"I said, tomorrow is another day, and the hell with it," the little lawyer said, "and let's get out of this highly refined joint and go on to the Casino."

At the end of a highly diverting taxi ride, he said, "And how about pale orange? Or taupe?"

He'd been right all along. She did giggle.

Two more lines of the song that had been bothering him off and on since he woke up that morning suddenly came into his mind.

> *Her eyes were blue, her hair was red,*
> *And her two lips were the same—*

He thought it would be interesting to find out her reaction to a rainbow.

"You sing, too!" Tamia Tabet purred.

"Flattery," Malone said happily, "will get you everywhere."

Otis Furlong was in the Casino's downstairs bar, gazing thoughtfully into an empty martini glass. He turned around to greet them and said, "From now on, every third round is on me, and what did you find out from the columnist?"

"It was another playboy," Malone said solemnly, "and another Delora Deanne."

Otis Furlong said, "Good God! That makes six of them!"

"No," Malone shook his head owlishly. "That makes none of them. No more Delora Deannes. All gone. Fact is, there never were any. Don't you know that? Delora Deanne was a myth. Myth Delora Deanne. But that was in another century and on another continent, or something."

"Malone," the bartender said, "you're drunk."

"And about time, too," Malone said, looking at his watch. "And I'll have Scotch and water, and a daiquiri for the little lady, and Furlong, I have news for you. Your ex-wife is missing."

The handsome photographer scowled. "What do you mean? How? Where is she missing from? What happened to her? How do you know?"

"One thing at a time," Malone said. He downed his Scotch, patted Tamia's hand, took out a fresh cigar, unwrapped it, lit it, and then said, "Maybe she isn't missing, but her voice is."

"Damn it, Malone—" Otis Furlong said frantically.

"The broadcast," Malone said. "I heard it. It was her voice, and it wasn't her voice. I mean—" He drew a long breath, started over and told of the Delora Deanne show, of the voice that had been so like Rita Jardee's, and yet not quite the same.

"But I heard it," Tamia said, in a puzzled voice. "And I didn't notice anything different."

"You didn't," Malone told her, "and probably untold thousands of listeners heard it and didn't notice the difference. But I did, and I know." He saw no point in adding just how long he'd been listening, rapturously, to the voice of Delora Deanne.

Otis Furlong, a little pale, said that he could hardly believe it, that Rita had never been known to miss a broadcast. But on the other hand, it might be true, and that anyway, it would be a good idea to find out. He added, "Let's go up to Rickett's and check. Dennis Dennis usually goes there after the show, and so does Henry."

"Henry Henry?" Malone asked hopefully.

"Just Henry," Otis Furlong said. "I don't know his last name. He produces the show."

They spotted Dennis Dennis and Henry at a table in a far corner of Rickett's, with a young woman in a cloudy gray-violet dress. Even with her back turned, and across the crowded room, Malone recognized Myrdell Harris. He'd known that it would be Myrdell.

Henry was a pale young man with thick-lensed glasses and what appeared to be a permanently worried expression. The expression was deepened by an added shadow of apprehension as the trio approached the table.

"Otis," Henry said anxiously, "I don't know what did happen. It was just one of those things."

"Rita simply didn't show up," Dennis Dennis said just as anxiously. "We phoned and phoned and couldn't locate her anywhere. She's never done it before."

"It was so late," Henry said. "I just had to go ahead and take a chance. Luckily, I remembered Myrdell, and I was able to reach her right away."

"Myrdell's a very talented, very promising actress," Dennis Dennis said as though he'd invented her himself.

"And I'm absolutely sure," Henry said, "*absolutely* sure, that nobody, but nobody, noticed any difference."

"Except me," Malone said, sitting down beside Tamia.

Myrdell gave him a vague, soulful look and said, "I do hope you liked me."

"The voice," Malone said, sighing, "was the voice of Esau. Or do I mean Jacob? I always mix them up. Anyway, I liked it." He pressed Tamia's hand and smiled at Myrdell.

"But that doesn't tell us where Rita is, you fools," Otis Furlong said angrily, his good-looking face white. "I'm going to telephone her apartment. Something might have happened to her."

"Still mad about Rita," Henry said sadly. He pressed Myrdell's hand and smiled at Tamia.

It seemed to be a very long wait before Otis Furlong came back. "She doesn't answer," he reported. "Nobody answers. I let it ring a long time, a long, long time."

Malone could have told him the phone wasn't going to answer. The little lawyer felt terribly cold, the cheerful glow of champagne, rye and Scotch had fled from him suddenly and completely. He felt a wild urge to tell them all the whole frightful tale, the hands and the feet, the gloves and the shoes, everything.

The voice, now. He wished he knew, and still didn't want to know, just what was going to be on Hazel Swackhammer's neat desk in the morning.

"For the love of something," Dennis Dennis exploded, "don't just stand there. And for the love of something else, don't look so awful about it. Nothing has happened to Rita. Nothing ever happens to Rita. Maybe she's just in the hospital. Maybe she's in jail. Why don't we go look for her?"

"Very good idea," Henry said. "We'll go look for her."

Otis Furlong said, "There's a joint on upper Clark Street where she hangs out sometimes—"

"Fine," Malone said. "Let's *all* go look for her."

Myrdell, it appeared, couldn't go along to help look. She glanced at her watch and said she was meeting someone in just a little while. Her eyes met Malone's as though he ought to know whom she was meeting, and why. The look puzzled him, and he didn't like it. No, he didn't like it at all.

With an assist from the driver, they all managed to crowd into one taxicab. Malone sat staring out the window, unhappily seeing snow-covered, moon-touched streets that had lost their magic for him now. Even Tamia Tabet snuggled confidingly close to him didn't make any difference.

Perhaps he should tell. No, he couldn't. Not yet, anyway. And especially not with that terrible, stricken look on Otis Furlong's face. The Clark Street establishment had a cheerful, neon-welcoming front, but it didn't cheer him up the least bit.

Until they found Rita Jardee.

She was sitting at a table at the back of the room, her red hair beckoning to them like a lighthouse beacon, her haggard, attractive face looking smugly pleased.

Otis Furlong reached her first, in long, almost leaping strides. He grabbed her by the shoulders, almost shook her, and gasped out, "Rita! I was afraid—something terrible had happened to you! Oh, Rita, darling, are you all right? Tell me you're all right, Rita!" He sank down beside her and said, "Oh, Rita, I do love you so!"

Dennis Dennis and Henry looked at each other solemnly and said almost in unison, "Rita is all right."

Malone sat down, pulled Tamia close to him and said, "Rita is all right."

Rita threw her arms around Otis Furlong's neck and said, "Darling! Don't ever leave me!" Then she pulled herself away and said firmly to Henry, "I'm through, understand? Through! No more mushmouth!"

Henry looked dubious for a moment and then said, "Well—"

Rita said, "I just suddenly reached the point where I simply couldn't stand it any longer. That awful copy, Dennis. That awful, awful copy!"

"That awful, awful, awful copy," Dennis Dennis agreed fervently.

"Sweet, soft, silvery snow," she mouthed. "Sweet silken dreams!" She revised the copy in words that would have put any network off the air in a hurry and probably forever. "I never wanted the job in the first place, but Otis coaxed me. I didn't want the job, I wanted Otis back again."

"You've got him," Dennis Dennis said.

"But I had to quit to get him," she said. "And that damn woman. Telling me where to go, how to act, what to do, and then griping about paying me any decent money. And that *stuff!* Silken soft, and sweeter than your sweetest dreams!" She added one very brief and very unpleasant word.

"I hate the sound of my own voice," she said. "Do you understand?" Her voice cracked and grew hoarse and shrill. She repeated, "I hate the sound of my own voice! There, that sounds better! I'm going to get a job as a hog caller!"

She gave a skillful imitation of a hog caller that would probably have gotten them all thrown out, except for Malone's hasty and expert intervention.

"Well, that's that," she said, resting her head happily on Otis Furlong's shoulder. "You're looking at a woman who's just retired from the radio business. Otis, do we have to get married all over again, and do we use the same ring?"

"A new ring," he promised her. "As big as Eva Lou's opal."

Again the song came back to Malone's memory, and he came up with two more lines.

> *A ring was on her finger,*
> *But I loved her just the same—*

"I know that song," Henry said. He added two more lines.

> *She was a lyin' woman,*
> *Delilah was her name—*

Malone leaned back contentedly and gazed at his glass. Delilah—Delora—what did it matter. Everything was all right. Everything was going to be all right. Rita was all right. Rita was right here across from him, purring like a tickled kitten, and showing no evidence of murder or mayhem.

Another thing struck him. Gus Madrid had vanished, sometime between the Casino and Rickett's. That could mean only one thing. Eva Lou had come home. Eva Lou had finally answered his phone call. Somehow, Eva Lou had turned up, as alive and well as Rita Jardee. True, there was the matter of repaying Gus Madrid, the enforcer, his five hundred dollars, since he, Malone, hadn't done the finding of Eva Lou. But he'd worry about that later.

A smart man like Otis Furlong would certainly find some way of piecing together a Delora Deanne on a televison screen. There was no doubt that all the Delora Deannes would be happy to be television stars, even if each one was only one-fifth of a star.

And the question of the column items was satisfactorily accounted for. And the little matter of the hands and feet sent to Hazel Swackhammer was something that must have some perfectly simple, logical, understandable and obvious explanation. It was just a small problem now of finding it, and he'd attend to that first thing in the morning. Meanwhile—

Rita Jardee gave another, and louder, hog-calling imitation, and the little lawyer took advantage of the resulting confusion to grasp Tamia Tabet firmly by the arm, slip quietly away and head for the door.

She looked at him admiringly and said, "My, but you're a busy man!"

"Not half as busy as I'm going to be," Malone said.

At that moment a waiter signaled to him. "Mr. Malone?"

Malone reached for his wallet, nodded toward the table, and said, "My guests."

It seemed that wasn't it. Mr. Malone was wanted, and urgently, on the telephone.

It was Jake's voice. And it sounded hoarse, desperate, and more than a little frightened.

"Malone—I've been trying all over to reach you. I traced you to Rickett's, and then someone said they'd heard someone say you were going to—"

"Calm down," Malone said, chewing his cigar. "Calm down! Where are you, and what's happened?"

"I'm in Myrdell Harris' apartment," Jake said. "And she's dead. Malone, you'd better get right over here."

Chapter Eighteen

Just when everything was going so smoothly. Too smoothly. He should have realized that and been wary. The little lawyer urged the cab driver to go faster, and leaned glumly back against the cushions.

Dennis Dennis and Henry had been delighted to take Tamia home. Too delighted. Malone scowled. There would be other nights, of course, but just the same—

He reminded himself sharply that Jake was the one to be thinking about now.

Finding Rita Jardee, plus the disappearance of Gus Madrid, had convinced him that the Delora Deannes were merely missing. Now he wasn't so sure. Rita Jardee might not have been included in whatever devilish plan there was to ruin Delora Deanne. Or she might have been later on the list, and simply picked this inopportune time to have an attack of hog-calling. Gus Madrid—anything might have happened to him.

Just as anything might have happened to Eva Lou Strauss, and Louella Frick, and Eula Stolz, and Gertie Bragg.

Another thought struck him. He felt certain that Rita Jardee wasn't going to be the silky voice of Delora Deanne any more, come what might. Even allowing for temperament, he knew determination when he met it face to face. And apparently Myrdell wasn't going to do any broadcasting either.

He was halfway up the elevator before he realized that the Jake Justus Television Production Company wasn't the only thing involved. There was, also, the matter of murder.

Jake met him at the door, his freckled face pale. "Thank God you're here," he said. "Thank God Helene isn't here. Thank God the doctor got here."

"Stop babbling," Malone said firmly, "and tell me what happened. Is Myrdell—"

"She's dead, all right," Jake said. "I was just sitting here. I was just talking with her. And suddenly she looked funny and died. Hazel Swackhammer called the doctor. They're in there now." He nodded toward the bedroom.

"Wait a minute," Malone said. He felt a little confused. He sat down and said, "Relax and begin at the beginning."

"I wanted to talk with her," Jake said. "I used the show as a reason. I thought I might find out more from her than you did. I mean, Malone—"

"Never mind what you mean," Malone said. "Go on."

"I telephoned her," Jake said. He paused to wipe his face with a crumpled damp handkerchief. "She said she was busy earlier, but she'd meet me here."

Then that was the appointment Myrdell had left to keep. With Jake. And incidentally with death.

"She was here when I got here. And so was Hazel Swackhammer. She gave me a hint that Hazel Swackhammer would go away. She lives in the same building. Hazel Swackhammer, I mean. A—an awesome kind of woman." He wiped his face again. "I waited for Hazel Swackhammer to go. Meanwhile we sat and we talked."

Malone asked, "What about?"

"Orchids," Jake said.

Malone opened his mouth and shut it again.

"It was all I could think of to talk about," Jake said defensively. "I wrote an article about them once and I happened to remember. Do you know how many different kinds of orchids there are? Or that some orchids—"

"Shut up," Malone said. He remembered where Myrdell Harris had kept her liquor, and poured Jake a stiff one. To be on the safe side, he poured a stiff one for himself.

"All right," he said, "you were all three talking about orchids. And then—?"

"She looked—funny," Jake said weakly. "For just a minute. And then she sort of—fell over. She was dead."

"How did you know?"

"Hazel Swackhammer said she was. She said she'd better call the doctor. Myrdell Harris' doctor. He's right here in the same building. She called the doctor and I put the—put her—in on her bed. Then Hazel Swackhammer went in to stay with her. Then the doctor got here. Then I got worried and I called you."

"And a good thing you did," Malone said. He took out a cigar, looked at it, put it away again. "How did she look the first time you saw her?"

"Hazel Swackhammer?"

"No, no, no," Malone said. He took the cigar out again, but he didn't light it.

"Oh," Jake said. He scowled. "She looked alive."

Malone sighed. "Jake, you'd better go home. Straight home."

Jake looked even more worried, and glanced at the bedroom door. "I don't know—"

"I do," Malone said. "No law says you can't leave a place where a person is taken ill. I'll explain for you. Just get out of here, go home and calm down. If there are any questions to be asked, you'll do better answering them later."

And there would be questions asked, he told himself. He felt certain of that. He fairly shoved Jake out the door.

After all, he told himself, there was no reason why Jake shouldn't leave. Myrdell wasn't even officially dead yet, to say nothing of being murdered. Jake had been here when she died, but so had Hazel Swackhammer, and as far as Jake officially knew, Myrdell Harris had simply been taken very ill, very suddenly.

His cigar had gone out, and he didn't bother to relight it, chewing on it savagely as he paced up and down the room. It had to be poison, some slow-acting poison. If she'd been stabbed, or shot, or strangled, Jake would have noticed it. He discarded that as a second-best thought, and decided it didn't have to be a slow-acting poison. Something she'd taken after she returned home? Had the three been having a drink when she suddenly toppled over? There weren't any glasses around.

Hazel Swackhammer had been with her before Jake arrived. He peered into the kitchen. No glasses in evidence there either. But someone could have been there ahead of Hazel Swackhammer. And if glasses had been used, Myrdell Harris could have tidily washed them and put them away, though she didn't seem like the domestic type. Of course, her unknown visitor could have done the washing up. Or Myrdell might have done it, undomestic type or not, because she didn't want it noticed that anyone had been there.

And there were so many different ways of poisoning, so infernally many different ways. Of course, once it was known what the poison was, things would be vastly simpler.

So much depended too on when Mydrell had arrived home. On what time Hazel Swackhammer had come in, and then Jake. The last two could be found out easily. The elevator boy would probably remember when Myrdell Harris had come home. Come home to die. The little lawyer shivered.

He tried to remember just when she had left Rickett's. Somewhere between eight and ten or eleven. He hadn't exactly been keeping track of time during the evening. But perhaps somebody had.

Then too, she might not have come straight home, might have made a stop on the way.

Dennis Dennis and Henry had been with her at Rickett's and during and before the broadcast. Any number of people could have been with her during the broadcast and long before

that. Jake and Hazel Swackhammer and possibly some unknown person had been with her after she left Rickett's. She
just could have seen Rita Jardee sometime along the course of
the evening. Or Otis Furlong. Or anybody.

It was all going to depend on how long it had taken whatever poison it was to take effect.

There was a handful of telephone call slips left on the desk
and he looked at them idly. They were all dated this evening,
they were spaced at ten-minute intervals, and all of them re-
quested Miss Myrdell Harris to call Mr. Dennis Dennis immediately at a number Malone concluded was the number of the
saloon where he'd left Dennis Dennis a while ago. He wondered if she'd ever made the call back.

The bedroom door opened and Hazel Swackhammer
came out, her ordinary face composed in what came close to a
polite expression of regret. Behind her came a tall, rangy,
loose-jointed man with a thick mane of snow-white hair, and
watery blue eyes behind thick glasses. He carried a doctor's
bag, and with him was a pleasant-faced, middle-aged man with
graying dark hair and a professional smile.

"Too bad," the tall man was saying. "But it wouldn't have
made any difference if I'd been called earlier. So don't distress
yourself, Mr. Justus."

"I'm not Mr. Justus," the lawyer said. "I'm Malone. John J.
Malone."

"Eh?" the doctor said. "You say Mr. Justus has gone
home?" One hand cupped his ear.

"No," Malone shouted. "I mean, yes, I mean, I'm John J.
Malone."

Hazel Swackhammer said helpfully, "This is Dr. Stonecypher. And his nephew Alvin." She roared, "Dr. Stonecypher,
this is Mr. Malone. My lawyer."

Dr. Stonecypher peered at him. "Must say you got a lawyer here fast. Heard of you, Mr. Malone."

"I just happened to drop in," Malone shouted. "Mr.
Justus went home. He was worried about his wife." Which was
certainly true.

He looked interestedly at the tall, white-haired doctor.
Dr. Alonzo Stonecypher was more than merely famous, he was
practically a legend. He'd been president of goodness knew
how many medical associations, he'd lectured everywhere an
audience could be rounded up, he'd been for years head of an

important medical school, and the Stonecypher Coronary Clinic, as well as a wing of an impressive hospital, had been named for him.

"Well, he doesn't need to worry about her life," Dr. Stonecypher said. "She's gone. I've expected it for a long time. Warned her any number of times. Nothing could have been done even if I'd been here earlier."

A new and incomprehensible idea was growing in Malone's mind. He stared at the elderly doctor and said, "Do you mean she died a natural death?"

"Eh?" the doctor said, and then, "I beg pardon?"

"He said, did she die a natural death?" nephew Alvin screamed into Dr. Stonecypher's ear. He said helpfully to Malone, "Of course she died a natural death."

Malone wiped his brow with the palm of his hand. He caught a chair and sat down. "Are you a doctor too?" he asked.

"No," Alvin Stonecypher said. "I'm an insurance salesman. I just take Uncle 'Lonzo around."

Dr. Stonecypher glared at Malone and said, "Are you implying that I don't know my profession, young man?"

"Oh, no," Malone said hastily. "No, no, no. Nothing like that." He tried to remember how long it had been since anybody called him "Young man," and couldn't.

"She had a congenital intra-atrial septal defect," Dr. Stonecypher said. He looked at Malone with pitying condescension for a layman's ignorance and said, "A defective heart."

Malone said, "No!"

This, curiously enough, seemed to mollify the white-haired doctor. "These cases go just like—that." He snapped his fingers and launched into a lengthy medical explanation, full of words Malone didn't grasp and tried desperately to remember. Then the doctor turned to Hazel Swackhammer. "Anything more you need? Notify her folks? Make the—arrangements?"

Hazel Swackhammer shook her head. "I'll do it," she shouted. Even her shout sounded efficient.

Dr. Stonecypher nodded, placated. "Well, everything's in order." He looked at his watch and said querulously, "Alvin, I want to go home."

After they had gone, Malone turned to his client. "I'm sorry—I must apologize for what I said. But—a sudden death—coming on top of—everything else—"

She lifted her shoulders slightly. "It's all right. I'd have thought the same thing if I hadn't known about Myrdell's illness."

"Well—" Malone looked at his dead cigar, laid it in a little blue porcelain ash tray. "Her family—"

"She hadn't any," Hazel Swackhammer said. "Known her for years. All alone in the world."

None of the girls who worked for Hazel Swackhammer seemed to have any family, Malone thought suddenly. He wondered if it had been planned that way. "Well—" he said again, and paused. "Well, I'll be glad to take care of the—the arrangements," he finished lamely, wondering why people didn't come right out and say what they meant, and be done with it.

"That," Hazel Swackhammer said, "will be very kind of you."

At least some little good might come of this totally—well, almost totally—ruined evening, he thought. Perhaps he would get back in the good graces of Rico di Angelo. He went to the telephone.

At first, Rico was angry at being wakened at such an hour. Then he was angry at being called by Malone.

"Whatever it is, Malone," he said firmly, "I—will—not—do—it!" He threatened to hang up.

"Wait a minute," Malone said hastily. "You don't understand—"

Things were straightened out at last. Rico promised to be over immediately. Indeed, he thanked Malone. But he hung up with, "Only, no monkey business, Malone, I warn you."

Hazel Swackhammer agreed that there was no need for Malone to wait with her until Rico di Angelo arrived. The little lawyer glanced at his watch and decided there was a bare chance he might still be able to salvage some of the evening. Dennis Dennis and Henry might not yet have gotten around to taking Tamia home.

He hurried down the elevator and ran right into Helene in the lobby.

"Malone! I've been looking all over for you. I finally trailed you here. Then I saw Jake come out, but he didn't see me. What's going on?"

"It's gone on," Malone said. "Jake came to see Myrdell Harris because he thought she might be an inside track to Hazel Swackhammer and selling the show—"

"I know that," Helene said impatiently. "And is she?"

"She isn't," Malone said. "Not any more." He told her, briefly and hastily, what had happened.

"And it was really a natural death?"

"Dr. Stonecypher said so," Malone said. "Dr. Alonzo Stonecypher."

She nodded, thoughtfully. "I know him. Malone—"

"I know," Malone said impatiently. "It's a shock. It's being natural, I mean. I thought the same thing. In a situation like this—a sudden death—" He began walking to the door, Helene right along with him. "Well, a murder wouldn't have been unexpected. But, Dr. Alonzo Stonecypher—"

She looked at him coldly, and had nothing to say.

"And a good thing, too," Malone said. "Because I have a date. I mean, I had a date. I may still have, if I can catch up with her in time."

Helene walked to her car, got in and slammed the door. "You! A time like this, and you worry about a date!"

She was gone, without even offering him a ride.

Chapter Nineteen

It was a thoroughly disreputable hour when Malone arrived at Joe the Angel's City Hall Bar. His search for Tamia Tabet had been long, tiresome, expensive, and unsuccessful and had involved buying drinks in a great many places. Now it was practically time to go home.

The place was deserted save for Joe the Angel himself behind the bar, a different city hall janitor at his regular table, brooding into his beer, and von Flanagan sitting on a bar stool and gazing moodily into his untouched drink.

The big police officer wheeled around as Malone came in and growled, "High time! I've been looking for you. Called your office three times. Called your hotel five times. Been here eight times. Looked in six different saloons in between times. Scared the daylights out of two floating crap games. Where the hell have you been?"

"Oh, just here and there," Malone said. He leaned on the bar, looked at his watch, and said, "Just gin now, no beer."

"Damn you, Malone. *Where are they?*"

"Should all be home and in bed by now," Malone said. "It's about time, too. Drink up, von Flanagan, and I'll buy." There were still two untouched hundred-dollar bills in his wallet. Maggie had doubtless made good use of one, and he had nearly half of another left. Perhaps Gus Madrid would accept that and wait a few days for the rest. Perhaps. Oh well, it still wasn't quite tomorrow, and the check from Hazel Swackhammer was in the mail.

"Malone, I swear by—" Von Flanagan's face began to turn scarlet. "Malone. For the last time. I'm giving you a chance only because you're an old friend. Where are they?"

"Where are what?" Malone said crossly, reaching for his gin.

"The hands and the feet!" von Flanagan roared.

Joe the Angel dropped his bar rag, picked it up, and stared at Malone.

Malone said, "Oh, that," very cheerfully. But the premonition of an unpleasant chill was beginning to creep into his bones.

"Because," the big police officer went on relentlessly, "we've got the rest. Torso and legs, anyway."

The little lawyer took his drink down in one gulp, and put his glass down very slowly and carefully while his hand was still reasonably steady.

"And the head," von Flanagan said. "Malone, what have you done with the head?"

Malone said nothing. He was beginning to wonder just what he was going to do with his own.

Von Flanagan drank his bourbon and began muttering bitterly, apparently to himself. The legal aspects of obstructing justice. Withholding vitally important information. Concealing necessary evidence. No consideration for years of friendship. Probably hiding out material witnesses. Making trouble and work for the whole police department. Ought to be tossed in jail. His voice trailed off at last into what became a deathlike silence.

Malone said nothing. He stared, bewildered, at nothing. Joe the Angel refilled both glasses and looked at Malone expectantly. Von Flanagan looked at Malone with a mixture of hopefulness and badly suppressed rage.

At last, in the icy silence, the city hall janitor drained his beer glass, rose, stretched, walked to the door, paused and said, "I remember once in the old country, they found a head. Like from a mummy. It was in a blue box." He went away, closing the door silently behind him.

"Box," Malone said suddenly. "Boxes. Lots and lots and lots of boxes."

"Malone," von Flanagan said anxiously, "are you all right?"

"No," Malone said. "Tell me about this torso. Where did you find it?"

"Klutchetsky found it," von Flanagan told him. "In a coffin."

Another box. Malone closed his eyes.

"It was in a storage warehouse," von Flanagan went on. "Night man, making his rounds, noticed it. Didn't think it belonged there. Called in. Klutchetsky got the call, went right to the warehouse. Opened up the coffin. Malone, it had been embalmed."

"Damn it," Malone said. "Of course it had been embalmed. I knew that."

"Fine," von Flanagan said. "But what else do you know?"

"I'm not sure," Malone said slowly, and very wearily. His stomach had decided to skip the wet concrete stage and turn directly into ice. "I'm not sure what I know and I'm not sure that I'm going to like it." He finished his gin in the hope that it would, at least, warm him a little. It didn't. He'd become painfully and suddenly sober now. "No, I don't like it even a little bit."

Von Flanagan said, "Well—" a little uncomfortably. He cleared his throat and said, "Well, Malone, I suppose we'd better go look at it."

"I suppose we had," Malone said miserably, and shivered a little.

They went out the door without bothering to nod good night to a worried Joe the Angel and got in von Flanagan's official car. Malone somehow managed to get a cigar lighted and puffed at it, looking out the window with unseeing eyes. He was terribly tired now, tired beyond all belief, and frightened, and very cold. There was unknown and unguessed-at horror in the darkened windows that they passed, horror in the deserted streets, horror in every light and every shadow. The walls knew it, and the alleys, and the winds that whistled around the corners knew it, and they whispered it back to him, over and over.

He said nothing, and he found himself trying to move very silently, his footsteps no more than quiet whispers as he followed von Flanagan down the seemingly endless corridors, through doorway after doorway.

The girl, whoever she was, had been beautiful. Malone took one long, despairing look, and closed his eyes for an instant.

"The hands," von Flanagan murmured hoarsely. "The hands, and the feet."

Malone glanced quickly, closed his eyes again, and said, "Yes. Yes, they could. But I couldn't swear to it. Not yet."

"There's no identifying mark of any kind," von Flanagan said. "Except this. Right above the knee. As though she'd habitually worn garters. Jeweled garters, Doc Flynn says. Even the very good embalming job didn't completely take out the mark."

Another line of the song began to run insanely through Malone's troubled mind.

She wore a diamond garter—

"Rings," Malone said. "Rings on her fingers."

"For the love of God, Malone," von Flanagan breathed, "this is no time for singing!"

The little lawyer shook his head. "The ring, von Flanagan. That was it."

Von Flanagan grabbed his arm and steered him quickly and firmly back through the dreary corridors, and out into the street. The night was beginning to vanish in the dawn now, a drab December dawn that threatened snow. Not soft and whitely falling snow this time, though.

"Don't you see, damn you," Malone said angrily. "There wasn't any ring." He paused. "Ring. The bird. The parakeet. Telephone."

"Malone," von Flanagan asked in an anxious voice. "Don't you feel well? Do you want to lie down somewhere?"

"I never felt better in my life," Malone said, lying in his throat. "And I never expect to. And where is the nearest telephone?"

Von Flanagan, his broad red face one big confused scowl,

pointed out an all-night lunchroom. Malone thumbed hastily through the telephone book for the number of Charlie Swackhammer's home.

The voice that answered was sleepy, then angry, and at last, bewildered.

"Do you know where Maybelle is?" Malone demanded roughly.

"Yes. Yes, of course I know where she is. And listen you, do you know what time—"

"I do," Malone said. "It's time for you to get up. Don't let Maybelle out of your sight. Do you understand? Don't let her out of your sight for as much as five seconds."

"All right," the cross, sleepy voice said. "All right, I won't. But what's the reason? What are you trying to do, Malone?"

"I'm trying to save her life, that's what," Malone said wearily. "Because she's the one who was going to be murdered."

He hung up and turned around to face von Flanagan, swaying a little with what was near exhaustion now. "There isn't going to be any head. And there hasn't been any murder. There isn't going to be any murder. That torso—"

"Death by natural causes," von Flanagan said. "Doc Flynn told me that already. It was—"

Before he could go on, Malone said, "Of course it was death from natural causes. I should have known it from the beginning. Because of the ring."

"Malone—" Von Flanagan paused, scowled, went on with, "But who was she?"

"Who knows?" Malone said in a curiously flat voice. "It doesn't matter now, von Flanagan. Somewhere, there's a coffin that was buried without a body in it. Or shortly to be buried. If you'll check with all the recent funerals of very beautiful young women, you'll find it." He shook his head, as though trying to clear it. "The ring," he repeated, whispering to himself. "That was the oversight."

"Are you *sure* you feel well?" von Flanagan said, the anxiety now turning into deep concern.

"Perfectly," Malone said. "Von Flanagan, you've got to believe me, now. I'll deliver the hands and the feet to you. But I can't do it before tomorrow. Understand?"

Von Flanagan nodded. He'd known Malone a long, long time. "What are you going to do in the meantime?"

"Things," Malone said, in that tired, listless voice.

"Various things. To check facts and conclusions. Ends that don't justify the means. Or something. Tomorrow, remember. And I'll deliver someone, too. But not to you."

Von Flanagan started to protest. Malone stopped him with a shake of the head.

"Because it's not in your department, von Flanagan."

Chapter Twenty

For a little while Malone stood on the windswept street corner, wondering what to do next. He thought about going back to his hotel, a tub full of hot water, a quick nap, a shave, and a change of clothes. Then he decided against it. He thought about ham and eggs, and fried potatoes, golden toast lavish with butter, about strawberry jam, about a pot full of steaming coffee. He decided against that too. He thought about the still half-full bottle of dollar gin in the filing drawer marked *Confidential*, but it too had no appeal for him now.

He went on to his office, slowly, wearily, unhappily. There was going to be trouble, and he hated trouble, for anybody. Especially, he reflected, for himself.

The office seemed more deserted than any place had ever been; the dim glow that came in through the windows sent unfriendly shadows moving over the floor. Malone quickly switched on every light in the room. It didn't help.

How could any place be so silent?

He sat thinking moodily for a while. There were things that he had to do. None of them unpleasant, but all of them important. All routine things. He considered sending for Maggie, and then decided to let her sleep. Somebody around the place had to get some sleep.

At last he lit his first cigar of what he had decided might as well be a new day. He was still sitting looking at it when the telephone rang, alarmingly loud in the dead silence.

It was Helene. "Malone! What are you doing at your office at this hour?"

"Never mind," the little lawyer growled. "What are you doing calling my office, or anywhere else, at this same hour?"

"Because I called everywhere else, and couldn't find you," she told him, with a calm serenity which, he knew, probably spelled trouble. "I called a lot of places, a lot of times. I left messages everywhere. Finally I just decided to try the office. Malone, come right out here. Because I need you."

"Come right out here where?"

"Rogers Park," Helene said.

Malone scowled at the telephone. "What the hell are you doing there?"

"Trying to talk my way out of jail," Helene said. "And I don't seem able to do it by myself. That's why I need you."

This time Malone swore at the telephone. Finally he said, "I'll be right out." He added unnecessarily, "Wait for me."

Well, at least it was a diversion. He managed to locate a taxi in spite of the hour, and caught a brief and uncomfortable nap on the way.

When he got there Helene not only looked serene, she looked almost pleased with herself. It was an expression Malone didn't like, no, not the least bit.

The charge, it seemed, was not just a little matter of speeding, but of assaulting an officer.

Malone looked at the officer in question, a big, burly, pink-faced man who might have been an ex-wrestler.

"Malone," the officer said, "she slapped me." He looked a little puzzled. "Then when we got here, she wanted me to apologize to her." With that, he looked not only puzzled but mildly hurt.

Malone felt not only puzzled, but mildly infuriated.

"Not only that," another policeman said, "while she was trying all those calls to reach you, she won practically all the money in the place playing blackjack."

"But I meant to give it back to you," Helene said virtuously. "That's why I didn't use it to put up bail or pay a fine or something."

Helene, Malone felt sure, had been having the time of her life. He sighed, went away, spent a little time on the telephone, talked to a few people, paid a small fine, and everything was settled.

Helene tucked her hand through his arm and gave the offended officer a smile that would probably have elected her mayor. He promptly offered to give the discussed apology. Helene waved it away with another smile, as Malone rushed her through the door. A few more minutes, he reflected, and they'd probably have offered to give the fine back.

Out in her car, he looked at her sternly and said, "I hope Jake beats you up. How did you get into this in the first place? And," he added hastily as she started down the street, "don't get pinched for speeding again here in the same territory."

"Well," Helene said, expertly weaving her way around pre-dawn truck traffic, "it was partly because of Myrdell. But partly because of Eula Stolz, too."

Malone sighed, relit his cigar, leaned back in his seat and tried to relax.

Helene told him, in detail, of her visit to the dreary little apartment where Eula Stolz had lived. "Malone, I had to talk to you, right away. All those clothes. She'd just gone off and left them, like—like the first two. But when I did finally find you—you told me about Myrdell. And I knew I had to find out about the last ones. I had Gertrude Bragg's address. So I decided I'd drive right out here. I was in a hurry. The cop stopped me. The rest," she said dramatically, "the rest you know."

"The rest, I don't know," Malone said. "You should have taken a ticket from him and gone on your way."

"I lost my temper," Helene said, looking as though she wouldn't lose her temper if someone burned down her home, wrecked her car, and threw rocks at Jake. "Well anyway, it's all right now. Or, that is—I still haven't done anything about Eula Stolz."

"And you're not going to do anything about Eula Stolz," Malone said, "or anyone else. You're going to go right home and stay there, I hope. You need to sleep occasionally too."

Helene sniffed and remarked that he was a fine one to talk about sleep.

"I've already had some," Malone said, thinking of the half-hour in the taxi. He looked long and admiringly at Helene. Her pale gold hair was beautifully in place, her face, with its exquisite profile, looked as though she'd just come from a long nap and the best possible beauty parlors.

"Eula Stolz is all right," he told her. "In fact, everybody is all right." Then he told her of the encounter with Rita Jardee the night before—had it been only that short a time ago?

"Which is all very well, except that it knocks the voice out of Jake's television show, when he gets it organized." This was no time to say *if*.

"With Myrdell gone—" She paused. "But when the time comes, Jake will talk Rita Jardee into providing the necessary voice. Jake," she said, with beautiful confidence, "could talk any woman into doing anything."

Malone hoped she was right, but reserved opinion.

"But the other girls, Malone—the ones that are missing—" She missed a truck's fender by inches and said, "Sorry, Malone," She went on, "And something still may happen to Rita."

"Listen, Helene—" He thought for a minute. "I'll fill in all the details in due time. But right now, you've got to take my word for one thing. All the Deloras are all right. Don't ask any questions now. Just believe me. In time, I'll prove it. Perhaps even today."

She drove in silence for a while. Then, "If that's the way things are—if some way can be found to make them all combine into one girl on a TV screen—then Jake—" Her voice trailed off into a hopeful silence.

"Then Jake has a show," Malone said. He threw away the cigar and thought about starting a new one. "Providing, of course, he has the mastery over women you credit him with having."

A few minutes later she swung the big convertible north on State Street. Malone protested that his office was in the opposite direction.

"I'm taking you home for breakfast," she told him firmly, "and don't argue. It's too early for anybody to be going to any office, anyway."

He thought that over and decided to give in gracefully. He did remind her that one speeding ticket in one day was considered par for the course.

"I'm worried about Jake," Helene said. "I'm worried about Jake worrying about me."

"Then why didn't you call him up hours ago?"

"Because," she said, with what seemed to Malone like perfect logic at the time, "I didn't want him to worry about me."

On the way up in the elevator, she murmured something about poor Jake, pacing the floor, not able to sleep, wondering

Introducing the first and only complete hardcover collection of Agatha Christie's mysteries

Now you can enjoy the
greatest mysteries ever written
in a magnificent
Home Library Edition.

Discover Agatha Christie's world of mystery, adventure and intrigue

Agatha Christie's timeless tales of mystery and suspense offer something for every reader —mystery fan or not— young and old alike. And now, you can build a complete hardcover library of her world-famous mysteries by subscribing to The Agatha Christie Mystery Collection.

This exciting Collection is your passport to a world where mystery reigns supreme. Volume after volume, you and your family will enjoy mystery reading at its very best.

You'll meet Agatha Christie's world-famous detectives like Hercule Poirot, Jane Marple, and the likeable Tommy and Tuppence Beresford.

In your readings, you'll visit Egypt, Paris, England and other exciting destinations where murder is always on the itinerary. And wherever you travel, you'll become deeply involved in some of the most ingenious and diabolical plots ever invented ... "cliff-hangers" that only Dame Agatha could create!

It all adds up to mystery reading that's so good ... it's almost criminal. And it's yours every month with The Agatha Christie Mystery Collection.

Solve the greatest mysteries of all time. The Collection contains all of Agatha Christie's classic works including *Murder on the Orient Express, Death on the Nile, And Then There Were None, The ABC Murders* and her ever-popular whodunit, *The Murder of Roger Ackroyd.*

Each handsome hardcover volume is Smythe sewn and printed on high quality acid-free paper so it can withstand even the most murderous treatment. Bound in Sussex-blue simulated leather with gold titling, The Agatha Christie Mystery Collection will make a tasteful addition to your living room, or den.

Ride the Orient Express for 10 days without obligation. To introduce you to the Collection, we're inviting you to examine the classic mystery, *Murder on the Orient Express*, without risk or obligation. If you're not completely satisfied, just return it within 10 days and owe nothing.

However, if you're like the millions of other readers who love Agatha Christie's thrilling tales of mystery and suspense, keep *Murder on the Orient Express* and pay just $9.95 plus postage and handling.

You will then automatically receive future volumes once a month as they are published on a fully returnable, 10-day free-examination basis. No minimum purchase is required, and you may cancel your subscription at any time.

This unique collection is not sold in stores. It's available only through this special offer. So don't miss out, begin your subscription now. Just mail this card today.

where she was, making telephone calls, going half out of his wits. There was a mist of repentance in her cornflower-colored eyes.

She opened the door to the apartment, stopped, and muttered, "The rat!" under her breath.

Jake was there all right. He was sitting very comfortably on the big divan, Otis Furlong on one side and Rita Jardee on the other. In front of them on the coffee table was a tray of bottles and glasses.

He smiled up at her as she came in and said, "Hello, darling. I was just beginning to wonder when you'd get in!"

Chapter Twenty-one

"But I had no idea it was so late," Jake repeated bewilderedly. "I got home and I had a drink, and I thought a while, and then they got here, and we talked, and I tell you," he said for now the fourth time, "I had no idea how late it was."

Suddenly he scowled. "Where have you been?" His face softened just as suddenly, turned a little pale. "Helene darling, are you all right?"

She looked at him with affection whose warmth fairly made the whole room glow. "Just a little traffic ticket. Malone fixed it all up."

Malone sat down in a comfortable chair and started to go to sleep. He moved quickly to a straight chair and sat bolt upright. If he let himself go to sleep now, he would go right on sleeping until sometime tomorrow, or quite possibly sometime next week.

"Myrdell—" Jake looked at him anxiously.

"It was natural causes," the little lawyer told him. "Something in her heart. Or something not in her heart. Anyway, it wasn't murder. I talked to Dr. Stonecypher."

Helene shook her head. "It should have been murder," she said. "It must have been murder."

"I agree with you," he told her. "Under the circumstances,

a murder was called for. But it wasn't one. And in any case, why would it have been Myrdell, if it had?"

Jake nodded. "It was the Deloras who were disappearing."

"Rita Jardee was jealous of her," Helene said, "because of her voice."

"But Rita Jardee didn't care about that any more," Jake said. "As of last night, she'd retired. And who else would have wanted to murder Myrdell Harris?"

"Who knows?" Malone said gravely. "Who knows indeed? But anyway, nobody did." He decided it was time to switch the subject off murder, and fast. "And about Rita Jardee—and Otis Furlong—"

"They came by to see me," Jake said, "because it was too early to go home. And because he wanted to talk with me about the process he's trying to work out."

Both Helene and Malone sat up expectantly. Helene poured a round of drinks and said, "Then, breakfast."

"It seems," Jake began. He began pawing through a handful of papers on the table, evidently emptied there some time earlier from his pocket. "I made a few notes as we talked." He picked up a paper cocktail napkin from the *Chez*, an empty match folder with some figures scribbled on it, and a slip of paper with a name written on it. "Sunflower Dan," he said, puzzled.

"Running in the seventh at Santa Anita," Malone said, "and a good horse, too."

Jake ignored him, found another scrap of notepaper, looked at it and said, "Legal angle. Malone."

"That's me," the little lawyer said.

"Pay scale," Jake went on.

"That's not me," Malone said.

Jake scowled at the paper for a minute, then said, "Oh, I know now. There's a legal angle, if what he is trying is a success. Can we legally show five girls on television—show four and hear one, I mean—and pass them off to the audience as one girl?"

They thought that over for a minute. "I don't know why not," Helene said at last.

Malone said, "I don't know. It might be misleading advertising, at that."

"The big question," Helene said, "is—can it be done?"

"The big answer," Jake said, "is yes." He looked at the

paper again. "It's pretty complicated. But it boils down to photographing every girl separately. Then painting out the part you don't want to have show, and finally you print the whole thing together. I mean, that's how I understand it."

"I can see how that would work for one picture," Helene said dubiously, "but for a movie film—"

"The whole thing has to be done for every picture on every strip of film," Jake said.

Malone shook his head. "It also sounds expensive."

Jake sighed and put away the paper. "It's not that it's so expensive," he said, "it's just that it costs so much. And let's have breakfast."

Helene had evidently read his thoughts of earlier in the morning, Malone reflected, as he lit an after-breakfast cigar. There had been ham and eggs, all pink and white and sunshiny yellow, there had been crisply fried potatoes, and a stack of golden brown toast, lavishly buttered. There had been strawberry jam, and a great deal of scalding hot coffee. He puffed deeply on the cigar and decided he was as close to being as good as new as he probably would ever get.

On his way back to his office, the thought of Gus Madrid rose up to haunt him like an unfriendly ghost. Probably a little harder to handle than a ghost, too. Gus Madrid was going to want his money back, unless by some miracle he, Malone, could convince him that he'd played an important part in the return of Eva Lou Strauss. The real trick was going to be proving to the hard-headed gunman that his money had been legitimately spent in a search for Eva Lou, and that he'd get the rest of it back as soon as Malone could raise it.

He decided on a quick stop at Joe the Angel's City Hall Bar, as the beginning of a softening-up process. If he paid Gud Madrid back what money he had left, he was going to need that recently re-established credit.

A moment after he'd walked through the door, he felt that the visit had been a mistake. Joe the Angel, alone in the place, shoved a rye and beer at him, and regarded him sourly. Even the parakeet seemed to glare at him a little more malevolently than usual.

"Drink your drink, Malone," Joe the Angel said gloomily, "and then go away. Go away and don't come back awhile." He turned his back.

"Now wait a minute," Malone protested. "Look here. I just sent your cousin Rico some very nice business—"

Joe the Angel wheeled around, sorrow in his eyes. "Malone. I do not know what it is you did. I do not know why you should do it to my cousin Rico, who is your good friend. But until you fix it up whatever it was you did, go away, Malone, and do not come back again."

Chapter Twenty-two

Maggie looked up from her desk as he came in, as though she sensed something had gone wrong. Malone threw his hat and topcoat at the couch and growled at her to get Rico di Angelo on the phone.

She came in a few minutes later and reported that Rico di Angelo was nowhere to be found, and that no one in his establishment seemed to know anything about anything.

Malone swore and sat scowling at his cigar, which had long since gone out. What could have happened? What could have gone wrong? Was it possible that Myrdell Harris had been murdered after all, and that Rico di Angelo had been the one to discover it? But that couldn't be possible. A doctor like Alonzo Stonecypher would hardly make a mistake like that. And certainly a doctor with his reputation and standing couldn't be bribed.

He told Maggie to keep trying, and settled down to worry in earnest. Gus Madrid had not called, which was good. He would undoubtedly call or turn up in person later, which was bad. No one else had called about anything, which could be good or bad. The mail hadn't come in yet.

He wondered if Otis Furlong's process would work. Then he wondered if Jake could talk Rita Jardee into returning as the voice of Delora Deanne.

Then there was the matter of the calls Dennis Dennis had made to Myrdell Harris. Whatever the reason had been, apparently it had been an urgent one. He picked up the phone and called Delora Deanne. No, Mr. Dennis hadn't come in yet. Yes, Mr. Malone, she did have his home address and phone number.

But Dennis Dennis wasn't at home either.

Well, he told himself at last, there was no point to just sitting here and getting nothing done. At last he lit a fresh cigar, sighed, and called Charlie Swackhammer. This time the answer was prompter, and a lot less sleepy.

Just a few things he wanted to know, Malone explained. About undertakers. Sorry, he'd meant morticians. Did they pal around together much, like lawyers and doctors and streetcar conductors, and so on?

He was gratified to be told that they did indeed, and that a finer bunch of fellows and pals couldn't be found anywhere. Oh sure, there was a certain amount of business rivalry, just like in any line from Ab to Zz. But as far as friendship and good times were concerned—well, he remembered a convention a few years ago, down in Miami Beach—

Charlie Swackhammer interrupted some highly colorful reminiscences to say, "What's going on, Malone? Maybelle's right here, and I'm watching her like she was the crown jewels, which she's just a little more valuable than, to me anyway. But what's this about her being murdered?"

"She isn't going to be," Malone said. "Not if I can help it. So don't worry."

He hung up, thought for a moment, then interrupted a busy and mildly profane Gadenski in what he was doing. Malone quickly offered apologies, tickets for the fights, and the use of a box at Washington Park when the races opened, reached for paper and a pencil, and said, "Now, about those girls—"

For a few minutes he wrote rapidly. Names, addresses, telephone numbers, and both important and unimportant details. At last he said, "Thanks, and if everybody was as good in his line as you are in yours, it would be a far, far better world, Gadenski," and hung up.

Then for the next few hours he sweated through a series of long-distance telephone calls, to Hollywood, California, to Little Rock, Arkansas, to a whistle stop in southern Ohio. He was thankful that he didn't have to call Havana, Cuba, though he was pleased that he'd been surprisingly right on that casual guess.

When he had finished, he leaned back in his chair, chewing on his cigar. Everything added up now, as far as the Delora Deannes were concerned. If he'd had any sense, he told himself, he'd have known it all along.

Jake chose that moment to arrive, and told the little lawyer that he looked appallingly smug, and what was this he'd muttered at breakfast about the Delora Deannes.

"That they're all alive and well," Malone said. He said it out loud this time. "I ought to have known it all along."

"Why?" Jake looked puzzled.

"The ring," Malone told him. "I should have known it because of the ring."

"What ring?" Jake demanded, in pure exasperation. He added that a good night's sleep wouldn't have done Malone any real harm.

"Eva Lou's," Malone said. "The opal. It was in every picture, it had almost become a trademark of the Delora Deanne hands. Otis Furlong told me himself that she could never get it off. That's when I should have known."

"I've seen it," Jake said. "In the pictures, I mean."

"That parakeet," Malone said. "The first time it said, 'Ring, ring, ring,' it made me think of something, but I couldn't quite figure what it was."

"Damn you, Malone—"

"The hands that came to Hazel by mail," Malone told him, speaking very slowly and patiently, "didn't wear any ring. There was no ring at all. And no sign of one ever having been worn."

Jake looked at him and said nothing.

"And then when I saw the jeweled garters," Malone said. "I mean when I didn't see the jeweled garters—"

Jake sighed. "All right. What jeweled garters, and where didn't you see them?"

Malone decided there was no reason not to explain, and went on to tell about Klutchetsky's grisly discovery, and the conclusions he'd drawn and passed on to von Flanagan.

"Any minute now," Malone said, "he'll call and tell me he'd found who the girl is. At least I hope he does. He owes me that much, after last night."

"But," Jake said, his freckled face a little pale, "but that's horrible."

"It is," Malone said. "The whole thing has been horrible.

Someone with a mind I'd rather not contemplate right now conceived and carried out the idea. To frighten Hazel—to put her out of business—to torture her—for some reason. Some reason of revenge, quite probably."

He drew a long breath. "This person—somehow, he or she found out when a very beautiful girl was going to be buried and managed to steal the body. The hands were sent to Hazel, and then the feet. The torso and legs were probably meant to be next. Just how, we'll never know. The head—that would have been the real problem."

He frowned. Last night, he'd thought of something, something of great importance. He'd almost told it to von Flanagan. Probably would have, except that it still wasn't altogether clear in his mind then. And whatever it had been, it seemed to be completely gone from him now. Oh well, he'd probably remember it in due time.

"There was another reason," he told Jake. "I should have known that the Deloras were all alive and well when I found out that Eva Lou had left all her gloves behind, and Louella had left all her shoes. I certainly should have tumbled to it last night when Rita Jardee was making like a hog caller, but I had other things on my mind."

"There must be a very fine line of reasoning there somewhere," Jake said, "but I don't get it."

"Very simple reasoning," Malone said. "The Deloras were all sick of their jobs. Sick of Hazel Swackhammer and her stinginess." When was that check going to get here, and how much would it be? "Sick of being anonymous. Eva Lou left her gloves behind because she was so damned sick and tired of posing her beautiful hands for photographs. Same thing with Louella and the shoes. And then Rita Jardee and her voice."

Jake nodded. "But why did they disappear?"

"They didn't," Malone said. "I know where they are." He noted a hopeful gleam in Jake's eye and went on fast. "Gertie Bragg dyed her hair back to its natural red—I'm told it's very becoming—and married a very rich millionaire. A hardware dealer from Little Rock, Arkansas."

"Hooray for her," Jake said.

"Eula Stolz," Malone said, "saw a chance to make important money in Hollywood, doubling in the figure for bathing beauties. Expects to do well, she tells me. Louella Frick went back to a farm in Ohio. Eva Lou Strauss took off for Havana and a rich boy friend. Changed her mind at Miami and came back to her other boy friend." Who would be coming along any time now. "And Rita Jardee—well, she's retired from radio. That's the lot."

"Nobody ever retired from radio," Jake said confidently. "And no woman would ever turn down a chance to be the star of a television show."

"One-fifth of a star," Malone reminded him.

Jake waved that aside. He looked at Malone with unconcealed admiration. "How on earth did you find out all this?"

"Oh," Malone said, with great modesty, "I just made a few telephone calls."

That was when Maggie appeared in the doorway, her face just a little more worried than usual. "Rico di Angelo, Malone. He's here."

He was here, and almost shoving Maggie to one side. He paused halfway across the room, planted his fists on his hips, and stood looking accusingly at Malone.

"You! And all these years, you are my good friend."

"I am," Malone said. "Now just a minute. Sit down. Have a cigar. Whatever it is, I had nothing to do with it."

Rico di Angelo did not sit down, nor did he take a cigar. "First you want me to cut off somebody's hands."

"No," Malone said. "No, no, no. Nothing of the sort. Nobody had any idea of doing anything of the sort. I just wanted to find out if it could be done. To—settle an argument." The argument had been with himself, but that had nothing to do with it.

Rico's silence and the expression of his handsome face showed exactly what he thought of that.

Malone decided to try taking the offensive. His voice became accusing. "Then," he said, sounding deeply hurt, "I send you a very nice piece of business, because of my friendship for you—" His voice trailed off weakly.

"And then," Rico di Angelo said bitterly, "you hold up my hearse and you steal the body."

Malone opened his mouth to speak, and shut it again. There simply didn't seem to be anything to say.

Jake said plaintively, "I do wish somebody would tell me just what *is* going on."

Rico di Angelo turned to him. "Too much is going on. First, this business of the hands. All right. That I will forget.

That I will believe Malone about. Then last night, a lady friend of his, she dies. Malone sends for me. All right. I go there. Everything is in order. The doctor, he has signed the certificate. Nothing is any kinds monkey-business. I make the arrangements with the lady who was the dead lady's boss. All right."

Jake looked at Malone and said, "Myrdell Harris?"

"Who else could it be?" Malone snapped.

"Then what?" Jake said to Rico di Angelo.

"Then on the way to my beautiful establishment on Division Street, somebody, he holds up my driver. He holds up my driver and me myself, and he steals the body. With a gun." He glared at Malone, and said, "Well?"

There still didn't seem to be anything to say. At long last, the little lawyer said feebly, "And then what did you do?"

"I went home and go to sleep," Rico di Angelo said. He seemed to be feeling a little better, his story told. He sat down, put his hat on his knee, and took out one of his own cigars. "Because I am your good friend, Malone, I want to find you before I tell the police. I try and try, and I cannot find you, and so I go home and go to sleep."

Malone muttered something about going home and going to sleep himself if the day kept up as it had started.

"Now," Rico di Angelo interrupted, "I have found you. And I have got to tell the police. This is not a good business to have happen. Not to my fine establishment."

"Believe me," Malone said earnestly, "believe me, Rico, I had nothing to do with it. This is the first I've heard anything about it. And I don't know any more about how it happened, or who did it, than you do."

Rico di Angelo turned to Jake as though for confirmation. He was beginning to look a little dazed. Jake nodded vehemently.

"Malone is telling the truth," Jake said. "And I'm in a position to know."

The baffled undertaker turned back to Malone, who also nodded vehemently.

"It might take me a little time," he told Rico, "but I could prove to you where I was every minute of the time between when I called you, and when you walked in just now. And," he added virtuously, "I certainly wasn't hijacking any hearses."

"But somebody did," Rico said anxiously.

"If it's the last thing I ever do," Malone promised him, "I'll find out."

"But now in the meantime," Rico said gloomily, "I have got to tell this to the police."

Jake frowned. "Look here, Rico. Is there any way you can put off notifying the police? Not for very long, perhaps just for a few hours?"

"Right," Malone said, nodding enthusiastically. "That way, it'll make it much easier to find out just who did do it."

"Besides," Jake pointed out, "if we find out, and we locate the body, you may never have to notify the police at all."

The reasoning appeared sound to Rico di Angelo. After a few minutes' thought, he nodded agreement. "I manage it. I explain that I am so upset that my assistant he has to take me home and put me to bed, and this makes my assistant so upset that he does not think of the police." He paused. "Or maybe easier and better, I change all the times around." He beamed at them both. "Don't you worry about it. I fix."

The briefly interrupted friendship was sealed again. Rico promised to tell Joe the Angel to say nothing about it to anyone. Jake and Malone promised to start immediately, finding out the identity of the hijacker, and the present location of the body.

At the door, Rico paused. "All is well." He smiled. "But, Malone," he added warningly, "I tell you. Do not do it again!"

Chapter Twenty-three

"Just when you'd found all the Deloras, too," Jake said bitterly.

"Leave me alone," Malone growled at him. "I want to think." After a moment he said, "Just why did you tell Rico not to notify the police right away?"

"Because I really did think you'd be able to find both the hijacker and the body," Jake said.

Malone sighed. "I probably can. But it may take a little

time. And Rico doesn't have much time. If he doesn't notify the police pretty soon, he'll be in the soup when they find out about it. If they find out about it," he added.

"The thing is, why?" Jake said. He lit a cigarette. "Not only who would want to steal Myrdell Harris' body, but why?" He paused. "Malone, actually I don't know why I asked Rico if he could stall notifying the police. It's kind of a hunch, and at the same time, not exactly a hunch, if you know what I'm trying to say. Something I know, and can't quite pin down, and maybe couldn't understand if I did pin it down, if you know what I mean."

"I know exactly what you mean," Malone said. He was experiencing exactly the same thing himself about the business of Charlie Swackhammer's bride-to-be. Nothing tangible made her appear to him as a prospective victim of murder. But something, just like what Jake had described. It was there, and still it wasn't there. And nothing he did, or thought, or found out, seemed to be bringing it into any better focus.

After a little while, Jake said, "Someone knew Myrdell Harris had been murdered, and wanted to dispose of the body before there was any chance of its being found out. Therefore, find the hijacker, and you find the murderer."

"But Myrdell Harris wasn't murdered," Malone reminded him. "Stolen body or no stolen body, you can't get away from that death certificate signed by Dr. Stonecypher." He added almost reverently, "Dr. Alonzo Stonecypher."

"Well," Jake said, "somebody thought Myrdell Harris had been murdered, and wanted to protect the murderer, and stole the body to get rid of it. In that case, find who wanted to murder Myrdell Harris, and then find who might have wanted to protect that person. It's as simple as that, Malone."

They played with that theory for a little while. It wasn't as simple as that. Someone, sometime this morning, was going to have to prowl Myrdell Harris' apartment, Malone reflected, and it was up to him to do the job. Furthermore, he didn't want Jake, or anyone else, along.

That reminded him, and he reached for the telephone. More and more he felt it would be helpful to know just why Dennis Dennis had been trying to reach Myrdell Harris the evening before, and if he'd ever succeeded.

The switchboard girl at Delora Deanne was sorry, but Mr. Dennis hadn't been seen nor heard from so far.

At that moment Helene breezed in, her usually pale face glowing from the cold. She smiled at them both, and wanted to know what was going on.

"Nothing much," Jake and Malone said, practically in unison.

They looked at her admiringly. She wore blue, a soft, dusty blue that intensified and reflected the bright blue of her eyes; the wide-brimmed hat that framed her face and pale-gold, shining hair was almost the exact shade of strawberry jam; her sleek furs were the color of a milky caramel. Her purse and her caramel-colored galoshes had small, absurd, rose-colored tassels.

"I don't believe either of you," she said cheerfully, "but go on with whatever you were saying."

"We were saying that things seem to be straightening out," Jake said.

"I don't believe that, either," she said. "And while you two wish-thinkers were sitting here theorizing, I've been doing something positive."

They looked at her silently and apprehensively.

"Shopping," she told them pleasantly, and Malone breathed again.

She indicated a frivolously wrapped package under her arm, and Malone's breathing was in more trouble. The wrapping was from a small and fabulously expensive Michigan Boulevard shop. It was the same wrapping that had covered the beautiful and terrible gloves he'd seen on Hazel Swackhammer's desk.

The difficult moment passed. Jake paid no attention to the box and said, "Now if Otis Furlong's process turns out to be in any way successful—"

The little lawyer saw an opportunity to keep them both busy and out of trouble for at least a while, and grabbed it fast.

"You know, in case it doesn't," he began thoughtfully, "I've been giving some consideration to that camera. The one Maggie's brother Luke has invented. From what I've been able to gather about it—it might solve the problem."

Jake and Helene looked at each other. After all, a camera with eyes—why not?

"It does sound like something," Malone went on encouragingly. Well, Maggie had said it had five eyes, hadn't she?

And there were five Delora Deannes, weren't there? Of course, one of them was an unseen voice, so the camera would have to have only four eyes. He tried to picture it in his mind, got into a state of hopeless confusion and abandoned the project.

"At least," he said, "it wouldn't do any harm to go and take a look at it." It would please Maggie, too.

After they had gone, Malone sat wondering about his next step. Myrdell's apartment? It had to be done, but somehow he dreaded it. Not the search itself, but what he might find.

It took the arrival of another visitor to make up his mind for him. Von Flanagan strode in, looking just a bit too friendly, and entirely too casual. He plumped down in the biggest leather chair and said, "I just happened to be in the building, and I just thought I'd drop in."

Malone knew perfectly well the only other tenant of the building who could have even a passing interest for the big police officer was the bookie down in the cigar stand. But he said amiably, "Always glad to see you. Well, usually."

Von Flanagan grinned, accepted a cigar, lighted it, and then said, "You got the tickets for the fights yet? Because if you haven't—"

"I'll tend to it," Malone said. He wondered just what von Flanagan was there for.

"About that business last night—" Von Flanagan paused, delicately flicked a totally imaginary ash from the end of his cigar. "Malone, it was like you said. We checked right away, fast. Coffin was still at the undertaker's place. Small place, fella name of Stoppenbach. Funeral's tomorrow. Won't need to be postponed or anything now. Girl name of Anna Ruth Cahill. Pretty girl, too. We got the torso back to him a'ready. Head was there all the time."

"Of course it was," Malone said. Again there was the sudden, cold chill, the ugly premonition. *But what was it?* The thing he knew and still didn't know, the combination of things he had to put together and couldn't quite remember.

Von Flanagan looked at him speculatively. "I wish you'd tell me what you're holding out. Malone, we've been friends a long time."

"The hands and the feet," Malone said, almost to himself. "You'll have them in time for the funeral. I promise. The Cahill family will never need to know a thing."

"That isn't what I mean," von Flanagan said. "It is, but it isn't quite enough. The rest of what you know, Malone."

Malone looked stubborn and said nothing.

"Damn it, I never wanted to be a policeman," von Flanagan said angrily. "I never would of been except that the alderman owed my old man money. I went to court and had the 'von' added to my name because I was sick and tired of being called an Irish cop. I never wanted to be promoted—"

The little lawyer sighed and leaned back. It was a story he'd heard before, and would, many times, again.

"—and one of these days I'm going to retire and get into something else—"

Malone was familiar with that, too. The choices had ranged from raising mink to running a dude ranch.

"—which reminds me, Malone."

A change had come into von Flanagan's voice. Malone sat up and paid attention.

"I want to talk to Jake. Now that he's a big-shot television producer. I've been thinking of it more and more. I think I could do a good television show, and I want to talk it over with him about what I want to do."

Malone opened his mouth to ask what kind of a show von Flanagan had in mind, and closed it quickly again.

"I used to be a very good amateur juggler," von Flanagan said modestly. "But that isn't quite enough. I'm thinking of something with more staying power."

This time, Malone couldn't resist. "For instance?"

"Well," von Flanagan said, "for instance, a different kind of quiz program. What do you think?"

Malone said gravely, "I think it would be a novelty. You ought to talk it over with Jake."

Von Flanagan beamed and nodded. "I knew you'd agree with me, Malone. But I'd do anything. I could probably be a pretty good actor, even. Just so I didn't have to be a cop." He shook his head sadly. "A cop, everybody tries to make things hard for you. Mix things up and complicate everything."

This was a familiar story to Malone too, and he knew just where to put in the right sympathetic answers.

"Like you holding out information on me. I could drag you down to jail right now, Malone. But you notice I'm not. Only because we've been friends for a long time."

And, Malone thought, because von Flanagan remembered from experience that it was safer to wait and see what was brought in.

"And like this babe found dead up in Lincoln Park this morning."

For the second time, Malone sat up straight and listened. "What babe?"

"We don't know yet. No identification on her. No marks on her to show cause of death. Doc Evans is working on her right now to find out what killed her."

"Interesting," Malone said, trying to sound bored.

"Cop noticed her, sitting up against a tree, magazine in her lap. Just sitting there. He wouldn't of paid any attention, except for the way she was dressed. House pajamas. Expensive ones, too. Kind of a smoky color—"

Chapter Twenty-four

If only one thing would go wrong at a time, Malone reflected, if only his carefully figured calculations could be upset in just one way at once, everything would be far, far easier.

He told the taxi driver to go to the Lake Shore Drive address, and tried to follow the printed card of advice to sit back and relax. The card also added, LET THE DRIVER DO THE WORRYING FOR YOU. He wondered how this cabdriver, one Maurice Dougherty, would feel about taking on his collection of worries.

The minute von Flanagan had gone, leaving an unskillfully veiled warning to show up with everything in a hurry, or else, he'd phoned Rico. The body had been found, he explained, and added the circumstances. Now, would Rico manage to hold off notifying the police for just about an hour?

Rico had assured him it could and would be done. He agreed to wait until Malone phoned him the word.

That would give him time to go through Myrdell's apartment in some detail. The minute von Flanagan had the body identified, he would head for the apartment like a homing pigeon in a rocket ship.

A few words with the building manager secured him the key, with no questions or difficulty. As Miss Harris' employer's attorney—the manager understood perfectly. In fact, he was rather glad not to have to take on the job of inventory himself.

Malone turned on the lights, looked around the apartment, and wondered just where to begin.

It would help if he had just the faintest idea of what he was trying to find.

Although it had been only a few hours since Myrdell Harris' body had started on the journey which ended in the police morgue by way of a tree in Lincoln Park, already the big, gracefully decorated rooms had a cold and empty feeling, as though no one had been in them for a very long time. Malone shivered a little, and decided to keep on his topcoat.

The apartment itself, the paintings on the walls, the furnishings, the clothes and accessories in the closets, the toiletries on the dressing table told him only that the late Myrdell Harris had had the very finest of taste and the means to indulge it lavishly.

Had Myrdell herself latched on to a wealthy playboy, like the Delora Deanne in Ned McKeon's column?

No, she wasn't exactly the type to attract one. Nor the type who, if she had attracted one, would have kept on with what must have been a thoroughly tiresome job.

Nor were there any signs of a regular masculine visitor, nor a sweetly signed photograph on the dressing table.

A wealthy woman, working for the pure pleasure of having a career?

Again no, not if the career included Hazel Swackhammer.

A thorough search of the drawers in the bedroom, her purse, and finally the desk drawers, revealed absolutely nothing.

He noticed a thick envelope that had been pushed through the mail slot, today's mail, arriving too late for Myrdell Harris to read. He picked it up, glanced at it, finally opened it. It was a regular monthly bank statement from the Chicago Trust and Savings Bank, with a handful of canceled checks. He glanced through them quickly. They meant nothing to him.

Checks for the rent, the maid, the grocery, a dress shop, a department store, a dentist.

He sat down on the upholstered divan and thought things over. Suddenly he realized that his search hadn't been worthless after all. The important thing was not what he had found, but what he hadn't found.

There weren't any bankbooks.

To make sure, he checked again: desk, dresser, every conceivable place a woman might keep bankbooks. There were none. But there had to be a checkbook, with its deposit book, if there were canceled checks. There could quite possibly be a savings account book as well.

He telephoned the bank. Yes, he was told after a long wait, Miss Myrdell Harris did have a savings account there, but they were not permitted to disclose the amount over the telephone.

The amount didn't matter. The missing bankbooks did.

Of course, it was just possible that she had kept them at the office, but somehow, he doubted it.

Then he realized that the telephone slips he'd noticed last night were gone. That mattered at least as much as the missing bankbooks.

While he was still puzzling over it, he heard sounds at the door, the faint scratch of a key inserted into the lock. Malone stiffened, stood up, and looked around quickly. Then he reminded himself that he had no reason to hide, even if there had been a place to duck into quickly. The door opened, a voice said, "The light's on," and Charlie Swackhammer came into the room, a woman at his side.

For a moment, everyone stared at everyone else. Then Charlie Swackhammer scowled and said, "Malone—what—?"

"I'm Mrs. Swackhammer's attorney," Malone said stiffly. "I was here last night. She asked me to make the arrangements for her, and I did. Sooner or later, an inventory—" He wasn't quite sure what he was saying. Because the woman on Charlie Swackhammer's arm was Delora Deanne.

What's more, she was the composite Delora Deanne. The same seraphic yet voluptuous face with its cloud of shining hair; there was also the slender, joyous body, swathed now in soft brown furs instead of swirling mists. There were the delicate, graceful hands, in pale blue gloves, one holding a cigarette in a slim, amber holder, and there were the tiny, high-arched feet, in cunningly designed high-heeled sandals that were the shade of pure maple sugar.

Cuddles Swackhammer said, "Startling, isn't it?" and beamed an introduction.

The vision said, "How do you do, Mr. Malone," in Delora Deanne's golden voice.

With a gigantic effort, the little lawyer finally managed to say, "Hello."

Cuddles Swackhammer beamed even more broadly. "I don't need to tell you, Malone, that Maybelle is—was—the original for Delora Deanne."

"Gertie's my sister," Maybelle said. "But I was always the one with the brains."

Malone had recovered himself enough to speak. "The brains, and the beauty," he said gallantly. "Outside of those two minor differences you could be twins."

She rewarded him with a smile that set his red corpuscles to moving like greyhounds around the last lap of the track.

"That's the big thing Hazel will never forgive me for," Cuddles Swackhammer said. "Hazel wanted to start this little business of hers, and I encouraged her. Helped her. Kept her out of my hair. Maybelle was the original model, at the beginning. Then I parted from Hazel. Not just because of sugar-pie here, but because Hazel was beginning to get on my nerves."

Malone nodded. Hazel Swackhammer could do that.

"But I kept on seeing Maybelle, and Hazel was violently jealous. Not because she cared any more about me. It was the other way. Maybelle had become Delora Deanne, and Delora Deanne belonged to Hazel. Hazel's the most jealous person I ever saw in my life. Wants to own everybody and everything completely, all by herself. So one day Maybelle got sore and quit. Looked for a while like Delora Deanne might go out of business. But Hazel found Gertie, latched on to the best-looking body and so on she could find to go with her, and kept right on a-going."

Malone had listened with half his mind. He'd realized something else. Myrdell Harris hadn't imitated Rita Jardee's radio voice, she had imitated the natural voice of Maybelle Bragg, the original Delora Deanne, and now the future Mrs. Swackhammer.

And at the moment, all he could think about was the Jake Justus Television Production Company. If Maybelle could be persuaded—and if Cuddles Swackhammer would agree—

He realized immediately it would be a losing battle before it started. On the one hand, Charlie Swackhammer was not going to let his new wife advertise his first wife's products, even though he received a big piece of the income. And on the other hand, Hazel Swackhammer was certainly not going to accept the ex-Delora Deanne as the future Delora Deanne. And finally, a brainy and beautiful girl who had just married a chain of undertaking parlors was hardly going to endure the long, hard work of a television production, even if she were going to be the star.

Still, there were the other Delora Deannes, who, with Jake's persuasive methods, could probably be assembled, and Otis Furlong's process which sounded as though it might work. As a last possibility, Maggie's brother Luke's camera.

He reminded himself sternly that this was hardly the time or the place to worry about the Jake Justus Television Production Company, important though it might be.

"If you don't mind my asking—" he began rather tentatively—"just what—"

"I do mind," Charlie Swackhammer said with surprising grimness. "But I don't suppose it will do me much good. I might as well tell you the works, the whole works." He sat down in the nearest chair, Maybelle close by him.

"To begin—" He paused a moment. "I don't suppose you'd want to have me as a client, Malone, in this whole—" he waved an all-embracing hand—"mess?"

The little lawyer thought fast. Just exactly how opposite a side of the fence was Charlie Swackhammer on from his ex-wife Hazel? There was a little matter of ethics involved.

"Well?" Charlie Swackhammer said, invitingly.

There was also the little matter of repaying Gus Madrid. The pleasant-faced Charlie Swackhammer didn't look as though he would strain at paying an immediate and handsome retainer.

But—a point of ethics, though a delicate one. Never change horses, he told himself firmly, even if they're about to lay golden eggs.

"I beg your pardon?" Swackhammer said.

"I just said," Malone told him, "that under the circumstances, I could hardly—" After all, that check from Hazel Swackhammer must surely be in the office by now.

The big man sighed. "I was afraid you'd feel that way. However—" His voice and expression left the subject wide open for future discussion, and Malone felt a little better. "What with Myrdell Harris murdered—"

"How do you know she was murdered?" Malone demanded. He added, "For that matter, how did you even know she was dead?"

Cuddles Swackhammer paused, scowled, and then said, "I telephoned her, and she was dead. I mean—" He paused again. "This morning. I wanted to talk to her—about something. I telephoned the salon. The girl at the switchboard told me. So we came here."

"All right," Malone said. "You found out she was dead. But how did you know she was murdered?"

There was a silence. Cuddles Swackhammer stared at him. At last he said, very slowly, "I—as a matter of fact—I didn't. I don't. It just seemed—" He paused again. "I don't know just how to put it."

Neither did Malone, and anyway, he wasn't going to help out, not right now.

"Let's put it," Swackhammer said, even more slowly, "that she was a likely person to be murdered."

"Fine," the little lawyer said more cheerfully. "Now we're getting somewhere. Why was she?"

"Oh, because—" Cuddles Swackhammer made an impatient gesture. "I don't know why you should be asking questions, or I should be answering them like this. It would be different if I were your client instead of Hazel."

More profitable, too, Malone thought unhappily. "You can believe me," he assured the big man earnestly, "that I'll respect your confidences just as though you were my client." He added lightly, "Who knows, you might be, some day."

The smile he got in return was a wan one. "All right, all right. And anyway, I haven't done anything wrong, and there's no reason why it shouldn't be known—now. Myrdell worked for me—in a sense. I mean—well, I needed to know how things were going at Delora Deanne. After all, I do own a big per cent of it. So I paid Myrdell, regularly, to keep me informed." He paused, thought, and added significantly, "Informed about everything."

Malone looked at him and waited.

"Yes," Cuddles Swackhammer said, nodding, "about the girls disappearing, and about Hazel getting those gruesome little packages in the mail. And I don't know any more about who sent them than you do." He made a gesture indicating there wasn't anything more to add. "That's why I assumed Myrdell was murdered. She knew entirely too much about everything that was going on, everywhere. And she liked money."

Malone nodded thoughtfully. The picture of Myrdell as a seller of information fitted in very well. So did a possible picture of Myrdell as a blackmailer. But blackmailing whom? Probably the person who had sent those gruesome little packages.

"The only trouble is," he said at last, "Myrdell Harris wasn't murdered."

He went on into details, his late-at-night trip to this same apartment, Myrdell Harris dead, and Dr. Alonzo Stonecypher in attendance and signing the death certificate. He omitted the minor fact of his having been the one to call Rico di Angelo. There was no point in telling a possible future client that he'd sent business to a rival.

When he'd finished, Charlie Swackhammer had nothing to say except, "I'll be damned!"

Malone nodded and said, "And that isn't the half of it." He went on to tell about the mysterious disappearance of the body, hijacked from Rico di Angelo, and its equally mysterious reappearance in Lincoln Park.

Charlie Swackhammer gave him a puzzled scowl. "It sounds impossible. But if it really happened, it isn't, is it? Also, it just doesn't seem to make sense."

"It doesn't," Malone agreed. Nothing in this whole affair made sense, so far. "Except—someone believed Myrdell Harris was murdered and wanted the police to find it out."

The three of them talked it over for a while and finally came up with only one conclusion, that it didn't make sense.

"But—you came here—?" Malone said questioningly.

"I wanted to look at Myrdell's bankbooks," Swackhammer said. "That's all."

Malone blinked at him. "Why?"

"Because—well, Myrdell might have been blackmailing someone. It would have shown in her bank deposits. I just wanted to take a look."

And, Malone thought, Charlie Swackhammer's own payments would have shown up in them, too. He said, "Well, you wasted a trip. They aren't there." As the big man's eyebrows raised a little, he went on. "I wasn't looking for them specifically, I was just going over things in general. I happened to notice they were gone." He started to say that he'd done everything but take up the carpets and pull down the wallpaper, and caught himself in time. That would be just a little too thorough for a mere general going-over.

"She kept them in the little center drawer of the desk," Swackhammer said. He strode over, pulled open the drawer, slammed it shut again, and said, "You're right, they aren't here. But why would anybody want to make off with her bankbooks?"

"For the same reason you did," Malone said boldly. "Because inexplicably large deposits might show up and have to be explained."

Cuddles Swackhammer glowered at him, and then suddenly grinned. "All right, that was it. I thought—any such connection between Myrdell and myself might prove embarrassing, if she was murdered." The grin faded. "She wasn't murdered. But her body—"

"We'll all know sooner or later," Malone said brightly.

Swackhammer nodded. "Oh, another thing, Malone. My key—you noticed I had a key to the apartment. It was only because—sometimes she'd have information and papers or something like that, and she'd have to go out herself, and she'd leave it for me."

"Of course," Malone said. Cuddles Swackhammer, he reflected, was a fast man with an explanation. He hoped the glorious Maybelle believed him.

There was obviously no reason to stay. The three of them rode downstairs in silence. Malone returned the key to the manager.

"I'd offer you a lift," Charlie Swackhammer said, "but we're going to pick up my cousin in Evanston, and—" he beamed—"and then, the ceremony is at four."

The little lawyer paused at the nearest telephone booth, called Rico di Angelo and told him to go ahead and notify the police, adding that he'd appreciate it if Rico could keep his name out of it. Not that that was going to do any good, he told himself glumly. As soon as von Flanagan started putting twos and threes together—

Oh, well, he'd worry about that later. As he started gloomily for his office, his only concern was—why hadn't he come right out and asked Charlie Swackhammer if he'd taken those bankbooks on an earlier visit and if so, why had he come back for a second trip?

But the call slips had been missing too. Perhaps the visitor who preceded him hadn't been Charlie Swackhammer after all but had been Dennis Dennis himself. That was one question he was going to have answered soon.

Chapter Twenty-five

"Malone," the elevator man said anxiously, "Miss O'Leary came out and told me to tell you about that man. Mr. Madrid, she said. He's waiting in your office. Him and his girl."

Malone nodded his thanks. He hesitated only a moment. No, better go ahead and get this over with. He'd stalled tougher creditors than Gus Madrid before, and probably would again.

Just the same, he hesitated another moment at the door. Then he drew a long breath and went right on in.

His face asked Maggie if there had been a check, and the slight shake of her head told him there hadn't. Well, he'd find a way to handle things somehow, before the day was over.

"Sorry to keep you waiting," he said affably, very affably. "An important client. Another important client."

"You and me, we'll talk business later," Madrid said. "Right now, I brought my girl down to see you. She's an intelligent type girl, and she's got something to tell you might be some good to you, I don't know."

Well, at least the money question was postponed, Malone thought with relief. He looked at the no longer missing Eva

Lou Strauss with interest and some curiosity as they were introduced. Yes, she fitted Dennis Dennis' description of her. And Otis Furlong's as well. "Just a generous, good-natured, lusty slob." Her yellow, just plain yellow hair, was much too frizzy, and she wore entirely too much make-up, but he liked her on sight, and was wholeheartedly glad to see her intact, beautiful hands and all.

"It was the phone call," Eva Lou Strauss said. She had a lazy, uneducated and thoroughly likable voice. "I didn' have no way a knowing it wasn' the up-'n-up. 'Sides, I was sick 'n tired of ole Hazel anyways and glad t'get outa there. Always thought I'd kinda like Havana, 'n I didn'. Thought maybe I'd kinda like Harold better'n Gus here, but I didn', so I said the hell, and I come right back. Glad I did."

"I'm glad too," Malone told her. "You have absolutely no idea how glad." He was pleased to see that the pair were holding hands. It occurred to him that a little drink might be in order, and it was.

"Like Scotch," Eva Lou said, favoring him with a wide, toothy smile. "Lika good slugga gin too, like this."

"Now," the little lawyer said briskly. "About this telephone call—"

"Like I tole ya. Thought it was the up-'n-up. Gus here, he says it wasn'. Hazel didn' call. Thought I was jus' up 'n gone. But I got the call, 'n I got the money, 'n Harold he was goin' t'Havana, so I up'n went. Wish I hadn', now, but Gus here, he says he don' care, so's I don' do it again." She turned the smile on Gus Madrid who returned one of his own, the first Malone had seen on his dour face.

"Let me get this straight," Malone said. "Hazel called you up and told you—what?"

"Wasn' Hazel," she repeated. "So Gus here says."

"That isn't important right now," Malone told her gently. "This person who either was Hazel or sounded like Hazel—"

Gus Madrid interrupted and said, "This party whom I think was not Mrs. Swackhammer, called up my girl here, Eva Lou, and told her she was fired."

"Tha's right." Eva Lou nodded. "Tole me she was goin' outa business. Was sendin' me money case I wanted t'take that trip I was always talkin' of, so when the money came over with a messenger that night, I up 'n went, 'specially, 'count of I was a little sore at Gus here anyway because—"

"Never mind why," Madrid said hastily.

"A'right. I was a little sore at Gus here. So I went. 'N then I came back." She smiled engagingly at both men. "An' I guess tha's all."

"I thought it was sort of funny," Gus Madrid said. "Because this Mrs. Swackhammer, she never seemed to be the money-giving-away type dame. And she didn't seem like she was going out of business. And then why would she send Eva Lou on a trip and then hire you to find out where she was?"

"Tell me," Malone said suddenly, "do you know Myrdell Harris?"

Eva Lou nodded. "That sorta drippy babe worked for Hazel? I knew her, sorta."

"Hazel Swackhammer's executive assistant," Malone said.

Eva Lou shrugged her shoulders. Suddenly her face brightened. "She does voices. Usta do Rita's, till Rita got sore 'n raised a big stink." She was really thinking hard now. "She coulda done Hazel's voice, you mean?"

Malone nodded.

"Bet you she won' do it no more," Eva Lou grinned. "Not when ole Hazel hears about she did this."

"She won't do it no more anyway," Malone told her solemnly. "She's dead."

His two visitors stared at him, wide-eyed.

"Just last night," Malone said. "It happened very suddenly." They could read further details in the newspapers, if they cared.

"Gee," Eva Lou said, her blue eyes round and shining, "Who murdered her?" Gus Madrid said nothing, but he looked interested. A kind of professional type interest, Malone thought.

"Nobody," Malone told them. "She wasn't murdered."

Eva Lou looked surprised, almost amazed. Gus Madrid simply lost interest.

"What made you jump to the conclusion—" He decided to simplify that. "What made you think she was murdered? Anybody ever threaten her?"

The big blonde shook her head slowly. "Huh-uh. Only, she was sorta stinky, y'know what I mean. Folks was always bein' sore at her. Rita, now, she 'n her hadda big fight. 'Cause Myrdell made the voice like Rita. An' they was fightin' over the picture man. Rita said she'd cut Myrdell up in li'l pieces, only she didn'. Not if Myrdell jus' died. All by herself."

Malone didn't like the expression Eva Lou had used. But, he reminded himself, that portion of the Delora Deanne problem was a thing of the past, except, of course, that he still didn't know who had done it to Hazel Swackhammer, or why.

Picture man. That would be Otis Furlong.

As though Eva Lou had been reading his mind, she said, "Myrdell knew sumpin' about him she said no babe'd ever look at him if she tole it, only I dunno what it was." She added, "The writin' fella, too, they had trouble."

Before she finished, Eva Lou had supplied practically every member of the Delora Deanne organization with ample reason for wishing that Myrdell Harris would, at least, drop dead. With the exception, that is, of herself, and Eva Lou didn't look as though she would harbor a grudge for more than thirty seconds, or even fifteen on a good sunny day.

Myrdell Harris had been threatening to tell Dennis Dennis' wife something that might have gotten her alimony increased. All of the Deloras hated her with one enthusiastic breath. Even Hazel Swackhammer seemed, according to Eva Lou's phrase, to act funny, where Myrdell Harris was concerned.

And Eva Lou found it amazing that, with all that accumulation ranging from mild dislike to fear and downright hatred, Myrdell Harris should have, as she put it, just up and died all by herself.

That seemed to be all the information Eva Lou Strauss had, or at least, wanted to contribute. As they left, Gus Madrid paused for a moment at the door.

"I'll be back to see you later, Malone," he said, and thus practically ruined the rest of the day.

After they had gone, Malone strolled over to the window and stood looking over the roofs covered with a combination of snow and soot. The sky was beginning to cloud again, heavy, dreary, unfriendly clouds.

Again there was that cold and unpleasant sense of something elusive, something just beyond his reach. And the even more unpleasant sense that he had no time to worry about it right now. Time was beginning to speed by entirely too fast. He still had to prevent—to prevent what? That was the maddening, elusive thing he didn't quite know.

Finally he returned to his desk, called Maggie, and told her to place three telephone calls, and fast. One to a whistle stop in Ohio, one to Hollywood, and one to Little Rock, Arkansas. As an afterthought, he added a fourth one, to Rita Jardee, if she was awake yet, or even if, as he very much expected, she was not.

Maggie raised her eyebrows and muttered something anxious about the telephone bill.

"I know, I know," Malone said wearily. "But it'll be a pleasant change, sending our messages by carrier pigeon. And think how hard it'll be for creditors to call us after the phone has been taken out."

She sniffed, went away and started making the calls.

The little lawyer was halfway through the last one when Jake and Helene came in. He waved them to chairs, and went right on talking.

"Thanks so much, Miss Stolz," he said at last. "That's just what I thought. Yes, of course you can keep the money. She gave it to you, didn't she?"

He hung up the phone and said, "Well, that's that."

"That's what?" Helene said suspiciously. "Maggie said you'd suddenly gone mad and were making phone calls all over the continent."

Malone ignored that. He said, "I've just found out a very interesting thing." He paused. "Why all the Delora Deannes suddenly up and disappeared, all at once." He paused again.

"Damn you, Malone," Jake began.

Malone waved him down. "They left because—Hazel Swackhammer called up every one of them and fired them. Because she was going out of business. But to make it up to them—she sent every one of them a thousand bucks." He smiled benignly at them and said at last, "All right. I don't believe it either."

Chapter Twenty-six

"Obviously, it's perfectly obvious," Malone said. He paused and scowled. That didn't seem quite like what he meant.

"We understand," Helene said sympathetically. "Just go on."

He smiled at her with his whole heart. "Myrdell Harris called up all five of the Deloras, making the voice like Hazel Swackhammer. Told them all she was going out of business, told them to take the little trips they'd been wanting or whatever, and sent each of them a grand by messenger. Naturally, all the Deloras took off."

"But the hands—" Jake began.

"Malone, the feet—" Helene began.

Both of them stopped suddenly, looked at each other, and then at Malone. He realized that he'd unthinkingly said entirely too much. With all his great care to keep Jake and Helene from finding out what the other knew, he'd gone and blurted out enough himself to give the whole show away.

Neither of them said a word. He wished, miserably, that they would. At last he got up and walked back to the window, clasped his hands behind his back, and stood looking dolefully at the first snowflakes that had begun to flutter down.

There was nothing he could say now, nothing he could do. Except possibly jump out the window, and the adjoining roof was only about two feet down, and covered with snow and mud. No, nothing except to stand here until eventually they went quietly away, probably never to return.

He didn't hear a sound behind him. He was damned if he'd turn around. He just stood there, not even hoping.

After a very, very long time, Helene's voice said, "You might as well come back, Malone, while there's still some of your gin left."

He turned around, went back to his desk, took the one very small drink that was left in the bottle and said, "A fine thing. A person goes and turns his back for just a minute, and his alleged friends drink up all his gin." He sat down, reached for a cigar and finally said, "Well, damn it, I meant everything for the best."

They were holding hands, he noticed with relief.

"All right," Helene said. "Myrdell Harris called up all the Deloras and told them to take off, and sent them lavish gifts of money—pretending to be Hazel Swackhammer. Take it from there, Malone."

"Well," he said a little weakly, "that's what happened." He told them about Eva Lou's statement and his subsequent telephone calls. He managed to get his cigar lighted on the third determined try and said, "The hands and the feet, Helene—"

"I know all about," Helen said calmly. "I mean, what von Flanagan discovered, and all the rest of it."

Malone stared at her. He muttered something about second sight, and a probable Welsh grandmother.

"Nothing of the sort," Helene said calmly. "Jake told me all about it. Everything."

The little lawyer glared at Jake. His lips formed the one word, "Judas!"

"I am not," Jake said hotly. "I didn't say a word until Helene told me about the visit the two of you made to Louella Frick's apartment yesterday."

Malone looked at Helene indignantly, and this time he couldn't say even one word.

"All right," he said at last. "Let's just say you told each other. The immediate question is—what was behind Myrdell Harris' suddenly getting rid of all the Deloras, at a total cost of five thousand dollars—an important detail for a girl who loved money just a little better than anything—and then going to all this business with the hands and the feet?"

"It's hardly what you'd call a girlish prank," Jake said.

Helene frowned. "Maybe the word isn't *Why*. It could be *Who*. Who was behind the whole thing?"

Malone nodded slowly. "Someone could have been in it with her. Or someone, more likely, was having her do the work." He paused for a little more thought, then picked up the telephone. "There's one way to find out."

He telephoned one Weasel Firman, an old friend and client, whose various ups and downs had ranged from selling shares in a uranium mine to running a small-time horse parlor. He'd helped Malone out more than once in the past by prying out information about the private financial affairs of clients and others. Right now, Malone wanted to know about Myrdell's bank account. Mainly, had there been any large withdrawals in the past week or so.

Satisfied, he hung up and said, "Good old Weasel. He says he can get it with one quick telephone call, and he'll call me right back."

"But whoever it was," Helene said, "Myrdell Harris or someone else—Malone, what was the reason, the idea, the purpose behind this awful—this awful, awful thing?"

"As Dennis Dennis would put it," Malone said, "this awful, awful, awful thing." He relit his cigar.

She ignored that. "It's like—" She paused. "I don't know what it's like. Maybe like voodoo. Or—" Her lovely face was pale. "Something you simply can't bear to think about."

Jake squeezed her hand tight.

"Well," Helene said, "at least I accomplished one thing today." She indicated the frivolously wrapped box. "I thought it was about time someone did something practical. Such as finding out who bought those fancy gloves Hazel got yesterday."

"So that's why you went to that store," Malone said.

She gave him an impish grin. "You don't think I'd spend seventy-five dollars on three pairs of underpants just because they came from Paris, do you?"

Jake muttered something about having an unemployed husband, and she pointed out that it was a worthwhile investment, in the circumstances.

"But who was it, damn it?" Malone demanded.

"I don't know yet. The girl who made that sale wasn't in yet. A shop of that size remembers such details. So I'm going back in a little while."

"Not, heaven forbid," Jake said fervently, "at seventy-five bucks a throw!"

Conversation languished until the telephone rang. It was Weasel Firman. Malone listened, and Jake and Helene kept very still.

"That was it," he said, as he hung up. "There haven't been any big withdrawals from either Myrdell Harris' very sizable checking or savings accounts. Just the usual number of fairly large deposits." He sighed. "I'm going to make this even harder," he said. "Two of the Deloras I called—Eula Stolz and Louella Frick—mentioned one thing. That the voice that fired them didn't sound exactly like Myrdell Harris imitating Hazel Swackhammer."

Helene said, "Oh Lord. Now we have someone imitating Myrdell Harris imitating Hazel Swackhammer."

"All we need," Jake said, "is to have it turn out to be Hazel Swackhammer imitating someone imitating Myrdell Harris imitating Hazel Swackhammer. Lord, my head aches."

Malone said unsympathetically, "You're making mine ache too. What did you find out about the camera?"

"Camera? Camera? Oh, yes," Jake said, "the camera."

"The camera with five eyes," Helene said.

Something began to stir in Malone's mind. "Go on," he said, leaning comfortably back in his chair and half-closing his eyes. "I'm hearing every word."

"Well," Jake said, "it's like this. The trouble is, this camera, which looks like a good idea otherwise, is just the reverse of what we need. It goes in five directions, like this—" he held out one hand—"and it takes five different pictures simultaneously. Whereas what we need is one camera that will take five girls—" He paused, looked at Malone accusingly.

"Eyes," Malone said, sitting up.

"You didn't hear a word," Jake said accusingly.

"I heard enough," Malone told him. He called Maggie and said, "Call up the Medical Association, or the *Herald-Examiner*, or somebody, and find out Dr. Alonzo Stonecypher's exact age."

"Malone," Jake demanded, "are you out of your mind?"

"I think I'm just beginning to get into it," Malone said. "If there's room."

Maggie came back in a very few minutes with the information that Dr. Alonzo Stonecypher was eighty-two years old on his last birthday, and did Malone want to know what day that was.

"Make a note of it," Malone growled. "We'll send him a birthday present of an ear-trumpet." He turned to Jake and Helene and said, "All this time we've all gone on the premise that Myrdell Harris died a natural death because Dr. Stonecypher had been treating her previously for the same ailment that he said killed her, that he was in attendance and signed the certificate, and that Dr. Stonecypher is more above reproach than rubies, or whatever it is I mean." He paused for breath.

"What we all missed," he said, "was the fact that Dr. Alonzo Stonecypher is eighty-two years old, so nearly blind that he mistook me for Jake, and has to be taken around by his nephew, and that he's as deaf as a whole fence full of posts."

There was a little silence.

"Well," Jake said, "I always did think she was murdered."

"You thought nothing of the kind," Malone said. "Like everybody else, you were surprised that it wasn't murder. But also like everybody else, you took the venerable doctor's word for it." He reached for the telephone.

Helene said, "But what are we going to do?"

"First of all," Malone said, "I'm going to call von Flanagan."

"Oh no, you're not," an indignant voice said from the door. "Save your money, Malone. Because I got tired of your stalling me along, and came up here to get the truth if I have to—oh, hello! I didn't see you!"

As the indignation faded out of von Flanagan's voice, Malone closed his eyes and breathed a quiet thanksgiving for Jake Justus and the whole television industry.

Chapter Twenty-seven

"And so," von Flanagan said, half an hour later, "for just those reasons, Jake, I have every reason to believe that a new kind of quiz show could be a success."

"You may have something there," Jake said, very solemnly and judiciously.

They'd listened to von Flanagan's life story—Malone for the second time that day and the fourth time in a week—to a discussion of the entire television industry in general, to the probable great advantages of a quiz program, also in general, and to von Flanagan's personal ambitions in particular.

"Soon as I get organized a little bit more," Jake told him. "Soon as I get a few programs going. Then we'll get together and really work this out." He felt a hundred per cent safe in saying that. By the time that stage of the Jake Justus Television Productions was reached, von Flanagan would either have found another ambition or, the way things looked right now, be eighty-two years old and not really care any more.

"Sure thing," the big police officer said, beaming. "Wonderful thing, having friends like you." He turned to Malone then, and his face became an odd combination of serious and puzzled. "And you, Malone—" He seemed to be trying to remember exactly what he had come there about.

"I was just about to call you," the little lawyer said quickly. "It's about that body that was found up in Lincoln Park."

"Sitting against a tree," von Flanagan added, his broad face darkening. "With a magazine." He scowled heavily. "The things people do to make my job hard for me. Now a nice simple murder I can understand—"

"The body's been identified, of course," Malone went right on, still quickly.

"You're damned right it has," von Flanagan said. His face was turning crimson now. "Malone, if you'd only told me about it in the first place. An old friend—"

Malone listened while von Flanagan went into one of his minor dissertations on friendship, and then said, "How was I to know who it was? Not until Rico di Angelo told me." He didn't mention just when Rico had told him, or just what. No point in stirring up unnecessary trouble when there was enough right now.

"Well—" von Flanagan said, about one-tenth mollified.

"That's why I was going to telephone to you," Malone said. He added, "If you don't believe me, just ask them."

Von Flanagan might pride himself on being the most skeptical man in Chicago, possibly in the hemisphere, but he would believe anything Helene told him, any time and under any circumstances.

"Well—" he said again. He took out his handkerchief and mopped his face. "And anyway, since it isn't my concern any more anyway, seeing as how she wasn't murdered—"

"But she was," Helene said explosively, and then looked worried about it.

Von Flanagan looked at her, and then at Jake, and then at Malone. "But—her doctor—"

"We know all about that," Malone said patiently.

"So," von Flanagan said. "The doctor signed the certificate. Too bad Doc Flynn had started work already."

"Better call him and tell him to keep right on," Malone said in a grim voice. "That's the whole point. In spite of the doctor's certificate, Myrdell Harris was murdered."

He went on into details, dwelling on Dr. Alonzo Stone-cypher, his age, his eyesight, and his hearing.

Von Flanagan listened and finally, convinced, nodded unhappily. "But Dr. Stonecypher, he ain't going to like it, us going ahead with the autopsy which we would have done if we hadn't of found out who the corpse was and all."

"Tell him," Helene said, with her sweetest smile, "that you didn't know who she was until the autopsy was all finished."

"Don't seem right," the police officer muttered, "but—" One hand picked up the telephone. "Mind if I use your phone?" He waited a minute on the wire and then said, "Doc? Go right ahead on that Lincoln Park babe. Yes, I know about that. Yes, I know he did. But officially you don't know he did. Yes, I do know what I'm doing. I hope I do. Oh, some kind of poison, I guess, that would make it look like whatever it was the doc said she died of. Yes, of course I take the whole responsibility."

He hung up, mopped his face again, and growled. "Always, I'm the one who has to take the responsibility. See what I mean about people making things hard for me on purpose?"

"Cheer up," Helene said. "This time, someone tried to make things easy for you."

"Who?" The look von Flanagan directed at Malone made it very plain that whoever it was, it wasn't Malone.

"The person who moved the body into Lincoln Park," Helene told him sweetly. "The person who thoughtfully rescued it from Mr. di Angelo's wagon, thereby preventing a murder from being concealed and a murderer going unpunished."

Von Flanagan looked skeptical and as though he wished the unknown thoughtful person had quietly stayed at home and watched television instead of messing around exposing murders and making more work for the whole police department.

"Sure," Jake added with enthusiasm. "Otherwise, you'd never have known about it."

Von Flanagan's expression said that would have suited him just fine.

Malone said, "Obviously, somebody knew Myrdell Harris had been murdered, or at least suspected it. But for some reason, unknown at this time, that person couldn't or wouldn't come forward. Or perhaps, simply couldn't prove anything. But this somebody did know that if an unidentified body turned up under rather unusual circumstances, the police department would have to do something about it. And that an immediate autopsy would be in order." He began unwrapping a fresh cigar.

"And just who," von Flanagan said suspiciously, "might this very thoughtful somebody be?"

"Who knows?" Malone said airily, lighting the cigar. He was beginning to have an unpleasant suspicion of his own, but he was keeping it strictly to himself.

Von Flanagan expressed his past, present and probable future opinion of Malone in no uncertain terms, and immediately apologized to Helene.

"Don't apologize," Helene said serenely, "you may be right."

Malone glared at them both and said nothing.

"This person—" Von Flanagan scowled. "This person couldn't be the murderer, because the murderer would be the one who didn't want the murder discovered. Therefore, the person who swiped the body and stuck it in Lincoln Park is somebody else."

"Naturally," Malone said. He aimed a smoke ring at the ceiling, and wished he felt as calm as he hoped he looked.

"So," von Flanagan finished in a roar, "that means I've got to find two different persons. And I don't even know yet how the babe was murdered, or why, or anything about it."

"Don't worry," Helene said consolingly, "we'll all help."

"That's why I'm worrying," he said indignantly. "The last time you three helped—" Suddenly he remembered the reason he was in Malone's office.

"Another thing," he snapped at Malone. "The other murder. Except that it wasn't a murder. Because it was a natural death."

"Stop being confusing," Helene said.

He paid no attention to her. "Malone, you swore—"

"And I will," Malone said. "Today." He didn't know how he was going to manage it or, at that moment, anything, but he did know he had to, and he would.

"Thank goodness," von Flanagan said, mopping his brow the third time, "it wasn't the head."

"The head," Malone said slowly. "It wouldn't have been the head." A new and somehow terrible note had come into his voice. He stared at them for a moment, not seeing them, not seeing anything. He rose and walked back to the window and looked out.

"Malone—" Helene began.

"Leave me alone," he murmured. "I've got to think."

They left him alone. It was one of those times when everyone felt Malone knew what he was doing, and Malone hoped he did.

Suddenly he turned around. "I should have known all along." He drew a long, slow breath. "I would have, if only so many extraneous things hadn't kept popping up to confuse me."

"For heaven's sake, Malone," Helene exploded.

"If you think you're confused—" Jake began angrily.

Von Flanagan simply stared.

The little lawyer looked tired and unhappy. He stood there for a moment, frowning. Suddenly he picked up the telephone and called the number of Charlie Swackhammer's apartment.

It was Maybelle who answered the phone, the original and unforgettable voice of Delora Deanne. Yes, Charlie was there. He'd been there all morning.

Charlie Swackhammer's booming voice wanted to know how everything was going.

"Fine," Malone said, hollowly, "just fine. I just wanted to make sure everything was fine with you?"

Charlie Swackhammer said, "Huh?" and then, "Oh," and finally, "Oh, sure. I'm not taking my eye off her for a minute—am I, Maybelle?"

Maybelle's voice came on with a touch of a giggle in it and informed that Charlie dear was guarding her as though she were the crown jewels.

"See that he doesn't stop," Malone said and hung up.

"And just what was all that about?" von Flanagan demanded.

Malone looked at him gravely. "Von Flanagan—"

The telephone rang. Malone looked at it for a moment as though the devil himself were at the other end of the line, then grabbed it off the hook. He listened to it for a half-minute, scowling.

Finally he said, "I'll be there as soon as I can," and stood looking at the phone for another half-minute before he put it slowly down on the hook.

Everybody started to ask questions at once. Malone shook his head at them.

"Client of mine," he said briefly. "Emergency." He reached for his topcoat.

"But damn it, Malone," von Flanagan said. "This other business—"

Malone looked at him firmly. "You said yourself, it wasn't in your department. It still isn't. This—other business—only delays it a little." He looked at his watch. He looked at Helene. "If you'll drive me—"

"A pleasure," Helene said, and looked it.

Von Flanagan started to protest, thought better of it, and settled for glaring at Malone all the way down in the elevator.

Once in the car, Malone said, "Rico di Angelo's. Fast."

The car moved out into traffic. Jake said, "What's his trouble?"

"Plenty," Malone told him. "First, a corpse that ought to be in his place wasn't. Now, a corpse that isn't supposed to be there, is." He sighed and added, "Dennis Dennis."

Chapter Twenty-eight

Dennis Dennis' body sat in a large upholstered armchair in the ornate waiting room of Rico di Angelo's strictly high-class funeral home. It looked a little surprised.

"You see?" Rico said accusingly.

Malone nodded and said that he saw. He shifted his un-lighted cigar to the other corner of his mouth and stared thoughtfully at the corpse.

"I went out," Rico di Angelo said. "I went out to talk with a friend of mine with the police. About that other body. I fix that all up good for you, Malone. I explain I don't tell them before because I am knocked very cold, and Joe my helper, he does not know what to do."

He scowled at Malone. "I fix everything up good for you, Malone, like you ask me, and what do you do? I come back here from seeing my friend with the police, and I find *him*."

Malone ignored that. He realized that for the time being,

at least, Rico was going to look at him with suspicion regardless of what happened.

"At least," Helene commented, "you're getting plenty of new customers."

He scowled at her too, which was unusual. "But I do not like it when they come walking in off the streets." He raised his voice and called, "Louie!"

Louie, his cousin and assistant, a short, swarthy, bucket-chested man, came in from the display room.

"Louie, you tell them how it is while I have gone to explain things to our friend with the police."

Louie accepted the cigar Malone offered, and explained simply that it wasn't his fault, that he'd never seen the man before, that he had no idea what had taken place, that his head hurt, that he was thinking of quitting this job, relatives or no relatives, and that he'd like to have a talk with Mr. Justus whenever the opportunity presented itself.

"My cousin Louie, he plays the cello," Rico said. "Not good. Tell them about your head, Louie."

"It hurts," Louie said balefully.

Rico shrugged his shoulders and said, "It is like this, Malone. I leave Louie alone here. This—this person—" he pointed to the late Dennis Dennis—"he came in. Said he was meeting someone. He sat down here. But in a different chair. Then Louie, he goes in the office. He sits down by the desk. He gets hit on the back of the head. After while he gets up off the floor. Nobody is around. He looks to see what is stolen. Nothing is stolen. He waits. I come back. I see this person. I go to speak to him. I see he is dead. So I telephone you, Malone. Then Louie tells me he is sitting in a different chair. Do I make it all quite clear?"

"Beautifully," Jake said admiringly.

"Except for a few points," Malone said. "Did Dennis Dennis go in the office, sneak up behind Louie and hit him on the back of the head, then come back here and sit down and die? And, from what?"

"And what was he doing here in the first place?" Helene demanded. "And who was he going to meet?"

"One thing at a time," Malone told her.

"He was hit on the back of the head too," Louie volunteered.

Malone walked around the chair and inspected the back of

Dennis Dennis' head. "Wouldn't have killed him," he reported.

"But what did, Malone?" Rico di Angelo asked despairingly.

The little lawyer sighed. "I'm gifted with many things, but second sight is not one of them. Have you called the police?"

Rico shook his head indignantly. "Naturally I have not. I called you, Malone. Because somehow you are mixed up in this. I look in his wallet, I see that he works in that same place as that girl did. So I know you are mixed up in this, and so, and because you are my good friend, I called you first."

"Good," Malone said, "and thanks. And go right on being my good friend, and call them now. And don't mention the fact that you did call me first. I'll handle them when they get here. But don't waste any more time, von Flanagan is unhappy enough as it is."

Rico went away to telephone and Helene said, "Have you any idea what killed him, Malone?"

Malone said, "No," and went on looking at the corpse.

"Do you know who he was going to meet, and why he was going to meet them here?"

Malone said, "No," again, chewing furiously on his cigar.

"Well, do you know—"

"No," Malone snapped, "I don't know. And stop bothering me, I'm busy."

Jake said mildly, "I know the layout here. In the office, Louie would have his back to the reception hall. Someone could have come in the front door without being seen—"

"Someone could have come in the back door, too," Rico said glumly, coming back from the phone. "When I came back from seeing my friend who is with the police, it is unlocked."

Malone nodded. "Someone came in through the front door or the back door, knocked Louie cold—probably watched for his chance—then came in here and knocked Dennis Dennis cold, and then finished him off."

"But how?" Helene said.

"And who unlocked the back door?" Jake asked.

Malone ignored them both, very pointedly.

"*He,*" Louie said stubbornly, "was sitting in another chair."

He pointed to it, another big upholstered chair next to an elaborately decorative table. It had its back to the office and to the rear room.

Malone sighed. "And why would *he* get up, unlock the back door, knock out Louie, come back and sit in another chair, then, I suppose, knock himself out and murder himself?"

"I never said he did," Louie said.

"And who says he's been murdered?" Rico demanded.

"The police will," the little lawyer said wearily. He gave the corpse an unhappy glance. "Who was in here this morning?"

Rico began holding up fingers. "Judge Touralchuk, about a lodge meeting. Mrs. Swackhammer, about the funeral. Mr. Swackhammer, a friend of mine, also about the funeral. My cousin Frankie, to borrow some money. A Mr. Furlong, a friend of the dead lady. And *him*." He pointed. He added reflectively, "I didn't tell any of them that the dead lady, she was not here."

"And I suppose any of them could have unlocked the back door," Malone said in a thoughtful voice. "And then waited till the coast was clear, come in and conked Louie and murdered Dennis Dennis."

"But how was he murdered?" Rico said. "Who says he was? To me, he only looks dead."

Malone sighed again and said, "Maybe the same way Myrdell Harris was murdered. She just looked dead, too."

"And who says *she* was murdered?" Rico seemed to be keeping his temper by main force. "The doctor, he wrote down—"

Malone said, "Never mind. It's too complicated to explain right now." To explain, or to understand, he reflected miserably.

"And aside from all that," Helene said suddenly, "it's too late to do anything about it now, but we've made a terrible mistake. We never should have called the cops. Rico's in enough trouble as it is. We should have taken *this* out of here, and let the police find it somewhere else. It might have done Rico out of a fine funeral job, but I doubt if he'd have made much profit anyway."

Rico looked a little brighter. "When I called the cops," he began, "I didn't tell them what it is for. We can move him away and when they come, I tell them it is because somebody hit my cousin Louie on the back of his head."

Malone shook his head. "No," he said firmly. "Very definitely no. Because for one thing, there's been enough body-snatching lately. And for another, von Flanagan would identify him, find out that he was a member of the Delora Deanne outfit and hence tied in somehow with Myrdell Harris, and Rico would still be in a spot."

Rico's face fell, but he nodded. "And anyway," he told Helene sadly, "it would be against the law."

That was when von Flanagan and Klutchetsky arrived. The big police officer looked suspiciously at everyone.

Helene beamed at him brightly. "You certainly got here in a big hurry. Rico just telephoned."

Von Flanagan looked a little puzzled. He pointed to the late Dennis Dennis and said, "Who's he?"

"The corpse," Malone said. "What else did you expect to find?"

"Well," von Flanagan said, "it's an undertaking parlor, isn't it? But what's he doing in that chair?"

"Just sitting there," Helene said.

Malone glared at her and said to von Flanagan, "That's the reason we telephoned you."

"Who telephoned me?"

"I did," Rico said. He added, "Malone told me to."

"All right. Why?"

"Because of him," Jake said, pointing to the corpse.

It took Malone a few minutes and a great deal of fast explaining to straighten things out. Then von Flanagan, an ominous growl in his voice, sent Klutchetsky to the telephone to round up the team he scornfully called the "experts." Finally he gave the corpse a desultory inspection, announced that someone had given the late Dennis Dennis a conk on the head but not a bad one, and that he hadn't been dead very long. Then he turned to Malone and demanded, "This your client?"

Malone shook his head.

"Then what are you doing here?"

"For that matter," Malone said quickly, "what are you doing here, if it wasn't because of Rico's telephone call?"

"I wanted to ask Rico some questions about Myrdell Harris' body," von Flanagan said. "Now that it's in my department, on account of it turning out she was murdered after all."

Rico opened his mouth, glanced at Malone, and shut it again.

"Well," Malone said quickly, and very smoothly, "Myrdell Harris was a friend of ours."

It wasn't exactly an explanation, but for a moment von Flanagan accepted it. Then his eyes narrowed. "You went tearing out of your office and asked her to drive you—" he jerked his head toward Helene—"because one of your clients had an emergency."

"Oh, that," Malone said. "That's all taken care of." He hastily shifted the subject to, "But I suppose you're mostly concerned with what happened here."

Everyone helped to explain except Louie, who had lapsed into a sour silence, limiting himself to muttered yesses and noes. The departure of Rico, the arrival of Dennis Dennis, the knocking out of Louie, the return of Rico and the discovery of the body. The fact that the back door had been unlocked was duly noted and the door examined by Klutchetsky. Somehow von Flanagan failed to inquire about the day's roster of visitors, Rico didn't volunteer the information, and Malone tactfully kept his mouth shut.

The experts came and began their dreary work. The story had to be told and retold again. An assistant medical examiner didn't care to venture a suggestion as to the cause of death; that would have to be determined by an autopsy. If then, Malone added to himself, thinking of Myrdell.

Finally von Flanagan turned on them and braced himself, his big face crimson. "I don't know why it is, but you people always go out of your way to make things hard for me." He gave a brief dissertation on the hardships of a cop. "And old friends of mine, too." He gave another dissertation on friendship, and how little it ever got anybody. "What I ought to do is lock up the whole bunch of you for obstructing justice." It wasn't a new threat.

Nobody said a word. There were times to answer von Flanagan, but this wasn't one of them.

"But I'm not going to do it," he roared at last. "Because somehow you'd find a way to make more trouble for me, even in jail." He glared at them, waved an arm toward the door.

"Go home," he said in a dramatic bellow. "That's all I want of you, understand? And it's an order. Keep out of my way. Keep out of my sight. *Go home!*"

The three fled.

Out on the sidewalk Malone wiped his face with a

crumpled handkerchief and said, "Well, that's a new angle from von Flanagan, anyway."

"Malone, what killed him?" Helene asked.

And Jake said, "Who did it, Malone?"

The little lawyer shook his head. "I don't know, and I don't know, and I don't know. For a little while I thought I did, but after this, I don't know!" He added, "And you heard what von Flanagan said."

Helene gave him a stricken look.

"Only," Malone told her reassuringly, "he didn't say just *whose* home."

Chapter Twenty-nine

"Don't bother me with questions now," Malone growled. He took out a fresh cigar, unwrapped it and stood there in the Division Street snow and slush staring at it. "It isn't that the questions bother me," he complained moodily, "it's that the answers are so hard."

Helene sniffed. "All right, Malone. But what are you going to do now?"

"Two things," he told her. "Two things simultaneously. And both of them have to be done right away. So, reluctant as I am to accept your help—"

He explained hastily. There had to be an immediate visit to the Delore Deanne offices, to pick up any loose ends of information that might be floating around there, before von Flanagan arrived on the same mission.

At the same time, there had to be an immediate search of the late Dennis Dennis' apartment. Because there just might be something, some hint as to the writer's private life, if he had one. Maybe a lead to his ex-wife. Something, anyway.

He gave them the address he had found in Dennis Dennis' wallet and added, "It's a second-rate apartment hotel on North Dearborn Street, not far from here. I happen to know the manager, name's Reilly. He doubles as day clerk, and he's probably there now. Tell him I said to let you in. And don't let von Flanagan find you if you can help it."

He waved down a passing taxi and was gone before Jake could finish a remark about how funny it was that Malone apparently knew all the apartment-hotel managers in Chicago, especially the second-rate ones.

The Astrid Arms apartment building looked as though it had never been anything but second-rate, and its years apparently hadn't been easy. The lobby, Helene observed, was dowdy, but not genteel. Not outright poor, but rather like a small-incomed widow who hadn't grown old gracefully.

The gray-haired, middle-aged Reilly leered pleasantly when Jake announced that they were friends of Malone, then grew grave when he explained their visit.

"Too bad," he said sadly, mentally marking Dennis Dennis' rent off the future ledgers. "Nice quiet young man, never had any parties, never gave any trouble. Too many murders going on, if you ask me. Suppose it'll be in the papers, too. Bad for the hotel. Oh, well." He produced the key and said, "Three-oh-two. Guess it's all right if Malone says so."

Helene remarked that Malone would also be just as happy if the police didn't find them there.

Reilly nodded as though he were used to the police and their vagaries, and said, "I'll call and warn you if I see them come in. There's a flight of stairs right around the corner of the corridor."

The gloomy little building seemed very quiet as they rode up the self-service elevator with its hand-lettered sign with instructions as to what to do in case of fire. Probably, Helene reflected, the occupants were all either people who slept all day, or who crept silently out to mediocre jobs early in the morning. She shivered and took Jake's arm as they walked down the worn carpeted hall.

Dennis Dennis' apartment was small, drab, and ordinary, like the building itself and its Mr. Reilly. There was one boxlike room with a folding bed—down and unmade, at the moment—and an assortment of badly worn cheap furniture—a desk, a sagging armchair, an end table, a magazine rack, and a couple of wooden chairs. The one window looked at another one exactly like it, but with the shade drawn, across a narrow airway. The scuffed rug had originally been of an Oriental inclination, and the one picture was a dust-streaked Maxfield Parrish reproduction.

There was a little box of a kitchenette, obviously used for nothing but coffee-making, and a bathroom with chipped tile and slightly tarnished faucets; there was a small closet with three built-in drawers and a rack from which hung a suit of clothes and a gabardine raincoat.

But there was nothing to indicate that Dennis Dennis or anyone else lived there, really lived there, that it was or had ever been anything more than a stopping-off place for sleeping, bathing, and changing clothes. Even the unemptied ash trays had a rented look.

There wasn't much to search. Helene sat in the sagging chair and watched Jake.

"Naturally," she observed as he opened the desk, "if there ever was anything here that told, or even hinted anything about the real Dennis Dennis, the murderer would have known about it and been here ahead of us."

"A fine piece of logic," Jake said, "and I'm proud of you. It occurred to me too. And probably to Malone. This is just to be on the safe side."

Helene glanced around the four bare walls. "It's a little sad. Dennis Dennis, writing poems, and living here."

"He undoubtedly didn't write them here," Jake said. "Or if he ever did, he carried them away with him. Poems, and everything else. There's nothing here about Dennis Dennis. Nothing about his ex-wife. In fact, nothing about anything."

"Too bad," Helene said regretfully. "I'd hoped there'd at least be a picture of his ex-wife. That woman has an unpleasant kind of fascination for me. Nobody could be that typical."

Jake shut the desk. "That's that. Unless, of course—somebody did get here first."

The telephone rang. It was Reilly. Jake hung up and said, "Time to go."

From around the corner in the corridor they could hear the elevator door open and close, and the sound of heavy footfalls. Von Flanagan's voice was muttering, "A guy in the radio business, living in a dump like this." A door closed.

"I was thinking the same thing," Jake said.

"You're forgetting the ex-wife," Helene reminded him.

"Nobody who knew Dennis Dennis could forget the ex-wife," Jake told her gloomily. "But even so, that's an awful lot of poverty for anyone with his job." He listened closely for a minute and then said, "Come on."

Helene took two steps down the stairs, paused, said, "Oh!" and then tried to smother a giggle.

Jake stared at her. "If there's anything funny that I've happened to miss—"

"My box," Helene said with a gasp. "The box of Paris-made panties, pink, blue and green, with real lace, at twenty-five dollars a pair." She caught her breath and said, "I left them. Back there. In Dennis Dennis' apartment." She paused and added, "Thank goodness, my name wasn't in them! But just the same—"

"Von Flanagan," Jake said. A slow grin spread over his lean, freckled face. "He's going to have a busy time figuring that one out. If he ever finds out the truth, he'll swear you did it on purpose." He looked at Helene searchingly. "Or did you?"

She sniffed at him and led the way down the stairs. The dreary little lobby was deserted except for the tired-faced Reilly, but through the dusty glass of the door they could see an ominously uniformed figure.

Reilly apparently took in the situation at a glance. He motioned them around the desk and into a tiny cubbyhole of an office. "Can't let a friend of Malone's get into trouble with the cops," he explained affably.

Jake nodded, and Helene beamed her thanks.

"For that matter," Reilly said, "can't let a friend of Malone's go thirsty, either." He produced three glasses and a half-empty bottle of cheap bourbon from a cabinet in the wall.

"Do tell us about Dennis Dennis," Helene said, shuddering a little as the bourbon burned its way down.

Reilly lifted his shoulders wearily. "Nothing to tell. Been here a year or so. No visitors. No parties. Not many phone calls. Not much mail." He refilled his glass and added, "No trouble." His voice indicated that he would be very happy to have more guests exactly like that. "Now you tell me about Dennis Dennis. Who murdered him?"

This time Helene lifted her shoulders. "Who knows?" she said owlishly.

Jake decided it was time to help out. "What time did Dennis Dennis go out this morning?"

"It was—let me see." Reilly squinted his eyes and wrinkled his forehead. "Oh, yes. Late. Not terribly, but late for him. About ten o'clock, in fact. I was thinking of ringing to see if he was awake, I knew he had to be at his job early. He got a telephone call. A couple of minutes later he went tearing out in a big hurry."

Helene's and Jake's eyes met and agreed that Dennis Dennis must have gone straight to Rico di Angelo's establishment without sparing any particular horses on the way.

"I don't suppose you noticed who called?" Helene said, very casually.

Reilly shook his head.

"Man or woman?" Jake asked helpfully.

Reilly didn't know.

They waited in silence for a while. Once Reilly stepped out to answer the telephone, twice he handed mail to outgoing guests. Then von Flanagan's booming voice and the clang of the elevator door sounded together.

"—not even a morning paper. Guy must've spent his time someplace else."

"Mmmmpf." That was Klutchetsky.

"I should of hung on to Malone. And those other two. They must be up to something."

Silence. Also Klutchetsky.

A long sigh. "Well, one thing," von Flanagan said in a happier voice, "we know one thing. He had one hell of an expensive girl friend. Now the first thing we got to do is find the babe who was going to get those very, very fancy pants—"

This time Jake's look at Helene was a long and somewhat anxious one. She shook her blond head and gave him her don't-worry-about-a-thing expression.

Von Flanagan was tossing a few more questions at the desk clerk, who'd gone back out front. He sounded tired, annoyed and baffled.

"Somewhere around ten," Reilly was saying in a bored voice. "I believe he had a telephone call before he left."

"No mail? No visitors? Nothing else?"

"No *sir!*" The manager of the Astrid Arms didn't seem to care much for the police.

He waited a minute after they'd gone, then strolled casually to the door and glanced up and down Dearborn Street. "All clear," he reported as he came back.

Jake and Helene thanked him profusely and started for the street. Suddenly Reilly called them back.

"Got something I'd rather give Malone than the police," he announced. "Malone's a friend of mine." He produced a small packet from behind the desk. "When Mr. Dennis came in last night—this morning—I was up. He asked me to keep this for him. Said he'd rather not have it around his room." He waved the packet in the air as he spoke, then handed it to Jake.

Helene said, "When he came in—what time was that?"

Reilly thought, shrugged his shoulders, finally said, "Must have been about four—five." There didn't seem to be anything unusual about his having made a night of it.

They thanked him again and examined the packet. It was a small manila envelope, loosely sealed, its metal clasp fastened. Jake took just a shade under ten seconds deciding whether or not to open it.

Inside were Myrdell Harris' missing bankbooks.

Chapter Thirty

Tamia Tabet looked a little tired, Malone reflected, but it was a nice, cuddly tired. He wanted at least to reach out and pat her cheek comfortingly, better yet, to snuggle her sleepy head on a protecting shoulder. He sighed deeply and confined himself to a smile that tried to convey the same idea.

He only hoped she wouldn't be too tired to pick up their date exactly where it had been interrupted last night.

Hazel Swackhammer, she informed him, wasn't in. She'd been in, yes. Then she'd gone out to see about poor Miss Harris' funeral, and hadn't come back. What time? Oh, she'd gone out about ten o'clock or so.

The little lawyer nodded and then said solemnly, "Dennis Dennis is dead."

Her eyes and mouth made little round circles of surprise. "Oh!" she said, and then, "Who murdered him?"

Malone blinked. "Now what makes you think . . ." he began.

Otis Furlong walked in from the next room and said, "Hullo, Malone, thought I heard your voice." He looked at Malone, at Tamia Tabet, at Malone again, and finally said, "What's what?"

"Dennis Dennis," Malone said. He didn't have time to add the word "dead."

"Murdered?" Otis Furlong said, frowning.

Malone nodded and said nothing. He reflected that, for some reason, whenever anyone died around the Delora Deanne establishment, everyone leaped to the conclusion that it was murder.

Tamia Tabet said, "How awful," in a shocked little voice, and Otis Furlong said, "Well!" as though he couldn't think of anything more appropriate on short notice. Neither of them seemed particularly grieved, Malone observed, or even surprised. Finally Furlong said, "Too bad," and took out his pipe.

Malone sat down on an exquisite little chair of delicate, gilded wrought iron and oyster-white satin, unwrapped a cigar, and told them briefly what had happened, skipping most of the details.

Otis Furlong frowned again. "Amazing," he said at last. "An undertaking parlor. Funny place for a murder. And besides, you know—Swackhammer Brothers—"

"I do know," Malone said and waited.

"Maybe a coincidence," Furlong said. He began filling his pipe, slowly and deliberately. "Undertaking business being mixed up in it." He paused and added, "Might make me a suspect. I used to work for an undertaker myself. Quite a bunch of them, in fact."

"Oh?" Malone said hopefully. There was a time to ask questions and a time to sit still.

"Ump. Taking beautiful naturally colored pictures of the dear departed, after they were all beautifully dressed and combed and made up. Beautiful pictures. The families used to buy a lot of them." He grinned wryly. "Beginning photographers have to do all kinds of jobs to get started."

Malone remembered something, and kept quiet about it.

"Matter of fact," Otis Furlong said, "that's how I happened to meet Hazel."

There was a little silence. The handsome photographer seemed to have exhausted the subject.

Tamia Tabet spoke up pertly. "I used to work for an undertaker myself. One of the Swackhammer brothers. I took care of the clothes. The laying-away clothes." That seemed to exhaust the subject for her too. But after a moment she added, "And Anna Hodges, who designs those lovely Delora Deanne jars and boxes used to work for a florist designing lovely funeral pieces."

"It'll probably turn out," Malone said gloomily, "that Dennis Dennis got his literary start writing epitaphs."

But no one seemed to know anything about how Dennis Dennis got his start.

Malone sighed. "His wife. Does anyone have her address? Has anyone here seen her? Does anyone here know anything about her?"

Neither of them did, beyond what Dennis Dennis himself had told Malone. Finally Tamia Tabet brightly offered to ask his secretary, and went away. The little lawyer turned to Otis Furlong.

"Tell me something," he said suddenly, deciding this was a time to come right out with things. "I heard a rumor that Myrdell Harris knew some unpleasant secret about you. With all that's happening around here, if you have any secrets, they'd be safer with me than—well, others."

"The police, you mean," Otis Furlong said, with another wry grin. "But I didn't murder Myrdell, and I didn't murder Dennis Dennis. And as far as the secret is concerned—I told you, photographers just starting out in life—sometimes have to turn to all sorts of ways of making a living—"

Malone nodded and let it go at that. He was afraid Otis Furlong might add that he'd included a few improvements of his own.

Tamia Tabet came back with the secretary, a dour, bored girl who seemed neither surprised at nor sorry about her boss' death, and who knew nothing at all about his ex-wife except that she cost an appalling amount in alimony payments. She didn't know much of anything about Dennis Dennis, either.

It appeared that no one did. Within an hour, Malone had talked with everyone in the Delora Deanne building, and what he'd learned fitted comfortably on the back of an old envelope. And Hazel Swackhammer still had not returned.

He went away unhappily, hoping Jake and Helene had had better luck, and not really expecting it.

In the taxi back to his office, he took out the scribbled notes and looked them over. So far, they didn't add up to much except a lot more questions to be asked.

No one had seen Dennis Dennis' ex-wife, knew what her name was, or had spoken to her. Nor had anyone ever seen a picture of her. There wasn't any address for her in any of Dennis Dennis' files, nor the name of anyone who might have been her lawyer.

No one had the faintest idea what Dennis Dennis' name had originally been, but everyone agreed that it had once been something else.

On the positive side, his birthday had been July 17, year unknown; this had been his first job—before that he'd had a couple of poems in *Poetry* Magazine; from various remarks he'd made, he was a Chicago product and had graduated from college here—some said Chicago University, some said Northwestern, and nobody knew what year; and he'd been with Delora Deanne for six years and two months.

The sum total was small, and time was short, and quite possibly the lines of inquiry he meant to follow would either lead him nowhere or mean nothing anyway, and in his haste he'd forgotten to confirm a second date with Tamia Tabet for that night.

And the snow was turning to rain.

Jake and Helene were waiting when he walked in his office, tired and thoroughly discouraged with it all, hurled his hat on the sofa and slumped down behind his desk.

"Nothing is ever that bad, Malone," Helene said gently. "And we didn't find anything else, but we found Myrdell Harris' bankbooks."

Jake handed them over and described the excursion in detail.

The little lawyer sighed and looked through them. "They show exactly what I thought," he said at last. "A number of large deposits over a considerable period of time. No big withdrawals. She didn't put up the money that was paid the Delora Deannes." He slid them into a desk drawer and slammed it shut, looking at it indignantly.

"The important thing about the bankbooks," he said at last, "was not what was in them, but who took them, and why.

Now we know Dennis Dennis took them and still don't know why."

"Or when," Helene put in.

Malone stared at her for a minute. "Yes we do. I do, anyway. It was some time last night. Because the telephone slips weren't there." He reached for a fresh cigar and said, "No, I am not addled by all this," and went on to explain about the telephone slips. "He must have kept on calling, and finally was told she was dead. Then he went up to the apartment and took the bankbooks out of there—and the telephone slips at the same time."

"Why?" Jake asked.

Malone glared at him.

"How did he get in?" Helene asked.

"With a key," Malone growled. "Everybody seems to have had keys to Myrdell Harris' apartment. Maybe she was his ex-wife."

"Malone," Helene said, "who *was* his ex-wife?"

"Myrdell Harris," Malone growled, "or Hazel Swackhammer, or one of the five Deloras. Don't bother me." He took the envelope out of his pocket, laid it on his desk, scowled at it, and said, "So far, that's all we know about the late Dennis Dennis."

"Not quite," Helene said cheerfully. "I have news for you, Malone."

She went on to tell him of leaving the package of Paris pants in Dennis Dennis' apartment, and of von Flanagan's interest in the discovery. Malone grinned briefly and then began to worry all over again.

"The label on the box," he said. "He may go to the shop and ask questions."

"I thought of that," Helene told him in her most serene voice. "I think of everything. So I went back to the shop. I looked very unhappy and told them my husband would probably beat me if he knew I'd paid so much for three pairs of underpants."

"He probably would, too," Jake said.

She ignored him. "So everyone swore they'd never, never tell anyone who'd bought them." She smiled sweetly and added, "I had to buy a dozen pairs of stockings to clinch it, but—"

Jake sighed, looked martyred, and said nothing.

"And while I was there," Helene went on, "the other girl came in. The one who'd sold that pair of gloves. In a place that size, purchases like that are remembered."

"Well?" Malone demanded.

"Naturally," she said, "it was Dennis Dennis!"

Chapter Thirty-one

"If only I'd had a lot more information," Malone said, "or a lot less." He thought that over and said, "If only I'd never heard of Delora Deanne. If only I'd never become a lawyer."

"That's von Flanagan's line," Jake said coldly.

Malone said, "If only I'd died in my cradle."

"Don't worry," Helene said, "you've got us."

He looked at her desolately and went right on worrying. That was the main trouble, he had them. If only it weren't for the Jake Justus Television Production Company and a prospective Delora Deanne show. He tried to tell himself that otherwise everything would be all right, that he didn't really care what had happened.

The telephone rang. Malone looked at it as though it probably had more bad news, and finally answered it. He listened, said once, "I'll be damned!" then, "Anything on the other one?" and finally, "Well, let me know."

He hung up and said, "Von Flanagan got a quick report on Dennis Dennis." He paused. "He was shot full of embalming fluid. While he was unconscious, but still alive."

There was a little silence. At last Jake said, "Well, it was an appropriate place for it, anyway."

Malone nodded. "Very. Which indicates that murdering Dennis Dennis may have been a spur of the moment affair. And by someone who knew that a shot of embalming fluid would be fatal."

They thought that over solemnly.

"Not entirely unpremeditated, though," Malone said suddenly. "Not something that happened in a sudden flare-up of rage."

"The kind you love to describe in front of a jury," Helene commented.

He ignored her and went on, "Rather, someone who trailed Dennis Dennis with the idea of murdering him, saw he was alone in Rico's except for the attendant, bopped the attendant, and used a tidy weapon which happened to be at hand on Dennis Dennis."

"After bopping him," Helene said. "Or to put it nicely, after rendering him unconscious."

He looked at her gloomily and said nothing. He rested his head on his hands and went right on saying nothing, for a long time. The little lawyer looked tired almost beyond endurance now, his eyes red, his face drawn.

Finally he looked up and said, in a kind of far-off voice, "I could probably have prevented this, you know." He drew a long, slow breath. "If one of my phone calls had reached him. If I'd only foreseen something of the sort."

"Malone," Helene said very gently, "you can't prevent all the murders, you know."

He looked at her gratefully. "No," he said, "and right now, I still probably have one to prevent."

He took the wrinkled envelope out of his pocket and stared at it. "There's a lot of things I need to know, practically right this minute. Dennis Dennis' real name. Name and location of his ex-wife. Details like that." He caught a suspicious look on Helene's face and said, "No, I'm not trying to get rid of you, I really do want to know all that. Because I want to locate the ex-wife. I don't know why, it just seems important."

"Anytime you don't know why a thing seems important," Jake said, "that means it definitely *is* important."

Malone let that go by him and said, "Nobody knows, or admits to knowing, the guy's right name. But here's a guess at his age, the length of time he's been with Delora Deanne, said to be his first job, the date of publication of a poem in *Poetry* Magazine, the fact that he's a Chicago product and went to college in Chicago, and that's about all there is to go on."

"It's enough," Jake said, reaching for his hat. "College registrars. Bureau of Vital Statistics. *Herald-Examiner* morgue. Most of it can be done on a telephone." He grinned reassuringly at Malone. "What's the good of having an ex-reporter for a friend, chum?"

"With a wife," Helene added, "who can drive a car places in a hurry?"

Malone loved them both and thanked them both from the bottom of his heart. Out loud he said crossly, "Well, get going, then."

The office seemed almost unbearably quiet after they had gone. He wished he knew just what to do next, or if he ought to do anything at all. He wished for a lot of things, including a sun-caressed beach in Bermuda. Or Hawaii. Practically the same place.

He sat brooding and feeling sorry for himself until a small nagging thought that had been annoying him all morning crystallized into a definite question, with an equally definite need for more information. Charlie Swackhammer had said, "I own forty-five per cent of Delora Deanne—but Hazel thinks I own fifty-five."

Who did own the other ten shares?

It was, he told himself furiously, one of the things he should have worried about a long time before and would have, he apologized to himself, if so many things hadn't kept coming up to distract him. For the second time that day he called Weasel Firman, and for the second time was told that the information would be along as good as immediately.

Well, now there was nothing to do but wait, while other people did his work for him. He told Maggie he'd gone to Chattanooga on sudden, urgent business, turned off the lights, locked the door, and settled down to a dream of tropic sands and beautiful native girls all looking exactly like the composite Delora Deanne and giggling like Tamia Tabet.

Then the pounding of the surf on the beach at Waikiki turned into a clamorous pounding on his office door, and the soft voices of native musicians were drowned out by Jake's bellowing to open up. He stumbled sleepily to the door, opened it, turned on the light, and stood there blinking at them and muttering something about hibiscus blossoms.

"Fine thing," Jake said indignantly, "here we work our fingers to a shadow for you, in this weather, and you go off to Hawaii. I've a good notion not to tell you about Dennis Dennis' ex-wife."

"I was thinking," Malone said, equally indignantly. He

stalked to his desk, sat down and said, "Well?" He started unwrapping a fresh cigar and added, "The ex-wife's name?"

"Zero," Helene said. "Miss Zero." As Malone stared at her she added with a malicious grin, "There isn't any."

"You mean you can't find her?"

"I mean Dennis Dennis never was married," she said smugly.

Malone looked, bewildered, at Jake, who nodded gravely. "It's the truth. We traced Dennis Dennis back to college. It was Northwestern, by the way. Majored in writing. Changed his name to Dennis Dennis. Lived in an alumni club. Sold two poems to *Poetry*. Got a job with Delora Deanne. Moved to a fairly good apartment hotel. Moved to the Astrid Arms. Talked very poor because of alimony to an ex-wife."

"But there wasn't any ex-wife," Helene said. "He made it all up."

"We checked thoroughly," Jake said. "He even spent his vacations in Chicago. No one ever saw a wife, let alone an ex-wife. No record of any marriage, no record of any divorce."

Malone stared at them for a long moment. Then he said, "I might have known it. She was entirely too perfectly typical to be real. Only a writer could have invented her." He beamed at them. "All that," he said admiringly, "in so short a time. And his right name, too. What was it?"

Jake lit a cigarette very slowly and then said, "Arthur Swackhammer."

This time the moment was a very long one. At last Malone said, "Are you sure?"

"Positive," Jake said. "Only son of one Gerald Swackhammer, deceased. The unsuccessful one of the Swackhammer brothers. There were only two, by the way. Charlie survives. Dennis Dennis' father left him enough to go through college and live for a year or so, and that's all."

"This I have to think over," Malone said. He scowled. "Did Hazel hire him as Dennis or as Swackhammer, and did she know it was really Swackhammer? And will she tell? How did his Uncle Charlie fit into all this? Will *he* tell? And why did Dennis Dennis—I like him better by that name—invent an ex-wife, and—"

There was a small silence. No one remarked that Dennis Dennis wasn't going to tell.

"And what was he doing with the money he said went for alimony?" Malone finished.

Helene said, "And we can't wait and tune in next week and find out."

At that moment, the phone rang. Malone grabbed it, listened, mumbled a few yesses and noes, finally said, "Thanks, Weasel," hung up and said, "We don't need to wait till next week to find out. He used the money buying stock in Delora Deanne. It was Dennis Dennis who owned that other ten per cent!"

Jake whistled. "And what does that mean?"

"Dennis Dennis owned the stock," Malone said. "Dennis Dennis worked it through Myrdell Harris. He also was one of the heavy contributors to her bank account. Then Dennis Dennis *did* take the bankbooks. He probably wanted to keep his transaction with her hidden—though he must have known her bank account would be checked up after her death. All this, and on top of it, Dennis Dennis was a Swackhammer."

"All of this," Helene repeated, "and on top of *that*, Dennis Dennis bought those gloves."

Jake said, "I begin to see what you mean that the more you find out, the less you know."

Malone stared at him and then said very slowly, "All these things are side dishes. They adorn the real thing, but they aren't the real thing itself. They aren't what I do know, and what I'd have done something about before if all this hadn't come up to distract me."

Before any questions could be asked, the telephone rang again. Malone listened, said, "Stay right there, I'm on my way," hung up, and said, "Come on."

They were in the corridor before Helene could gasp, "Where, Malone?"

"Hospital," Malone said, leading the way into the elevator, "Come *on!*"

"*Who?*" Jake demanded.

Malone simply said, "I didn't expect this. Something like it, but—"

"*Malone*—" He didn't answer.

Down on the sidewalk, Gus Madrid was shoving his way through the crowd. "Malone, wait," he called.

"Later," Malone called back. "I'll talk to you later."

Once in the car, he said, "Helene, lose him if you can."
He gave her the address of the emergency hospital.

The snow was coming down hard now. "In this," she said,
"I could lose anybody. I can hardly see my hand in front of my
face."

"If you put your hand in front of our face," Jake said anxiously, "how are you going to see to drive?"

She ignored that. "Tell us, Malone."

"Charlie Swackhammer," Malone said tersely. "Smashed
up his car. Not hurt much. That's all I could gather."

"And his bride-to-be?"

Malone caught his breath. "That's just it," he said. "She's
disappeared. She's gone."

Chapter Thirty-two

During the nightmare drive through the thickly falling
snow, Malone tried once more to add up everything in his
mind. Not that it mattered too much, he reflected once or
twice, when any moment now might be his last.

It all fitted together perfectly now. Then he looked at the
pattern again and decided that no, only half of it was there.
The murder of Myrdell Harris and the hijacking of her body
seemed to be another picture entirely, and carved up—he
winced at his own expression—with a different jigsaw.

Or was it? He got back to the original, to the main picture
again. Myrdell Harris had found out, in her own peculiar way
of finding out things, just what was going on at Delora Deanne's. That was why she'd made it a point to get better acquainted with him. Because, he reasoned, she had figured
there would come a time to sell her information to the highest
bidder.

It followed, then, that she must have tried blackmailing
her murderer, with unfortunate results.

Helene whisked the big convertible around an icy corner,
and the little lawyer covered his eyes.

"It's not that I'm worried about my neck," he complained, "but I've got my duty to my client to worry about."

"Don't worry," Helene said consolingly, "we're almost there."

And so was he, Malone told himself, so was he. Almost to the finish of this—if he had reasoned it right. And he must have. There could be no other way.

The convertible slid to a screaming stop in front of the emergency hospital entrance. An instant later, Gus Madrid's black sedan slid to a stop behind them.

"Damn!" Helene said furiously, and then, "Good driver, that boy. Never mind, Malone, go on in and tend to your client. I'll take care of Rover boy here." She began to get out of the car.

"But Helene—" Malone began weakly.

"I said never *mind*. Go *on*."

Malone went on. He found Charlie Swackhammer waiting in a chair in the lobby. One arm was in a sling, a rakish bandage went around his head, but the pallor on his normally ruddy face appeared to be purely one of anxiety.

"Malone!" he said, and then, in a cracked voice, "*Maybelle!*"

"We'll find her," Malone said grimly. "Don't worry. Tell me what happened."

Charlie Swackhammer groaned. "It happened so fast, Malone." He shook his head.

"Accidents usually do," Malone said. "But just tell me how it happened, and where."

"In the park," Charlie Swackhammer said. "We were driving up through the park. Through the snow. Then a car came up behind us. I thought it was trying to pass us at first. All of a sudden I realized it was drawing pretty close. It was trying to shove us off the road. We were going pretty fast." He closed his eyes for a minute. "If I hadn't been going fast—"

"Never mind," Malone said quickly. "If someone was really after you, it wouldn't have made much difference."

Swackhammer nodded slowly. "Was after me, all right. Thought for a minute—a second, I guess—was trying to sideswipe us. Then I saw a tree." He paused. "Then I hit the tree." He paused again. "That was all."

"All right," Malone said. "Let's get you pulled together. What's about Maybelle?"

"I don't know," the big man said miserably. "She's gone. I was knocked out for a minute. I don't know how long. Not very long, I guess. But when I did come to, Maybelle was gone. She just wasn't there. Just *gone*."

For one horrible moment, Malone was afraid Charlie Swackhammer was going to blubber.

"Malone, she hadn't been hurt. There wasn't any blood. Except mine, from a cut here." He pointed to his forehead. "The car wasn't smashed much. I sprained my wrist and I cut my head, that's all that happened to me. Some people came by and then the police came, and they brought me here. But Maybelle, she's gone, Malone, and I don't know where she is."

Malone started to say, "I think I do," then changed it to "I told you not to worry. We'll find her." He added, "Just how much did you tell the police?"

"Not much of anything. I was dazed, I guess. Then I didn't tell them about Maybelle. I don't know why, I just didn't. As soon as I could, I called you."

"And a good thing you did, too," Malone said modestly. "The situation couldn't be in better hands."

For some reason, Charlie Swackhammer didn't look any better.

"First we'll find Maybelle," Malone said, with perfect confidence. Find Maybelle, and then wind up everything else, and then worry about paying back Gus Madrid. And how to finance another and probably more successful date with Tamia.

He went to the public telephone and called Tamia first, but not about the date. It was, he told her, a little matter of information. Just who was in the Delora Deanne building, and how long had they been there? And Otis Furlong? Fine. He was going to be there himself before long. Roughly, a half-hour or so.

"Hazel is there," he told Charlie Swackhammer, "and Otis Furlong. Came in about the same time. From lunch, I suppose." He realized that so far that day he hadn't even begun to think about lunch.

"But Maybelle—"

"Isn't there," Malone said. "So first of all, we're going where she is."

Heaven help him if he was wrong, he reflected, as he guided Charlie Swackhammer out to the car. Help him, and most of all, help Maybelle. Because right now he could think of no other possible answer.

Gus Madrid was still there, but he was leaning against the car, chatting companionably with Jake and Helene. He looked up as Malone arrived.

"Malone," he began. "That money—"

"Look," Malone said, helping Charlie Swackhammer into the back of the car, "you've got to wait. This is something that has to be tended to right this minute."

"I'm in a hurry too," Gus Madrid said. "Now listen, Malone. I been talking all this over with the lady here. And I'm a reasonable type guy. I want you should keep the money I give you for finding my girl. Even if you didn't find her. You was trying to, and it wasn't your fault she came back of herself."

Malone forgot Charlie Swackhammer and everything else for a mad moment. He opened his mouth to speak, closed it again, finally said, "No, let me give back half of it," and immediately hated himself. Half was exactly what he had left. But his wallet was already out.

"No," Gus Madrid said, shoving the wallet back. "I said you should keep it, I said."

"I insist—" Malone began, but more weakly.

"Shut up, both of you," Helene said, "and get in, Malone. You two can play Alphonse-Gaston some other time. This other thing is urgent." She smiled and said, "Good-by, Mr. Madrid."

Gus Madrid flashed the second smile Malone had ever seen on his face, waved good-by and called after them, "Don't forget our date, Mr. Justus."

"You don't need to tell me, Jake," Malone said sympathetically. "Does he want to dance or sing?"

"Act out his life story," Jake said.

Malone gave Helene the address of the Lake Shore Drive apartment building where Hazel Swackhammer lived and where Myrdell Harris had died, patted Charlie Swackhammer's shoulder comfortingly and said, "Don't worry."

A few blocks later he said to Helene, "But just exactly what did you say to Gus Madrid?"

She drove on in silence.

Finally Jake said, "She wouldn't even tell me, Malone."

At the building, Malone said, "Let me out here. Do any of you know where the service elevator is?"

"I do," Charlie Swackhammer said.

"Good," Malone said, almost adding that he'd thought so. "I'll meet you at 405. Myrdell Harris' apartment." He dodged any further questions by ducking into the building fast.

He paused briefly at the manager's office. To his relief, there was no difficulty about the key, though the manager did look a trifle dubious at first.

"Mrs. Swackhammer did say that she wanted the apartment left untouched—not even dusted—until she was through with it."

Malone nodded. "Of course. The inventory. But I promise it isn't going to take very long." Nor would it, he thought, as far as he was concerned.

"Of course, the police did go through it earlier—I'm sure I don't know why, but Mrs. Swackhammer said it was perfectly all right. They were very nice and quiet about it," he added.

And didn't find anything, Malone added to himself.

He let himself into the now familiar living room and glanced around. Everything was exactly the same as it had been earlier in the day. Even to the feel, the cold, lonely feel that it had taken on after the death of Myrdell Harris. He decided he didn't want to do any further exploring until the rest were there.

They came along in a rush. "All right, Malone. Now that we're up here—"

Silently he led the way into the bedroom. He had to have guessed right about this, he told himself, he absolutely had to. There wasn't any other way.

Maybelle Bragg was there all right, very quiet and still, in the exact center of the beruffled bed where Myrdell Harris had died so short a time before. For just one fraction of a second, his heart stopped. Had he been wrong, was he too late? Then he bent down and felt her pulse.

He straightened up and said to Charlie Swackhammer, "See? I told you not to worry. She's perfectly all right. Or she will be, as soon as whatever dope she's been given wears off."

Then he sat down, hard, on the nearest chair.

Chapter Thirty-three

"If you say, 'I told you so,' just once more," Helene said between clenched teeth, "I shall shriek, Malone."

He smiled at her, but it was a wan smile. "I can't seem to think of anything else to say, right at this minute." He took out a cigar and began unwrapping it very carefully.

Maybelle Bragg, her lovely hair loose on the pillow, still slept the heavy sleep of the drugged in the next room. Malone had sunk into the most comfortable chair in the living room to catch his breath. The day was not anywhere near over yet.

A doctor had been sent for. Not, Malone had specified, Dr. Alonzo Stonecypher. Charlie Swackhammer sat on the divan, his head resting on his hands. Helene was prowling restlessly around the room, and Jake had thoughtfully raided the pantry, declaring that everybody present needed a drink, especially himself. Helene had commented, after one taste, that the drink Jake had made would probably wake up Maybelle without the help of a doctor, and stopped just short of the unfortunate comment that it would undoubtedly even wake the dead.

"But how did you know, Malone?" Charlie Swackhammer said at last. "How did you know she was here?"

The little lawyer toyed with the idea of claiming either inside information or second sight, and decided to tell the truth.

"It was a lucky guess," he admitted. "Because this seemed the most logical place. There had to be some connection between this and the—the Delora Deanne business. Just as there had to be some connection between this and the Myrdell Harris—death."

175

He turned to Charlie Swackhammer. "Whoever shoved you into that tree, did it with one intention, kidnaping Maybelle. When she comes out of it, she'll be able to tell who it was. Too bad you didn't get a good look at the car or the driver."

"It was snowing," Charlie Swackhammer mumbled, shaking his head. "And it all happened too fast."

"But why, Malone?" Helene demanded. "And why bring her here?" She added, "Of all places."

"Of all places," Malone told her, "this was the safest. Because no one was going to come here, and the kidnaper knew it. Myrdell Harris' body had been removed. The police had been through here. The manager wasn't going to let just anybody in here, not even the maids. That's why it was the one really safe place and, to me," he went on, "the one really obvious place." He lighted his cigar and tried to look modest.

Helene said, "But who else would know about this place?"

"Anybody and everybody connected with Delora Deanne," Malone told her.

"I still don't understand," Swackhammer said. "Why kidnap Maybelle?"

"To murder her," Malone said, "at a convenient time and place."

"Malone," Helene said very softly, "there's still another and very important *Why*. Why murder Maybelle?"

Malone knew, and he didn't even like to think about it. "I'm damned if I'll tell you," he said. "At least, not right now." He added, "And anyway, she's safe." He looked at his watch. "I'm going on over to the Delora Deanne building," he announced. "You three stay right here until the doctor gets here and takes over."

Helene objected. She'd be very happy to drive Malone to where he was going. Jake didn't object out loud, but he looked definitely wistful.

"You two stay right here," the little lawyer said, and he said it sternly.

He paused at the telephone booth in the lobby and made two telephone calls. One of them was to von Flanagan. Would the police officer meet him at the Delora Deanne offices in, say, half an hour? If he did, everything would be cleared up once and for all. He hung up on von Flanagan's burst of agitated questions, and hoped he'd been telling the truth.

Then he made a second call on impulse. If it succeeded, it was going to be interesting. If it didn't—not much would be lost.

He thanked his luck that a taxi was waiting, in spite of the snow. He relit his cigar, looked out the window, and tried to admire the snow and the trees, but without success. What had Dennis Dennis written? *Sweet silver dreams, Delora! Snow will not harm your soft smooth skin—*

Well, nothing was going to harm Maybelle Bragg now. Thinking about it made him feel a little better. But there was still much to be accounted for. Including the matter of Myrdell Harris, which still didn't entirely fit into the picture he had drawn in his mind.

He paused a moment at the top of the marble steps that led to the cream-and-rose doorway just off Michigan Boulevard, crossed his fingers once for luck, and went on in.

Tamia Tabet smiled at him pertly from behind the gilt-and-ivory desk. "Malone! How wonderful!"

He gave her the best smile he could muster, apologized profusely for being so suddenly called away on business the night before, made another date, this one for tonight, and asked for Hazel Swackhammer. Hazel Swackhammer was in Dennis Dennis' office. Tamia Tabet showed Malone the dimple in her left cheek again.

He looked at her admiringly, but right now his heart wasn't in it. There was no sign of von Flanagan so far. He looked at his watch. Ought to be here fairly soon now.

Then he went up the lovely little stairs to the second floor and back to Dennis Dennis' unadorned and business-like office. Hazel Swackhammer was there, staring thoughtfully at the empty desk.

"I'm very sorry—" he began a little hesitantly.

"Naturally," she said. "So am I." If she was, she didn't show it, or anything else. "It was unexpected."

All of that and more, Malone agreed inwardly. Unexpected, perhaps unnecessary.

He tried another tack. "If there's anything I can do—"

"No," she said. "Everything has been done."

He looked at her carefully. Yesterday she had seemed tired and just a little anxious. Today she seemed tired and, somehow, just a little relieved. He wondered.

In what seemed like an amazing burst of complete

confidence she went on. "I've made the necessary arrangements—" there was that word again, he thought—"for after the
police are through. There didn't seem to be anyone else."

"His ex-wife?" Malone asked cautiously.

Hazel Swackhammer indicated Dennis Dennis' desk. "No
one seems able to find out anything about her." The expression
on her face would have been a grin on anyone else. "Frankly, I
don't believe there was one."

Malone did grin. "Neither do I. Especially as he wasn't
using the money to pay alimony."

This time a long, silent look passed between them.
Nothing needed to be said, and Hazel Swackhammer didn't
like to use up unnecessary words.

"Frankly," she said, "I was in no position to—buy him out.
I needed to raise money myself, to pull Delora Deanne out of a
temporary slump. And when it came right down to it, he
wasn't as interested in money as he was in helping run Delora
Deanne."

And, Malone thought silently, having every copywriter's
dream of a completely free hand.

"He seemed to be confident he could raise it," she told
Malone. "So, you see—?"

Malone shook his head.

"Well," she said, "yesterday I reached an agreement with
Mr. Dennis, whereby he became a partner in Delora Deanne."
That was that, and intended to cover everything.

"And—now?" Malone asked delicately.

"In the agreement we signed," she told him, "the surviv-
ing partner would inherit."

He refrained from remarking that Dennis Dennis'
murder, coming on the heels of the agreement, was a little too
tidy.

At last she said, in her flat, ordinary voice, "We might as
well go down to my office."

There was nothing to worry about, Malone told himself
firmly. Maybelle Bragg was safe. Jake and Helene were there,
and so would be a good reliable doctor in a few minutes.

All the Deloras were alive and all in one piece and safe,
except that none of them were Deloras any more and quite
possibly never would be again, unless Jake's persuasive powers
were all that he claimed them to be.

And so there was nothing to be unhappy about any longer, no reason for this unaccountable weariness and depression.

Hazel Swackhammer opened her office door and ushered Malone inside.

There was a box on the desk.

It was a gay little box, a bright, yet pale, blue, tied with rosy ribbons that matched the simple lettering *Nelle's*. It was a hatbox.

Malone gripped the edge of the desk and looked at Hazel Swackhammer. He saw her homely—no, not homely, ordinary—face turn pale, slowly and horribly, saw her mouth sag loosely, saw her eyes stare and then begin to close. He thrust out a hand to catch her as she fell, eased her into a chair, and stood looking at her closed eyes and slackened jaw.

Finally he untied the ribbon, slowly and very carefully. He smoothed it out and laid it on the desk. Then he lifted the blue lid with its rosy lettering, even more slowly.

There was nothing in the box but a hat.

After a little while Malone lifted it out gently and looked at it admiringly. It was a very merry and minxy little hat, with a wreath of small, smiling flowers, a bit of ribbon, and a tiny wisp of a just slightly playful veil.

Suddenly there were heavy footsteps behind him, and he turned around in time to see von Flanagan in the doorway, Klutchetsky at his side.

"There was a hat in the box," Malone said.

"What the hell did you expect to find?" von Flanagan growled. "A nest of bunny rabbits? Season passes to the hockey meets? It's a hatbox, isn't it?" He snorted indignantly. "And what's the matter with her?"

"A faint," Malone told him, "a real one. Probably her first." He picked up the hat. "The finger of fate," he said. "The *fine* finger of fate. The clutch of circumstances. Something. Not," he added reflectively, "that I wouldn't have managed as well without it."

"Malone," von Flanagan said, "sit down. Don't *you* faint."

The little lawyer sat down gratefully. Right now he needed to stall for time, just a small bit of time.

Hazel Swackhammer had opened her eyes again. Now she sat absolutely still in her chair, her hands gripping its arms tightly, a little color—but not much—slowly creeping back into her gray, expressionless face. Her whole body seemed to be frozen into complete rigidity, her eyes were like balls of ice.

There was a sound at the door and Malone looked up to see Charlie Swackhammer standing there, a little breathless.

"I got here as soon as I could." He looked around, stared at the desk, and said, "What's that? What's going on here?"

"A hatbox," Malone said calmly. "And everything's going on here. How's Maybelle?"

"The doctor's staying with her," Charlie Swackhammer said. "She'll be all right in an hour or so, when she wakes up." He added, "The Justuses stopped in the lobby, to talk to that Furlong fellow."

Malone nodded as though none of it were important, picked up the hat, turned to Hazel Swackhammer and said, "You see? There's nothing to worry about. In fact, there never was."

The look she gave him was such that he hoped frantically the iron wasn't all going to melt and give way at once. Tears began to slide down her face, probably her first in a very long time.

"Please," von Flanagan said, breathing hard, his broad face red, "will somebody—Malone—explain something?" He nodded toward Hazel Swackhammer. "And what's the matter with her now?"

"She's happy," Malone said, taking out a cigar. "You don't have to believe me, and I wouldn't blame you if you didn't believe me. But it's because there was a hat in the box."

Chapter Thirty-four

Malone sat with his eyes closed for a few moments. He was terribly tired now, more than he had ever been before or ever wanted to be again. And the whole thing wasn't over with yet, not anywhere near over with.

At last he looked at von Flanagan. "You'll find the hands and the feet," he said in a toneless voice, "right here, in the top left-hand drawer of the desk." He took out a dusty and crumpled handkerchief and wiped his face.

Von Flanagan stared at him, at Hazel Swackhammer, at the desk, at Charlie Swackhammer, back at Malone again, and barked a couple of orders to Klutchetsky, who took the boxes out very gingerly, carried them away as though they contained the very latest in thermal bombs, and came back a few minutes later, still a little pale.

"There won't need to be any commotion about this, of any kind, von Flanagan," Malone said. "The Cahill girl's people still won't ever need to know. Nor will the newspapers. No one needs to know, not ever."

Hazel Swackhammer had been given a sip of brandy that Jake had providentially found somewhere. Now she sat in her chair, not moving nor speaking, but with her eyes, brighter now, watching everything, and the marks of tears still on her face.

Von Flanagan looked around the room, rubbed his left ear, and said, "But what's with the hatbox?"

"Only had a hat in it," Malone said, "because Charlie didn't have the chance he expected to provide the head. Did you, Charlie?"

Charlie Swackhammer stared at him stupidly.

"And Maybelle won't be able to tell what happened to her, will she?" Malone went on ruthlessly and fast.

"No," Charlie Swackhammer said, taken by surprise. "She—" He caught himself and said inadequately, "I don't know what you mean."

"Never mind," Malone said. "I do. And von Flanagan does, too. And Hazel. She knew it all along."

Von Flanagan had the face of a man who'd been just about to speak, and had caught himself just in time.

But Helene who, with Jake, had arrived in the doorway, said, "Knew *what*, Malone?"

"Why," Malone said easily, "that Charlie Swackhammer had planned to murder Maybelle, and sending those little—offerings—to Hazel was a kind of reverse build-up."

In the silence that followed, Charlie Swackhammer turned white, then red, then white again. Finally he said weakly, "Prove it."

"I can, and I will," Malone said in a serene and confident voice he didn't feel at all. "From the way the whole thing was planned and carried out, it had to be either Charlie or Hazel. I thought it was Hazel, setting herself to destroy the business she'd built so that no one else could have it. Sending all the Deloras away, making it appear that they'd been murdered— or worse. Planning to murder Maybelle, the real Delora, so that Charlie Swackhammer couldn't have her too, and setting the stage for it just as it was set."

He took time out, a long time out, to light his cigar.

"Or," he said, "it could have been Charlie. First, trying to scare Hazel out of business. Second, building up to Maybelle's murder in advance. Figuring that other people were bound to think just as I did at first, and pin it on Hazel."

Charlie Swackhammer muttered something that sounded like "Perfectly ridiculous." Malone ignored him.

"He never intended to marry Maybelle, or he'd have done it before," Malone said. "So Ned McKoen's column guess wasn't far off at all. She was blackmailing him. Blackmailing him into matrimony."

Charlie Swackhammer said, "Now look here, Malone." The big, round-faced man laughed a little hoarsely and said, "It's ridiculous, I said, perfectly ridiculous. If I didn't want to marry Maybelle, I didn't need to. In this day and age, who's afraid of a breach-of-promise suit? Besides, I could have afforded to buy her off."

"Leave Maybelle out of this for a minute," Malone said. "The presents Hazel got through the mail and by messenger. You can't deny that, because I have proof. Any more than you can deny you paid Myrdell to impersonate Hazel over the phone and send all the Deloras packing. I know all about that, too."

"I suppose Myrdell—" Charlie Swackhammer stopped, glared at Malone and said angrily, "All right. I admit it was a pretty shabby practical joke. But it wasn't murder." He glanced involuntarily at von Flanagan.

"You're right," Malone said in a soft voice. "It isn't in his department."

Von Flanagan cleared his throat and said, "Transporting a body or any part thereof without a permit." He paused. "But I suppose you have a permit."

"There!" Charlie Swackhammer said triumphantly. He added, "And Maybelle hasn't been murdered, and I hadn't any reason for murdering her. Furthermore," he said, even more triumphantly, "I certainly wouldn't murder her when she's my alibi for the murder of Dennis Dennis!"

"Oh," Malone said. He looked at the other man long and thoughtfully. "So you know Dennis Dennis was murdered?" He paused a moment. "Second sight, no doubt?" he added pleasantly.

Von Flanagan moved a step closer.

"You were seen there, you know," Malone said, daring everything, and waiting breathlessly.

"I went there to see about poor Myrdell's funeral," Charlie Swackhammer said.

"Oh," Malone said again. "You even know where the murder took place. It must be second sight." He paused. "Who suggested meeting there, you or Dennis Dennis?"

Charlie Swackhammer opened his mouth to speak, and shut it again, but his mouth had formed the word, "Neither—"

"For that matter," von Flanagan growled, "why did this guy go to Rico's place?"

"I told you—" Charlie Swackhammer began.

Malone said quickly, "Following Dennis Dennis."

"But why did Dennis Dennis go there?" von Flanagan roared.

There was another silence until Hazel Swackhammer said, "I told him to. I got to thinking things over. It seemed to me there had been something strange about Myrdell's death. Something—too opportune. I didn't want to be involved myself, and I knew he knew his way around morticians. I thought he could nose around and perhaps find out something."

It was, Malone reflected, the most he'd ever heard her say. He noted and approved her choice of the word "mortician." "There you are, von Flanagan."

He drew a long, deep breath and plunged in, hoping he was going to reach land. "I'll give you all of it. From the beginning."

Von Flanangan regarded him coldly and said nothing.

"Actually," the little lawyer said slowly, "the murder of Dennis Dennis wasn't in the original plan at all. Actually, I don't think any murder was." He beamed winsomely at Charlie Swackhammer and said, "You can stop me, of course, if I'm too wrong."

Charlie Swackhammer scowled at him silently.

"But Dennis Dennis owned ten per cent of Delora De-

anne—enough to make a big difference considering that the
rest was divided two ways. He was dickering both ways, with
Hazel and with Charlie." He'd almost said "Cuddles." He
brushed a cigar ash off his vest and went on. "Meantime,
Charlie started a campaign to scare Hazel out of business. It
might even have been successful if she hadn't been very
smart," he said modestly, "and called me in. But—as long as
the face of Delora Deanne was safe, the rest could be replaced
by other models. And Hazel knew Maybelle would never come
back to being Delora Deanne. So—there was a definite
threat—" He glanced at Hazel Swackhammer.

"This morning," she said. There seemed to be more life in
her voice now. "I should have told you. But by that time I'd
made an arrangement—as you know. Dennis Dennis said he
could handle the threat and—everything else."

Malone nodded. "He was going to handle it," he said
grimly. "He was going to raise money to put into Delora Deanne by blackmailing Charlie Swackhammer. A very good
idea, too. But Charlie Swackhammer paid him off with a pre-
mature shot of embalming fluid."

He looked happily at von Flanagan who looked right back
at him unhappily.

"I don't get it," the big police officer said. "Mind you, I'm
not saying you're wrong, I'm just saying I don't get it. Like
why, for instance?"

Malone sighed and said slowly and very patiently, "Because Dennis Dennis was blackmailing him, that's why."

"With what?" von Flanagan said, scowling. "All right, so
he did pull those stunts on the little lady here. I'll go along
with you that it wasn't very gentlemanly, and a very objection-
able thing to do, I'll admit, but he wasn't breaking any law. You
heard him say so yourself, he had a permit for—" he drew a
long breath—"transporting a dead body or any part thereof—"

"Von Flanagan," Malone said gently. "Are you forgetting
what business this man is in?"

After a moment von Flanagan said, "Well—"

"Suppose you were the Cahill girl's parents?" the little
lawyer went on. "Suppose this whole thing came out in the
papers? Even if what he did isn't illegal, it certainly isn't going
to do the Swackhammer Brothers Undertaking Parlors any
good."

"They'd be ruined," von Flanagan said, nodding. "Ruined."

"You chose a mild word for it," Malone told him. "And remember, Charlie Swackhammer *is* Swackhammer Brothers. And it's a million-dollar business, too."

Hazel Swackhammer said, "That's right. He always looked on Delora Deanne as—pretty small potatoes. Something between a hobby and a sideline."

"Profitable enough that he'd want to get hold of it, after it had been built up," Malone said. "But Swackhammer Brothers is the big tree—even if it does have some biggish branches— and Charlie here didn't want to see it cut down in its prime." He glanced at Charlie Swackhammer and observed, with a certain approval, that here was a client who wasn't going to have to be told to shut up and let a lawyer do the talking.

"And not only because of the profits," Malone pointed out. "Charlie here is a man who takes pride in his profession." He turned to Jake. "Remember the way he talked about formulas he'd developed, and all that sort of thing?"

Jake nodded, started to go into detail, and changed his mind fast. If Delora Deanne cosmetics were based on those formulas, the less said the better. This was no time for him, or anyone, to cast a shadow on Delora Deanne.

"As a matter of fact," Malone said, "that was what really convinced me it was Charlie, and not Hazel. Dennis Dennis' means for blackmail was all that hanky-panky with a beautiful anonymous body. It wouldn't have been nice for Hazel, if she'd been the one, and the facts had come out. But it wouldn't have gotten her into any serious trouble, and it certainly wouldn't have put her out of business. But Charlie, here—" He paused.

"There simply wouldn't have been any Swackhammer Brothers business any more," Helene said softly. "Not any more, ever."

"And there won't be now," Malone said. "And that's what Dennis Dennis realized the minute he found out what Charlie Swackhammer had been up to. It was just the biggest and best hold anyone could have. It wasn't too hard for Charlie Swackhammer to trail him this morning. And Rico di Angelo's undertaking parlor looked like a good, quiet place—and appealed to the kind of whimsical mind that would send Hazel those gruesome little gifts."

He paused to relight his cigar and Helene said, "Maybelle—"

"Maybelle told me over the telephone that he'd been with her every single minute," Malone said. "He was right at her elbow when she did. Obviously, he gave her some simple little excuse for saying it—and just as simple a little excuse for having been away an hour or so. But he had to make sure that she wouldn't trip him up later, and he was glad to get rid of her anyway."

Helene shivered.

At last Charlie Swackhammer spoke. He said, "Now look, Malone!"

The little lawyer paid no attention. He had to reach that other shore now. "He took Maybelle to the apartment on some pretext, had a drink with her, doped hers of course, and left her there to finish off when the right opportunity came along. She'll confirm that when she comes to. Then he faked the accident to set up another alibi. He didn't realize," he added, "that I'd figure out right away where she was."

He abandoned his cigar in the nearest ash tray and began unwrapping a new one with relaxed, loving care. "It was all beautifully planned," he said admiringly.

At that moment a change came over von Flanagan's face. It wasn't a pleasant change.

"All this is very fine," he said coldly, "all this is a very fine explanation and I don't doubt it's true. Only it doesn't even begin to explain what happened to Myrdell Harris.

"Furthermore," the big police officer growled, "it doesn't even begin to explain who stole her body out of Rico di Angelo's hearse and then parked it sitting against a tree in Lincoln Park with a magazine on its lap."

There was no emotion on anyone's face except von Flanagan's.

"And it was a beautifully planned murder too," von Flanagan said, his voice beginning to rise. "Even to having the babe's doctor be a respectable old coot who could just about see the end of his own nose and maybe hear a cannon go off if it was right beside his ear."

Before Malone could think of anything to say, Charlie Swackhammer finally found his voice. "You can't pin that on me. Maybe you can bring me to trial over Dennis Dennis' murder, but with a good lawyer—" He paused. "But as far as

Myrdell Harris is concerned," he went on, "I can prove where I was every minute of the day yesterday and last night, and not by Maybelle, either. I couldn't have murdered Myrdell, and I didn't have any reason to murder her, and I didn't murder her."

"And I imagine you can prove it," Malone said smoothly.

Von Flanagan glared at both of them. "Okay, maybe he didn't murder her. Only somebody did, and somebody moved the body."

All Malone could think of to say was, "Yes."

"I think," von Flanagan said, with the air of a man who has come all the way to the end of his patience and started back, "I'll take you down to headquarters for questioning. All of you."

"Why bother?" Malone said. "Why not settle everything right here and now? Assuming, of course, that anyone here had anything to do with it."

Von Flanagan thought that over. "Okay with me, Malone, if it can be done."

Malone slid the wrapping from his fresh cigar, blew the wrapping accurately toward the wastebasket, and lighted the cigar slowly and lovingly. Everybody watched him as though they expected him to turn it into a rabbit.

"In the first place," Malone said, "why was Myrdell Harris murdered?"

Von Flanagan said, "I don't answer the questions, I ask them. You tell me." He thought it over. "All right, Malone, who did murder Myrdell Harris and hijack her body, and why?"

"I don't know," Malone said cheerfully.

Von Flanagan raised his eyes to heaven, opened his mouth, and remembered just in time that there were ladies present.

"Well," he said, "who else was around this babe before she died, near enough to of slipped her poison?"

Malone thought for a moment. There was, he decided, no reason to conceal anything. "She was at the broadcasting studio," he said. "There were any number of people around—musicians, actors, technicians, and so forth. After the show went to Rickett's with two people from the studio—the writer and the producer."

He flicked an ash from his cigar and went on. "Otis

Furlong, the photographer, and I joined them at Rickett's. We went on to another place from there, but she didn't go with us. She had an appointment at her apartment." He hesitated just a moment, then went on, "The appointment was with Jake."

Von Flanagan looked at Jake, and then back at Malone. He didn't say anything.

"Jake went to keep the appointment—"

"Let him talk for himself," von Flanagan growled.

"Okay," Jake said. "I went there. On business. Business about a television show, in case you care. Mrs. Swackhammer and Myrdell Harris were both there when I arrived. She suddenly collapsed and died after I got there."

"And any number of people," Helene put in, "could have been there before Jake arrived."

"Yes, and what's more," Jake said, "she could have stopped anywhere along the way between Rickett's and her apartment, and been with practically anybody."

Von Flanagan seemed to be trying to look in three or four directions at once.

"You forget another thing," Malone said, very smoothly. "Jake doesn't know exactly when she died. She collapsed, and Jake carried her into the bedroom while Mrs. Swackhammer sent for Dr. Stonecypher. But she might only have fainted."

There was a little silence while everybody considered that new idea.

"Jeez!" Klutchetsky said unexpectedly, making everyone jump. "Maybe the old doc done it himself!"

Von Flanagan gave him a very cold and very silent look.

"You see?" Malone said.

"No," von Flanagan said somberly. "I don't see a damn thing. Except that any one of a couple hundred people, maybe, could of give her poison. That's what I mean about everybody tries to make it hard for the police department."

"It seems to me," Hazel Swackhammer said, "that you can't tell very much until you know just what kind of poison it was, and how long it would take to work."

"Now there," von Flanagan said to Malone, "is the first thing said that makes any sense. There is a smart lady, Malone." He added, "If by any chance Doc Flynn's finished by now—"

He picked up the phone and called. Everybody waited, half-breathless. His end of the conversation consisted mainly of "yes," "no," and "what," but his face changed slowly to bewilderment and then to incredulity. At last he hung up.

"Well," he said at last, "Doc Flynn says it wasn't any kind of poison. No poison at all. Turns out she died of exactly what it was the old doc said she died of."

Helene gasped. Jake mumbled something about eighty-two not being so old after all. Charlie Swackhammer looked relieved; Klutchetsky looked puzzled. Hazel Swackhammer didn't move a muscle.

"So," Malone said, "you haven't a thing more to worry about, von Flanagan. None of this business about Myrdell has gotten out to the papers, luckily. You can just send her body back to Rico di Angelo and forget the whole thing ever happened."

For one moment it looked as though von Flanagan was going to hug everybody in reach. He drew a long, happy breath. Then suddenly he looked at Malone.

"But wait a minute," he said. "What about the body being stolen and turning up in the park? What about that?"

Malone shrugged his shoulders. "Why worry?" he said. "That didn't get in the papers either. It can stay a secret between the bunch of us. After all, von Flanagan, it isn't in your department."

"Just the same," von Flanagan said, "who did it?"

Malone's gaze met the big police officer's in a long, understanding look.

"That, von Flanagan," he said very solemnly, "is one thing I suspect we'll never, never know."

Chapter Thirty-five

Now that it was over, Malone felt the weariness and the utter melancholy coming back. He'd watched von Flanagan escort a glowering and silent Charlie Swackhammer off to jail. He'd managed to congratulate Hazel Swackhammer on the solution of all her problems, and had heard her say something about seeing him later, that first she had to look after Maybelle Bragg.

He'd reminded Tamia Tabet of their date for the evening, and even that failed to lift his enthusiasm more than a little. Now he waited dismally in the little blue-and-gilt reception room while Jake and Helene had one last word with Otis Furlong.

"I didn't get a chance to really talk with you before," the handsome photographer said to Jake. "Everything was in such an uproar." He looked a little anxious. "I hope this won't affect Delora Deanne in any way."

"It won't," Malone said reassuringly. "I don't think anything could."

Otis Furlong nodded. "I suppose you're right. And anyway, other people need photographers, and heaven knows, she didn't pay much. But Jake, about that process—"

The three of them looked at him hopefully.

"It'll work all right," he said. "No question about it. I added a few simple ideas of my own, of course."

"Of course," Jake echoed.

"And the cost," Otis Furlong said. "I figured that all out too. It'll run to, roughly, around $196,500 for a half-hour program. That," he added, "is just for the technical work, you understand. You'll have to add the talent and so forth on top of that, of course."

"Of course," Jake said again.

Out in the car Helene said, "Just the same, I bet it's a wonderful process, and I bet it would work just fine, and now where are we going next?"

"After that," Jake said, "Joe the Angel's. And don't say a word to me until we get there."

Nobody said a word until they were comfortably settled, with three rye-and-sodas lined up in front of them.

"Now, Malone," Helene began.

He turned to her. "You first. Just what did you say to Gus Madrid that made him get so noble about his money? Not," he added, "that I'm not going to send him back what's left of it anyway. Not only as a matter of ethics, but because he's a good man to have on your side."

Helene looked straight up in the air and said, "No dice, Malone. I promised him I wouldn't tell." She added a remark of her own about ethics.

The little lawyer said, "All right, then I'll tell you." He paused, looked at her, and said, "You promised not to tell me, or anyone, that he'd held up Rico di Angelo, stolen Myrdell Harris' body, and put it against a tree in Lincoln Park."

Helene lit a cigarette very airily and went on saying absolutely nothing.

Jake stared at Malone and said, "For the love of Mike, Malone. What made you think she did it?" He paused. "Or rather, had Gus Madrid do it?"

"Because," Malone told both of them, "I've known Helene for a long time, and I know the fine way her mind works. Because when she left me at the door of Myrdell Harris' apartment house the night of her death, she was in a tearing hurry."

He drew a long breath. "And because," he finished, "she turned up much later in the Rogers' Park police station, where she'd conveniently provided herself with the alibi she'd inevitably need when embarrassing questions began to be asked later."

"You taught me that alibi dodge yourself," she said accusingly. "Remember your telling me about that time you had a client of yours get himself arrested for speeding and—?"

"Never mind," Malone said hastily. He sipped his drink, relit his cigar and said, "The only thing I want to know is, just why did you do it?"

She sniffed. "Because I had sense enough to remember right away that Dr. Alonzo Stonecypher was nearsighted, deaf, and at least eighty-two years old."

"Well, you were basically right," Malone said, "even though you were absolutely wrong."

The little lawyer looked into his half-empty glass and sighed deeply. True, the whole Delora Deanne situation and the murder of Dennis Dennis were cleared up to everyone's satisfaction, including even his own. True, he had another date with Tamia Tabet for tonight, and there was no reason he could foresee why this one should be interrupted so unhappily. He was going to send Gus Madrid back the rest of his money, with a note for the balance, but his credit with Joe the Angel was on a firm footing again and would undoubtedly cover tonight's expenses.

And there was the long awaited check from Hazel Swackhammer coming in.

Just the same, he wasn't happy. The Jake Justus Television

Production Company was still without a program. Otis Furlong's process for producing a composite televised Delora would doubtless work, but it was out of the reach of any advertising budget except perhaps Fort Knox. Maybelle, the original Delora, was alive and in one piece, but she'd made it plain that she'd retired.

He'd solved his own problem; he'd failed Jake. Jake and Helene both. And there didn't seem to be anything he could do about it.

He was still sitting there brooding, with Jake, Helene and Joe the Angel silently respecting his mood, when Hazel Swackhammer walked in. There was actually an expression on her face. Indeed, she even looked pleased.

"I went to your office," she said, "and your secretary told me you'd be here. She sent these over."

"These" were a small but important package he'd purchased earlier that day and left forgotten on his desk, and an envelope, check-size.

"Please," Hazel Swackhammer said, holding out her hand. He gave her the envelope and watched while she opened it, took out a pale green oblong, tore it into bits and dropped it in the ash tray. From the corner of his eye, he saw that it had been a ten-dollar oblong.

"I'll write you another," she told him. "One you deserve. But we'd better wait a while before deciding on the amount. Because right now I'd probably say, make it as much as you want."

He wasn't mistaken. She was smiling. Not much of a smile, but recognizable.

By mutual consent, they adjourned to a booth in the back room. There, Hazel Swackhammer said admiringly that Malone had handled a tricky situation very nicely, yes, very nicely indeed. She couldn't have done better herself, and she was considered an expert at such things.

Malone murmured a thank you, and said modestly that it had really turned out to be a much simpler situation than it looked to be at first glance.

Joe the Angel broke up the admiration society by offering drinks on the house. "Because, old friends." He beamed at Malone. Hazel Swackhammer said that yes, a small sherry would be very fine right now.

The little lawyer looked at her thoughtfully. Even the fact

that she'd both thawed and unbent to what, in her, was a downright exuberant degree didn't make her pretty nor anywhere near it. But his heart warmed to her. A very plain woman, her life dedicated to making more fortunate women even more beautiful. No wonder she all but worshiped the Delora Deanne she'd created out of nothing. And with the only helping hand she'd ever had attached to her own wrist.

She did her best to return the smile he gave her, and said, "I still don't know how you knew it was Charlie."

Malone said, "Because of the hat."

"Yes," Jake said, "how's about that? What gives about the hat, Malone?"

Malone said, "If Hazel—if Mrs. Swackhammer here—had been behind all that monkeydoodling with the gruesome little gifts, she'd have reacted entirely differently to the hatbox. But when she saw that hatbox on her desk, she thought she knew what was in it—and she fainted."

He paused and added thoughtfully, "I think I'd have fainted myself, if I hadn't known what was in it."

"You knew?" Hazel Swackhammer said.

"Naturally," Malone said, rolling the cigar around between his fingers. "I sent it."

Helene said, "I might have known. And I thought it was coincidence."

"John Coincidence Malone," Jake said.

"And a quick telephone call on my way to Delora Deanne's," the little lawyer said. "A telephone call to Nelle's Millinery. Up to then, it was all a guess." And that reminded him. The first guess, the first giveaway, that he hadn't quite tumbled to for a very long time. The ring.

He felt in his pocket for the package Maggie had sent over, excused himself, and walked over to the parakeet's cage. The bird regarded him balefully as he unwrapped a birdseed bell, hung it in the cage, and said, "For services rendered."

The parakeet pounced on the bell, which gave a sharp, off-key jangle, jumped back on his perch, and shrieked triumphantly, *"Telephone!"*

"See?" Joe the Angel said happily. "Very rare bird."

The word "telephone" reminded Malone of his date with Tamia Tabet. He looked at himself in the bar mirror. Tired, a dusty, unshaven face with eyes that were red-rimmed from lack of sleep. Hair that hadn't been combed since sometime yesterday. A tie that had crept up under one ear. A wrinkled suit. A dirty shirt.

Not a thing that a good barber and a fresh suit of clothes wouldn't fix in a hurry. But his spirits failed to rise, the weariness seemed to be in his bones. He went back to the table, sighing.

Jake, Helene and Hazel Swackhammer were talking animatedly about television. Malone slipped quietly into his chair and waved to Joe the Angel for service. Suddenly he realized that Hazel Swackhammer was talking exactly like a prospective sponsor, and Jake exactly like a prospective producer, and they seemed to be getting along fine.

"—and Maybelle is perfectly all right, and as soon as she's recovered from all this, she is going back to being Delora Deanne again after all—"

The world immediately brightened as though someone had pulled a master light switch. There would be a Delora Deanne television show. The Jake Justus Television Company would be booming. Helene would be paid back her investment, and Jake would never, never know where it had come from. Everything was wonderful.

He listened a little more intently, and suddenly realized just what Hazel Swackhammer was saying. It had absolutely nothing to do with Maybelle Bragg. He went on listening.

"—to advertise Delora Deanne on television ought to be both different and dignified. So as I was saying—a new angle on a quiz program—"

Dear Mystery Maven,

Satisfy your taste for the murderously mysterious, indulge your urge to unravel the most baffling puzzle, revel in intrigue and suspense, find out who *really* done it! Subscribe now to **The Bantam Deadline**, Bantam's new Mystery Newsletter—published quarterly and mailed to you—FREE OF CHARGE.

Take a peek behind the mask of your favorite Mystery Maker in revealing Author Profiles. Get the inside dope on mysterious pleasures to come with the publication of titles ranging from classicly delicious Murders Most British, to the finest and hardest-boiled All-Americans. And—be the first to hear about Special Mystery Offers—Contests, Fabulous Prizes (including a Mystery Tour to England), and other *very* mysterious doings!

Send in your coupon now—if you think you can bear the suspense!

☐ 25789-7 **JUST ANOTHER DAY IN PARADISE,**
Maxwell $2.95

Fiddler has more money than he knows what to do with, he's tried about everything he'd ever thought of trying and there's not much left that interests him. So, when his ex-wife's twin brother disappears, when the feds begin to investigate the high-tech computer company the twin owns, and when Fiddler finds himself holding an envelope of Russian-cut diamonds, he decides to get involved. Is his ex-wife's twin selling high-tech information to the Russians?

☐ 25809-5 **THE UNORTHODOX MURDER OF
RABBI WAHL,** Telushkin $2.95

Rabbi Daniel Winter, the young host of the radio talk show "Religion and You," invites three guests to discuss "Feminism and Religion." He certainly expects that the three women, including Rabbi Myra Wahl, are likely to generate some sparks . . . What he doesn't expect is murder.

☐ 25717-X **THE BACK-DOOR MAN,** Kantner $2.95

Ben Perkins doesn't look for trouble, but he isn't the kind of guy who looks the other way when something comes along to spark his interest. In this case, it's a wealthy widow who's a victim of embezzlement and the gold American Express card she gives him for expenses. Ben thinks it should be fun; the other people after the missing money are out to change his mind.

☐ 26061-8 **"B" IS FOR BURGLAR,** Grafton $3.50

"Kinsey is a refreshing heroine."—*Washington Post Book World*

"Kinsey Millhone . . . is a stand-out specimen of the new female operatives." —*Philadelphia Inquirer*

|Millhone is| "a tough cookie with a soft center, a gregarious loner." —*Newsweek*

What appears to be a routine missing persons case for private detective Kinsey Millhone turns into a dark tangle of arson, theft and murder.

Look for them at your bookstore or use the coupon below:

50 YEARS OF GREAT AMERICAN MYSTERIES
FROM BANTAM BOOKS

Stuart Palmer

"Those who have not already made the acquaintance of Hildegarde Withers should make haste to do so, for she is one of the world's shrewdest and most amusing detectives." —*New York Times*
May 6, 1934

☐ 25934-2 THE PUZZLE OF THE SILVER PERSIAN (1934) $2.95
☐ 26024-3 THE PUZZLE OF THE HAPPY HOOLIGAN
(1941) $2.95
Featuring spinster detective Hildegarde Withers

Craig Rice

"Why can't all murders be as funny as those concocted by Craig Rice? —*New York Times*

☐ 26345-5 HAVING WONDERFUL CRIME $2.95
"Miss Rice at her best, writing about her 3 favorite characters against a delirious New York background."
—*New Yorker*

☐ 26222-X MY KINGDOM FOR A HEARSE $2.95
"Pretty damn wonderful!" —*New York Times*

Barbara Paul

☐ 26234-3 RENEWABLE VIRGIN (1985) $2.95
"The talk crackles, the characters are bouncy, and New York's media world is caught with all its vitality and vulgarity." —*Washington Post Book World*
☐ 26225-4 KILL FEE (1985) $2.95
"A desperately treacherous game of cat-and-mouse (whose well-wrought tension is heightened by a freakish twist that culminates in a particularly chilling conclusion." —*Booklist*

For your ordering convenience, use the handy coupon below:

Special Offer
Buy a Bantam Book
for only 50¢.

Now you can have Bantam's catalog filled with hundreds of titles plus take advantage of our unique and exciting bonus book offer. A special offer which gives you the opportunity to purchase a Bantam book for only 50¢. Here's how!

By ordering any five books at the regular price per order, you can also choose any other single book listed (up to a $4.95 value) for just 50¢. Some restrictions do apply, but for further details why not send for Bantam's catalog of titles today!

Just send us your name and address and we will send you a catalog!